BETWEEN THE DARK AND THE DAYLIGHT

Between the Dark and the Daylight…

by

RICHARD MARSH

Author of "The Beetle: A Mystery", "The Joss: A Reversion", "Curios", "The Datchet Diamonds", "Philip Bennion's Death", etc.

Introduction by Paul Fox

𝕶𝖆𝖓𝖘𝖆𝖘 𝕮𝖎𝖙𝖞:
VALANCOURT BOOKS
2011

Between the Dark and the Daylight by Richard Marsh
First published London: Digby, Long & Co., 1902
First Valancourt Books edition, 2011

This edition © 2011 by Valancourt Books
Introduction © 2011 by Paul Fox

ISBN-13 978-1-934555-83-5

Composition by James D. Jenkins
Published by Valancourt Books
Kansas City, Missouri
http://www.valancourtbooks.com

INTRODUCTION

Forging Identities: Craft and Graft in Richard Marsh's
Between the Dark and the Daylight

THE twelve short stories composing Richard Marsh's *Between the Dark and the Daylight* present the reader with a conundrum. From the mundane to murders from beyond the grave, from international plots to middle-aged romance, Marsh's collection seems to maintain little sense of unity, neither stylistically nor in terms of content. The tales are as motley a bunch as the crowd of misfits that arrive at the home of the narrator in the opening story, "My Aunt's Excursion". That Marsh was, in more ways than one, a prodigal talent, publishing around eighty novels and story collections at an average of around three volumes a year over almost three decades, might suggest to the reader that the seemingly haphazard combination of tales was a simple case of the author churning out and packing off to his publisher whatever quirky compositions flowed from his prodigiously fertile imagination. Unlike the country curate whose cupboard overflows with unaccepted manuscripts in his story "Skittles," Marsh clearly did not allow *his* ideas to accumulate and gather dust before sending them on in written form to editors. Perhaps the key to making sense of the stories as a collection lies in the question of their author's life, not in the sense of his intentionality but in his *personality*, for Marsh, like so many of the characters in his writing, had a secret and one only recently discovered.[1] It may well be that making sense of Richard Marsh himself might shed some light on his collection of tales.

Richard Marsh was born Richard Bernard Heldmann in St. John's Wood, London in 1857. He was the son of a Joseph Heldmann, a German-Jewish convert to Christianity, and Emma Marsh. In 1880 he began contributing adventure stories to G. A. Henty's weekly-published quality boys' paper, *Union Jack*, and was surprisingly quickly promoted to a position as joint-editor in 1882. By the summer of the following year his contributions to the

Union Jack abruptly stopped and Henty announced that Heldmann had ceased to be associated with the paper in any way.[2] Minna Vuohelainen has revealed that Heldmann's final serial, "A Couple of Scamps," was dropped by Henty when the story concluded inappropriately, considering the paper's readership, in violence and the supernatural.[3] A disagreement between the editors presumably over this subject led to Henty's notice of his colleague's departure. Heldmann's grandson, the author Robert Aickman, in a 1966 biography of Marsh entitled *The Attempted Rescue*, revealed that his grandfather would revive his literary career in 1888, publishing under his mother's maiden name. What had happened to Heldmann between 1883 and 1888 has until recently been a subject for much academic speculation, Aickman being the first among a number to suggest that some "problems" with women might have been occurred, Vuohelainen that he might have had some financial trouble with the law.

Callum James has recently revealed what had actually been occurring during at least part of this period.[4] From at least early 1883 to his arrest in 1884 on two charges of obtaining goods and money under false pretenses, Heldmann had traveled under false names and was living in high style, writing checks to the value of £2000 (a princely sum) only to abscond from various hotels and towns without his bills being honored. James has discovered this local newspaper's description of Heldmann's behavior in one small, Welsh town:

> The gossips of Llandudno have had a rare time of it recently recounting the adventures of a swindler of the "high-toned" sort. It appears that about a week ago a fashionably dressed, good-looking young man arrived at Llandudno. From the hour of arrival he put on the airs of a gentleman; by general deportment, not less than by elaborate get-up, seeking to impress upon the public that he could behave as one "to the manner born". He went to the Imperial Hotel but subsequently engaged apartments for a time at a very respectable house in Chapel Street. Having made sundry enquiries he intimated the fact that "my luggage will come over from the Imperial—aw, and please give the portah this shilling. Where can I purchase the best wines?" [...] [H]is custom was to take breakfast at eleven in the morning and dine at 6.30pm. For

several days he "lived like a Lord", ordering in plenty of "stuff" from various tradesmen and had dinner parties *ad libitum* as some of the young gentlemen in the town can testify.[5]

Heldmann had chosen to live far beyond his means, impatient to spend money he presumed his successful career would some day soon earn him. He was sentenced to eighteen months hard labor which he served seemingly without further incident. But his reputation was, of course, ruined. When he finally resurfaced as an author, he did so, rather ironically, if necessarily, under a new name.

It was not Heldmann's first brush with the law or with knowledge of how one's reputation and name might suffer when one breached societal expectations. His father had been part of a very public bankruptcy hearing when Heldmann was a child, ultimately having to leave his career as a businessman to become a schoolteacher. Vuohelainen has shown what his father suffered in the face of public opinion, or prejudice more accurately.[6] She notes that Heldmann Sr. had been swindling his wife's relatives who were also his employers and business partners and that he would suffer from thinly veiled attacks upon his Jewish ethnicity in the pages of *The Times*. His son would undoubtedly have known if not remembered what his family—his father in particular—had gone through, and would take the opportunity to shed his own past identity after his release from prison. His ancestry was a potential social burden to which had now been added his own conviction for fraud. And so he began his new career publishing sensational literature this time for adults rather than boys under his mother's family's name. He would not look back.

If Henty's break with Heldmann could presumably have been as much about his young co-editor's lifestyle as a dispute over literary taste, it is a lifestyle that would inform the themes and plots of Marsh's stories for the whole of his subsequent career. His books are full of questions about identity, mistaken and forged, tales of criminal acts and court cases, "get rich quick" scheming, and explorations into the relationship of personal morality and public ethics to the conventions and strictures of late-Victorian society. And whatever the case with Henty might have been,

Richard Marsh would within a few years become one of the most successful writers of his day, his bestselling novel, *The Beetle*, outperforming Bram Stoker's *Dracula* in 1897 when both books were published. *Between the Dark and the Daylight*, published in 1902, examines the craft of the storyteller through examining craft itself in all its myriad forms: subterfuge, deception, legerdemain, the deliberate and unwitting disguising of identities, the subtle graft required of the criminal-artist at work. The book's title points to the liminal identity of many of its characters existing on the outskirts of social acceptability, the moments of shocked recognition before understanding finally dawns, and those marginal human desires and activities that are impossible to categorize in the black-and-white world of late-Victorian mores.

In "Miss Donne's Great Gamble" Marsh confronts the latter question most obviously. The eponymous heroine is a very normal, middle-aged woman who has recently come into an unexpected inheritance which allows her to leave her job at a young ladies' school. Traveling on the continent, she meets—and keeps meeting wherever she travels—an American gentleman, Mr. Huhn, who eventually makes his affection for her known but in a manner which contravenes Miss Donne's social expectations as to how such "adventures" should occur; indeed, whether "adventures" of this kind are even socially acceptable at all. Confused in her wishes to both avoid offence to her suitor and to return a gift he has given her, she attempts to pen a letter to him several times. She thinks to herself that "to combine these opposite desires and intentions within the four corners of one short note was a puzzle". Inasmuch as this statement might be taken as a reflection upon Marsh's own views in his collection of stories, the choice of tales presenting various moral perspectives and shifting senses of clearly identifiable conventionalities and virtues, Miss Donne's consideration can equally be taken as an epigraph to the craft of her own author. Later on, Mr. Huhn will admit to the object of his affection that sometimes black and white "merge so imperceptibly into one another that it's hard to tell where the conjunction begins. You want keen sight to do it". It is his own keen sight and even keener experiences that Marsh will bring to bear in his collection.

Mr. Huhn's position is very similar to that of the Vicar, Mr.

Harding, in "Skittles," the following story in *Between the Dark and the Daylight*. The latter gentleman, we are informed, "was one of those people who are possessed of the questionable faculty of being able to see both sides of a question at once". Marsh himself, both as author and man, seems to have existed like the tales in his collection in the grey areas between conventional mores and social offence. Like so many of the personalities he penned, he negotiates the complex of twilight spaces between what is acceptable and that which is beyond the pale. It seems that his characters' misdemeanors and crimes are always eminently forgivable, from kleptomania in "Mitwaterstraand" to murder in "A Relic of the Borgias"; from post-mortem theft in "The Haunted Chair" to plotting and causing international war in "La Haute Finance". Being caught elicits, unsurprisingly, a certain sympathy from the authorial voice. The one crime recounted in *Between the Dark and the Daylight* that seems to be truly unacceptable occurs in "Skittles" and it is an artistic one. But even that is forgiven, in a manner, at the story's conclusion.

The opening story of *Between the Dark and the Daylight* is narrated by a young, London sophisticate, a typical gentleman-about-town enjoying life in the metropolis who is unexpectedly visited by his harridan of an aunt up from the country, a bunch of misfits in tow, with a mind to see the city. "My Aunt's Excursion" is a humorous tale, a succession of disasters befalling the day-tourists as they are guided as best he can, and despite his aunt's interference, by the young man. The aunt's party is initially nine, excluding herself and her nephew, before a ruddy gentleman all bonhomie and charm attaches himself to the group and more specifically to one of the young, pretty and giddy maids who is part of it. The final tally of twelve does not remain constant, the group's composition reorganizing itself as several members come and go, collapse or lose themselves, have to be pried from shop windows or manhandled from public houses. The initial plan suggested by the aunt is marked as ridiculous by her nephew, the number of places she wishes to visit a physical impossibility in the time allowed. Calculating the relationship of each place to the other, the narrator states that they should simply proceed straight to the Crystal Palace, unaware that tens of thousands of others are

making their way there at the same time to celebrate Foresters'
Day. Much confusion ensues.

At the conclusion of this first story the aunt is robbed, her
identity literally stolen, and, her tickets gone, she now has to pay a
second time for the return to Cornwall on behalf of all but two of
her charges: the young Stephen Treen and the alcoholic Matthew
Holman have been lost. They show up unharmed two days later
as do thereafter the stolen train tickets that the aunt has had to
repurchase. The twelve members of "My Aunt's Excursion" will
be numerically mirrored in the collection's second story, "The
Irregularity of the Juryman". The "hero" of this tale is one of
twelve jurors who finds himself playing a much greater role in
the story and trial of a lost will than he had initially expected. The
part he takes is constantly referred to as "irregular" throughout,
the jury's other members being affected by his place within the
jury box as much as his part in the narrative of the case they
are expected to judge. Mr. Roland initially resents the fact that
he has been chosen, detests his fellow jurors, falls asleep during
the barristers' statements, refuses to eat the fare provided by the
court at lunchtime, and behaves, generally and overly-particularly,
about as badly as a gentleman might behave. Finding himself a
very important part of the events he has been asked to adjudicate
upon changes his attitude entirely. The usually oh-so-ordinary
Philip Roland becomes the most significant and irregular part of
the story he has attempted to ignore.

Between the Dark and the Daylight is a collection of twelve
stories and, despite Miss Donne's warning that to suggest certain
possibilities can be to carry the doctrine of probabilities too far,
the replication of the number of stories by the number of people
on the day-trip and in the jury box is surely not insignificant. "My
Aunt's Excursion" makes it quite apparent that the young narrator's
attempt to maintain the integrity of a constantly shifting collection
of disparate personalities is hopeless. Like his shepherding the
herd of misfits in that story, the reader must make allowances for
Marsh's always shifting perspective within his compendium of
tales. The relationship of each story to each adapts and reorients
our perception of the whole just as Mr. Philip Roland's unusual
role in "The Irregularity of the Juryman" will ultimately shift the

court's assessment of the narrative it is considering along with its adjudication. As the plotline shifts our own attention alongside the unraveling of the story's mystery, Marsh's craft is revealed as one which attempts to repeatedly "shock" the reader into a new manner of approaching his characters; the title of each section of Mr. Roland's story announces a new individual who "is startled," adding a new perspective for both reader and characters upon the story as a whole. The process of reading *Between the Dark and the Daylight* is one in which we are constantly challenged to assess our own sense of absolutes, our sureties about identifying individuals and their moral qualities. As each of the twelve stories is finished, the collection as a single text must be reappraised, for each story necessitates a shift in our impression of its place in relationship to all the others.

In "My Aunt's Excursion," one of the group of characters brought up from the wilds of Cornwall for the day and the last to be introduced to reader and narrator alike is a Mr. Poltifen. This gentleman's appearance is described as "suggestive of pugnacity" and in the course of the day the suggestion is shown to be quite accurate. Mr. Poltifen carries about with him a dozen books bound up in a leather strap, seven of which the narrator tells us, having good reason to be made aware of this in the course of the outing, are a "History of London". He is a self- and aunt-professed authority upon the city, but not only is he overheard multiple times reporting falsely upon some detail of London's history, he also ironically complains several times that he finds the narrator's chosen course for their excursion lacking in any educational benefit. He states that he would have left his books at home if he had known beforehand that so many sights would be left unseen, a promise that the narrator wishes he had actualized. The idea that the teeming, multifaceted life of the city portrayed in "My Aunt's Excursion" can be detailed in a series of history books is revealed as simply a misguided and erroneously reductive view of London's real identity. Like the crowds on the streets, those who throng the rail terminals through which the party pass, and the Foresters' teeming at the Crystal Palace, the mass of people into and from which members of the party move at will (and sometimes against their will) is the reality of life in the city. The Aunt's laughable itinerary, based upon a ridiculously simplified view of a complex, dynamic metropolis, is no doubt based upon the dusty books and dry chagrin of Mr. Poltifen: each ignores the vibrancy of life in London. And even the party itself, a "simple" group of lower-class rustics, is much more complex than the Aunt and, initially, the narrator presumes. Their personalities are as individual as their intentions and they simply cannot be maintained as a group no matter what authority seeks to impose itself upon them. In the end, to see the party as a whole is as inadequate as Mr. Poltifen's and the Aunt's view of London: each is a complex and shifting entity, unidentifiable for more than a moment and irreducible to a simple, controllable body.

So with Marsh's *Between the Dark and the Daylight*. To summarize any single story does not do justice to the collection as a whole. To presume upon the reader's experience is to neglect the dynamic individuality of each personality's perspective as it approaches and makes its way through a shifting series of altering viewpoints. To maintain a single interpretation of the collection as a whole is to neglect the fluid allegiances and momentary insights that the relationship of each story to every other suggests. The idea of an authoritative reading is constantly undermined by the characterization that Marsh presents in his texts. In every story expectations are dissolved, shocks abound, authoritarian figures are made ridiculous, and social "norms" are undercut and shown to be inadequate to the complexity of life. That the aunt at the end of the day literally loses her proof of identity, that all her expectations and her control over others is dissolved in the reality of the excursion's chaos, is only the first example of the dangers of reductive perspective in the collection. In "Mrs. Riddle's Daughter," "Nelly," and the gentler "Em," Marsh relates stories in which mistaken identities occur precisely because of preconceived notions of society and individuals. The first of these stories deals, like "My Aunt's Excursion," with a young, worldly-wise gentleman dealing with a harridan aunt's authoritarian principles. Unlike the first story in this collection, "Mrs. Riddle's Daughter" suggests a potentially much harsher result for characters when confronted by those who wish to control our sense of who we are in the world and, by extension, what we do in it. A "Woman Crusader" attempts to control her daughter's love of the theater, beating her as a child, locking her in her room with no food when she is older, and sending her to a puritanical Girls' School when she is of age. Mistaken identity and the masks that we wear before others is the motivating theme of the plot.[7] That society itself through its "crusading" moral authority requires us to act the roles we are given while living our "real" lives secretly, is shown ultimately to be the most immoral of systems. Life itself, as Miss Donne realizes in her great gamble, is simply too complex to be reduced to a set of abstract moral or social principles.

The question of the actor's craft, the ability to misdirect the gaze of society and reader alike, is part of Marsh's skill, and one, as suggested before, that he was most particularly capable of exterior to the world of letters. Forging a sense of who we are in terms of both manufacturing ourselves and fooling others is par for the course in *Between the Dark and the Daylight*; indeed, the distinction between the two is often, as Mr. Huhn suggested, not an issue of black and white. It is when characters cede control over their identity to others that calamity occurs. In "Mitwaterstraand" a newly-wed husband discovers that his wife—the picture of Victorian innocence—is actually an inveterate kleptomaniac.[8] Marsh divides the story into two sections: "The Disease" and "The Cure". No one considers the young wife capable of crime and it is only when she is falsely accused of theft that she is "cured". But the story is not as simple, perhaps, as it first appears. The father of the new bride fails to tell his son-in-law of his daughter's affliction prior to the marriage. It is only the husband's presumption and announcement that his wife stole a collection of diamonds that "cures" her in the end. But is the disease that is cured kleptomania or the expectation of society that certain actions should be hidden, that identity should be authorized by mores exterior to the reality of the individual? It is only when the husband publicly announces his wife's "guilt" that she is "cured"; in other words, she need no longer *appear* to be that which she is not. The "shock" that cures her is the truth. She is no longer obliged to act a role that has been written for her by social convention. Crime and its necessity is often, it seems, as much a product of how society obliges us to be seen as it is the voluntary action of an independent individual.

"Nelly" suggests another rendition of the relationship between authority, identity, fraud, and deliberate disguise. Mr. Gibbs, after some years abroad, returns to England where he attempts to find his erstwhile love with whom he has lost contact some time before. Coming across a painting in a gallery entitled "Stitch! Stitch! Stitch!" he believes the model is his Nelly. Through the painting's artist he discovers her address and finds her there on the verge of suicide, starving in a garret. Putting her coldness and bitterness down to the harsh life she has had to lead, Gibbs intends marriage. After she has postponed the nuptials twice already, on the morning of the wedding Nelly disappears and, in the course of his wandering the streets of London, Gibbs is accosted by a vulgar, slovenly fishwife who, it turns out, is the "real" Nelly. Returning in shock with this woman to meet her husband and five children, Gibbs finds the "Nelly" he had intended to marry is the new lodger. They are joyfully reunited, "Nelly" admitting that she has grown to love Gibbs and that she could not enter marriage having conned him. The conclusion of the story marks "Nelly's" shock when she is introduced to the woman she has been mistaken for, the "original" Nelly from Gibbs' past.

Artifice runs rampant through "Nelly," the art of duping another for one's own gain, the power of the imagination to provide us with what we desire, the adoption and mistaking of identity, and the manner in which art renders impressions that are at odds with reality. The coincidence of Gibbs meeting the real Nelly who has accepted the escaped fraudster as a lodger might seem to be authorial clumsiness of the first order. But the construction of the narrative highlights the manner in which art can compose life in the manner we choose and for our own ends. Just as Gibbs "discovers" Nelly in the painting (whose title accentuates the tacking together of various seemingly disparate threads or strands), so Marsh allows the reader to discover the art of identification by "stitching up" a coincidence that challenges our expectations. Forgery becomes truth when Gibbs appreciates that the Nelly of his imagination has much more in common with the fraudulent identity of his would-be wife than the slattern the "real" Nelly has become in the intervening years since he last knew her. The shock of the "new" Nelly at the story's conclusion suggests that each individual will

see the world the way they imagine it; Gibbs' belief that the two
share some resemblance is tantamount to an insult to his new love.
In the end, reality itself is no more an authority to be followed
than harsh aunts or dictatorial mothers. Marsh appears to point
out that art and artifice are truths more amenable to human desire
and that the power of the aesthetic imagination affords more to
life than the authority of any social realism.[9]

Perhaps the most extraordinary story in *Between the Dark and
the Daylight* is "Exchange is Robbery," a title that obviously reflects
upon the rest of the collection when questions of character and
the imposition of identity by social authority are so important. It
is the tale of Messrs. Golden and Ruby, jewelers to the aristocracy,
and the discovery that their stock of diamonds has been exchanged
for paste fakes. Initially thinking that the Duchess of Datchet is
to blame for the crime, accusations are made and a much more
complex case than they (or we, the readers) initially assumed
is uncovered. The social masks that are worn in the story are
constantly torn away until, at the conclusion, a cross-dressing
servant, the lover of the Duke of Datchet's one-time mistress, is
revealed to be the fake Duchess who has been perpetuating the
thefts. Even by Marsh's standards, the shock of the denouement
for a late-Victorian reader is difficult to imagine: an aristocrat's
mistress forms a liaison with a cross-dressing servant who in turn
impersonates the selfsame aristocrat's wife in order to perpetrate
a diamond swindle of enormous proportion. The dissolution
of gender and class distinctions, of everyone's expectations
by the effeminate and beautiful young crook, is art at its finest.
The accepted roles and rule of society are shown to be the very
framework that allows for its own deconstruction. The culprit at
the conclusion will leave a photographic triptych revealing the
process of his "change" from a handsome, liveried servant into
a dainty Duchess of the realm. The exchanging of identifiable
roles—class, gender, legal and romantic—is a matter of grand
artifice both on a fictional and an individual level. The authority
of society is left in shreds by an artistic parvenu, a magician who
leaves the stage and the secret of his trick to an unappreciative
audience.

The final story in *Between the Dark and the Daylight* is the only one in the collection that ends in tragedy. As such it warrants investigation as to why Marsh might conclude with this tale when all the others are wound up to the satisfaction of those characters with whom we, as readers, sympathize. "A Relic of the Borgias" is a tale of murder, both intentional and accidental. The narrator of the story, Mr. Benham, is witness to the death of an acquaintance, a womanizing scoundrel who is, unknown to all at the time, poisoned by a woman he throws over for another; the murder "weapon" is Lucrezia Borgia's poisonous cameo ring. The murderess marries her former affianced and will bequeath a manuscript describing the properties of the ring to Benham at her death in childbirth. Not knowing what to do, Benham decides to keep the secret safe since all those immediately concerned with the murder are now dead. He sensibly believes that no good will come of revealing what has occurred in the past. The story leaps forward in time to the now grown child's eighteenth birthday when, accidentally and despite Mr. Benham's best efforts, the unfortunate young woman unwittingly kills herself by putting the ring upon her finger. She cries "Mamma" and drops dead. And with that Marsh's collection of stories abruptly concludes.

The daughter's final cry immediately forces the reader to confront the conception the girl has of her parent, one we know to be a murderess. The mother-murderess conflation is one of the most extreme binaries one might conceive for a woman. The mother not only has murdered a former lover, but now her own child, making the dual conception of her identity even more horrendous. But why such a tragic ending to *Between the Dark and the Daylight?* The answer may lie in Mr. Benham's refusal to reveal the truth of the murder and the truth of the identity of the criminal when he has the opportunity to do so. He does not reveal the truth because of his desire to leave society without it, to avoid disturbing the social framework. He refuses to query the reason why a man was murdered and a system permitted that allows such men to use and abuse women. It is not that Marsh is acting as an apologist for the crime—the woman's hysterical laughter is described as verging on the insane—but rather as an interrogator querying the acceptance of the mask that social authority itself wears and the tragedy that can ensue when the face behind the mask is never revealed. All the characters who artfully construct fake identities are finally unmasked for what they are: Mrs. Riddle's hypocrisy becomes evident, as does the Aunt's false authority on her excursion; Miss Donne eventually follows her emotions rather than act the role society dictates for her; in "Mitwaterstraand" the "cure" for the young kleptomaniac arrives when she is mistakenly denounced as a thief; the curate is afforded another chance when his artistic crime is revealed by the Vicar in "Skittles". Each of these stories ends, to varying degree, happily. It is only in "A Relic of the Borgias" that a character's true identity remains hidden at the story's conclusion and it is the only story that ends in tragedy. Marsh finishes with a death because, excepting supernatural events such as those related in "The Haunted Chair," with death comes an end to the attempted imposition of identity by social authority as surely as it concludes our ability to forge identity from the metal of our own personalities. This forging of our characters may be considered criminal by the majority of authoritarians in Marsh's texts, but society seemingly obligates us to endeavor such artistic responses. That is, in the end, the only authentic act for their author.

Paul Fox
Abu Dhabi

July 12, 2010

PAUL FOX is currently an Associate Professor at Zayed University in the United Arab Emirates and specializes in late-nineteenth century aesthetics and Decadent literature. He has previously edited and introduced Gabriele d'Annuzio's *The Intruder* and M.P. Shiel's *Prince Zaleski*, both published by Valancourt Books. He is currently editing and introducing John Lane's *Keynotes* series for republication.

NOTES

[1] The biographical information is drawn from the recent investigative research of Minna Vuohelainen and Callum James to whom I am indebted.

[2] This notice appeared in the *Union Jack*, on the 5th June, 1883.

[3] See Minna Vuohelainen, "Richard Marsh's *The Beetle* (1897): a late-Victorian popular novel". *Working with English: Medieval and Modern Language, Literature and Drama* 2:1, Literary Fads and Fashions (2006): 89-100.

[4] See Callum James, "*Why* was Richard Marsh?" *Wormwood* 14 (2010): 40-45.

[5] *North Wales Chronicle*, February 23rd 1884.

[6] See Minna Vuohelainen, "Richard Marsh". *Working with English* 2:1 (2006): 89-100.

[7] Many of Marsh's views about the actor's craft on the social stage are suggestive of Oscar Wilde's essay, "The Truth of Masks". The conceit of the criminal as an artist, an idea appearing in several stories in *Between the Dark and the Daylight*, was also portrayed by Wilde in his essay "Pen, Pencil and Poison".

[8] Much recent late-Victorian criticism has examined the authoritative taxonomies of "disease," particularly as they relate to questions of gender.

[9] Wilde again, in his essays "The Decay of Lying" and "The Truth of Masks," may here have been an influence upon Marsh's thoughts.

Between the Dark and the Daylight . . .

My Aunt's Excursion

"THOMAS," observed my aunt, as she entered the room, "I have taken you by surprise."

She had. Hamlet could scarcely have been more surprised at the appearance of the ghost of his father. I had supposed that she was in the wilds of Cornwall. She glanced at the table at which I had been seated.

"What are you doing?—having your breakfast?"

I perceived, from the way in which she used her glasses, and the marked manner in which she paused, that she considered the hour an uncanonical one for such a meal. I retained some fragments of my presence of mind.

"The fact is, my dear aunt, that I was at work a little late last night, and this morning I find myself with a trifling headache."

"Then a holiday will do you good."

I agreed with her. I never knew an occasion on which I felt that it would not.

"I shall be only too happy to avail myself of the opportunity afforded by your unexpected presence to relax for a time, the strain of my curriculum of studies. May I hope, my dear aunt, that you propose to stay with me at least a month?"

"I return to-night."

"To-night! When did you come?"

"This morning."

"From Cornwall?"

"From Lostwithiel. An excursion left Lostwithiel shortly after midnight, and returns again at midnight to-day, thus giving fourteen hours in London for ten shillings. I resolved to take advantage of the occasion, and to give some of my poorer neighbours, who had never even been as far as Plymouth in their lives, a glimpse of some of the sights of the Great City. Here they are—I filled a compartment with them. There are nine."

There were nine—and they were about the most miscellaneous-looking nine I ever saw. I had wondered what they meant by coming with my aunt into my sitting-room. Now, if anything, I wondered rather more. She proceeded to introduce them individually—not by any means by name only.

"This is John Eva. He is eighty-two and slightly deaf. Good gracious, man! don't stand there shuffling, with your back against the wall: sit down somewhere, do. This is Mrs. Penna, sixty-seven, and a little lame. I believe you're eating peppermints again. I told you, Mrs. Penna, that I can't stand the odour, and I can't. This is her grandson, Stephen Treen, aged nine. He cried in the train."

My aunt shook her finger at Stephen Treen, in an admonitory fashion, which bade fair, from the look of him, to cause an immediate renewal of his sorrows.

"This is Matthew Holman, a converted drunkard who has been the worst character in the parish. But we are hoping better things of him now." Matthew Holman grinned, as if he were not certain that the hope was mutual, "This is Jane, and this is Ellen, two maids of mine. They are good girls, in their way, but stupid. You will have to keep your eye on them, or they will lose themselves the first chance they get." I was not amazed, as I glanced in their direction, to perceive that Jane and Ellen blushed.

"This," went on my aunt, and into her voice there came a sort of awful dignity, "is Daniel Dyer, I believe that he kissed Ellen in a tunnel."

"Please ma'am," cried Ellen, and her manner bore the hall-mark of truth, "it wasn't me, that I'm sure."

"Then it was Jane—which does not alter the case in the least." In saying this, it seemed to me that, from Ellen's point of view, my aunt was illogical. "I am not certain that I ought to have brought him with us; but, since I have, we must make the best of it. I only hope that he will not kiss young women when he is in the streets with me."

I also hoped, in the privacy of my own breast, that he would not kiss young women while he was in the streets with me—at least, when it remained broad day.

"This," continued my aunt, leaving Daniel Dyer buried in the depths of confusion, and Jane on the verge of tears, "is Sammy Trevenna, the parish idiot. I brought him, trusting that the visit would tend to sharpen his wits, and at the same time, teach him the difference between right and wrong. You will have, also, to keep an eye upon Sammy. I regret to say that he is addicted to picking and stealing. Sammy, where is the address card which I gave you?"

Sammy—who looked his character, every inch of it!—was a lanky, shambling youth, apparently eighteen or nineteen years old. He fumbled in his pockets.

"I've lost it," he sniggered.

"I thought so. That is the third you have lost since we started. Here is another. I will pin it to your coat; then when you are lost, someone will be able to understand who you are. Last, but not least, Thomas, this is Mr. Poltifen. Although this is his first visit to London, he has read a great deal about the Great Metropolis. He has brought a few books with him, from which he proposes to read selections, at various points in our peregrinations, bearing upon the sights we are seeing, in order that instruction may be blended with our entertainment."

Mr. Poltifen was a short, thick-set individual, with that in his appearance which was suggestive of pugnacity, an iron-grey, scrubby beard, and a pair of spectacles—probably something superior in the cobbling line. He had about a dozen books fastened together in a leather strap, among them being—as, before the day was finished, I had good reason to be aware—a "History of London," in seven volumes.

"Mr. Poltifen," observed my aunt, waving her hand towards the gentleman referred to, "represents, in our party, the quality of intelligent interest."

Mr. Poltifen settled his glasses on his nose and glared at me as if he dared me to deny it. Nothing could have been further from my mind.

"Sammy," exclaimed my aunt, "sit still. How many times have I to request you not to shuffle?"

Sammy was rubbing his knees together in a fashion the like of which I had never seen before. When he was addressed, he drew the back of his hand across his mouth, and he sniggered. I felt that he was the sort of youth anyone would have been glad to show round town.

My aunt took a sheet of paper from her hand-bag.

"This is the outline programme we have drawn up. We have, of course, the whole day in front of us, and I have jotted down the names of some of the more prominent places of interest which we wish to see." She began to read: "The Tower Bridge, the Tower of London, Woolwich Arsenal, the National Gallery, British Museum, South Kensington Museum, the Natural History Museum, the Zoological Gardens, Kew Gardens, Greenwich Hospital, Westminster Abbey, the Albert Memorial, the Houses of Parliament, the Monument, the Marble Arch, the Bank of England, the Thames Embankment, Billingsgate Fish Market, Covent Garden Market, the Meat Market, some of the birthplaces of famous persons, some of the scenes mentioned in Charles Dickens's novels—during the winter we had a lecture in the school-room on Charles Dickens's London; it aroused great interest—and the Courts of Justice. And we should like to finish up at the Crystal Palace. We should like to hear any suggestions you would care to make which would tend to alteration or improvement—only, I may observe, that we are desirous of reaching the Crystal Palace as early in the day as possible, as it is there we propose to have our midday meal." I had always been aware that my aunt's practical knowledge of London was but slight, but I had never realised how slight until that moment. "Our provisions we have brought with us. Each person has a meat pasty, a potato pasty, a jam pasty, and an apple pasty, so that all we shall require will be water."

This explained the small brown-paper parcel which each member of the party was dangling by a string.

"And you propose to consume this—little provision at the Crystal Palace, after visiting these other places?" My aunt inclined her head. I took the sheet of paper from which she had been reading. "May I ask how you propose to get from place to place?"

"Well, Thomas, that is the point. I have made myself responsible for the entire charge, so I would wish to keep down expenses. We should like to walk as much as possible."

"If you walk from Woolwich Arsenal to the Zoological Gardens, and from the Zoological Gardens to Kew Gardens, you will walk as far as possible—and rather more."

Something in my tone seemed to cause a shadow to come over my aunt's face.

"How far is it?"

"About fourteen or fifteen miles. I have never walked it myself, you understand, so the estimate is a rough one."

I felt that this was not an occasion on which it was necessary to be over-particular as to a yard or so.

"So much as that? I had no idea it was so far. Of course, walking is out of the question. How would a van do?"

"A what?"

"A van. One of those vans in which, I understand, children go for treats. How much would they charge, now, for one which would hold the whole of us?"

"I haven't the faintest notion, aunt. Would you propose to go in a van to all these places?" I motioned towards the sheet of paper. She nodded. "I have never, you understand, done this sort of thing in a van, but I imagine that the kind of vehicle you suggest, with one pair of horses, to do the entire round would take about three weeks."

"Three weeks? Thomas!"

"I don't pretend to literal accuracy, but I don't believe that I'm far wrong. No means of locomotion with which I am acquainted will enable you to do it in a day, of that I'm certain. I've been in London since my childhood, but I've never yet had time to see one-half the things you've got down upon this sheet of paper."

"Is it possible?"

"It's not only possible, it's fact. You country folk have no notion of London's vastness."

"Stupendous!"

"It is stupendous. Now, when would you like to reach the Crystal Palace?"

"Well, not later than four. By then we shall be hungry."

I surveyed the nine.

"It strikes me that some of you look hungry now. Aren't you hungry?"

I spoke to Sammy. His face was eloquent.

"I be famished."

I do not attempt to reproduce the dialect: I am no dialectician. I merely reproduce the sense; that is enough for me. The lady whom my aunt had spoken of as "Mrs. Penna, sixty-seven, and a little lame," agreed with Sammy.

"So be I. I be fit to drop, I be."

On this subject there was a general consensus of opinion—they all seemed fit to drop. I was not surprised. My aunt was surprised instead.

"You each of you had a treacle pasty in the train!"

"What be a treacle pasty?"

I was disposed to echo Mrs. Penna's query, "What be a treacle pasty?" My aunt struck me as really cutting the thing a little too fine.

"You finish your pasties now—when we get to the Palace I'll see that you have something to take their place. That shall be my part of the treat."

My aunt's manner was distinctly severe, especially considering that it was a party of pleasure.

"Before we started it was arranged exactly what provisions would have to be sufficient. I do not wish to encroach upon your generosity, Thomas—nothing of the kind."

"Never mind, aunt, that'll be all right. You tuck into your pasties."

They tucked into their pasties with a will. Aunt had some breakfast with me—poor soul! she stood in need of it—and we discussed the arrangements for the day.

"Of course, my dear aunt, this programme of yours is out of the question, altogether. We'll just do a round on a 'bus, and then it'll be time to start for the Palace."

"But, Thomas, they will be so disappointed—and, considering how much it will cost me, we shall seem to be getting so little for the money."

"My dear aunt, you will have had enough by the time you get back, I promise you."

My promise was more than fulfilled—they had had good measure, pressed down and running over.

The first part of our programme took the form, as I had suggested, of a ride on a 'bus. Our advent in the Strand—my rooms are in the Adelphi—created a sensation. I fancy the general impression was that we were a party of lunatics, whom I was personally conducting. That my aunt was one of them I do not think that anyone doubted. The way in which she worried and scurried and fussed and flurried was sufficient to convey that idea.

It is not every 'bus which has room for eleven passengers. We could not line up on the curbstone, it would have been to impede the traffic. And as my aunt would not hear of a division of forces, as we sauntered along the pavement we enjoyed ourselves immensely. The "parish idiot" would insist on hanging on to the front of every shop-window, necessitating his being dragged away by the collar of his jacket. Jane and Ellen glued themselves together arm in arm, sniggering at anything and everything—especially when Daniel Dyer digged them in the ribs from behind. Mrs. Penna, proving herself to be a good deal more than a little lame, had to be hauled along by my aunt on one side, and by Mr. Holman, the "converted drunkard," on the other. That Mr. Holman did not enjoy his position I felt convinced from the way in which, every now and then, he jerked the poor old soul completely off her feet. With her other hand my aunt gripped Master Treen by the hand, he keeping his mouth as wide open as he possibly could; his little trick of continually looking behind him resulting in collisions with most of the persons, and lamp-posts, he chanced to encounter. The deaf Mr. Eva brought up the rear with Mr. Poltifen and his strapful of books that gentleman favouring him with totally erroneous scraps of information, which he was, fortunately, quite unable to hear.

We had reached Newcastle Street before we found a 'bus which contained the requisite amount of accommodation. Then, when I hailed one which was nearly empty, the party boarded it. Somewhat to my surprise, scarcely anyone wished to go outside. Mrs. Penna, of course, had to be lifted into the interior, where Jane and Ellen joined her—I fancy that they fought shy of the ladder-like staircase—followed by Daniel Dyer, in spite of my aunt's protestations. She herself went next, dragging with her Master Treen, who wanted to go outside, but was not allowed, and, in consequence, was moved to tears. Messrs. Eva, Poltifen, Holman and I were the only persons who made the ascent; and the conductor having indulged in some sarcastic comments on things in general and my aunt's *protégés* in particular, which nearly drove me to commit assault and battery, the 'bus was started.

We had not gone far before I had reason to doubt the genuineness of Mr. Holman's conversion. Drawing the back of his hand across his lips, he remarked to Mr. Eva—

"It do seem as if this were going to be a thirsty job. 'Tain't my notion of a holiday——"

I repeat that I make no attempt to imitate the dialect. Perceiving himself addressed, Mr. Eva put his hand up to his ear.

"Beg pardon—what were that you said?"

"I say that I be perishing for something to drink. I be faint for want of it. What's a day's pleasure if you don't never have a chance to moisten your lips?"

Although this was said in a tone of voice which caused the foot-passengers to stand and stare, the driver to start round in his seat, as if he had been struck, and the conductor to come up to inquire if anything were wrong, it failed to penetrate Mr. Eva's tympanum.

"What be that?" the old gentleman observed.

"It do seem as if I were more deaf than usual."

I touched Mr. Holman on the shoulder.

"All right—leave him alone. I'll see that you have what you want when we get down; only don't try to make him understand while we're on this 'bus."

"Thank you kindly, sir. There's no denying that a taste of rum would do me good. John Eva, he be terrible hard of hearing—terrible; and the old girl she ain't a notion of what's fit for a man."

How much the insides saw of London I cannot say. I doubt if any one on the roof saw much. In my anxiety to alight on one with room I had not troubled about the destination of the 'bus. As, however, it proved to be bound for London Bridge, I had an opportunity to point out St. Paul's Cathedral, the Bank of England, and similar places. I cannot say that my hearers seemed much struck by the privileges they were enjoying. When the vehicle drew up in the station-yard, Mr. Holman pointed with his thumb—

"There be a public over there."

I admitted that there was.

"Here's a shilling for you—mind you're quickly back. Perhaps Mr. Poltifen would like to come with you."

Mr. Poltifen declined.

"I am a teetotaller. I have never touched alcohol in any form."

I felt that Mr. Poltifen regarded both myself and my proceedings with austere displeasure. When all had alighted, my aunt, proceeding to number the party, discovered that one was missing; also, who it was.

"Where is Matthew Holman?"

"He's—he's gone across the road to—to see the time."

"To see the time! There's a clock up over the station there. What do you mean?"

"The fact is, my dear aunt, that feeling thirsty he has gone to get something to drink."

"To drink! But he signed the pledge on Monday!"

"Then, in that case, he's broken it on Wednesday. Come, let's get inside the station; we can't stop here; people will wonder who we are."

"Thomas, we will wait here for Matthew Holman. I am responsible for that man."

"Certainly, my dear aunt; but if we remain on the precise spot on which we are at present planted, we shall be prosecuted for obstruction. If you will go into the station, I will bring him to you there."

"Where are you going to take us now?"

"To the Crystal Palace."

"But—we have seen nothing of London."

"You'll see more of it when we get to the Palace. It's a wonderful place, full of the most stupendous sights; their due examination will more than occupy all the time you have to spare."

Having hustled them into the station, I went in search of Mr. Holman. "The converted drunkard" was really enjoying himself for the first time. He had already disposed of four threepennyworths of rum, and was draining the last as I came in.

"Now, sir, if you was so good as to loan me another shilling, I shouldn't wonder if I was to have a nice day, after all."

"I dare say. We'll talk about that later on. If you don't want to be lost in London, you'll come with me at once."

I scrambled them all into a train; I do not know how. It was a case of cram. Selecting an open carriage, I divided the party

among the different compartments. My aunt objected; but it had
to be. By the time that they were all in, my brow was damp with
perspiration. I looked around. Some of our fellow-passengers
wore ribbons, about eighteen inches wide, and other mysterious
things; already, at that hour of the day, they were lively. The crowd
was not what I expected.

"Is there anything on at the Palace?" I inquired of my neighbour.
He laughed, in a manner which was suggestive.

"Anything on? What ho! Where are you come from? Why, it's
the Foresters' Day. It's plain that you're not one of us. More shame
to you, sonny! Here's a chance for you to join."

Foresters' Day! I gasped. I saw trouble ahead. I began to think that
I had made a mistake in tearing off to the Crystal Palace in search of
solitude. I had expected a desert, in which my aunt's friends would
have plenty of room to knock their heads against anything they
pleased. But Foresters' Day! Was it eighty or a hundred thousand
people who were wont to assemble on that occasion? I remembered
to have seen the figures somewhere. The ladies and gentlemen
about us wore an air of such conviviality that one wondered to what
heights they would attain as the day wore on.

We had a delightful journey. It occupied between two and three
hours—or so it seemed to me. When we were not hanging on to
platforms we were being shunted, or giving the engine a rest, or
something of the kind. I know we were stopping most of the time.
But the Foresters, male and female, kept things moving, if the
train stood still. They sang songs, comic and sentimental; played
on various musical instruments, principally concertinas; whistled;
paid each other compliments; and so on. Jane and Ellen were in the
next compartment to mine—as usual, glued together; how those
two girls managed to keep stuck to each other was a marvel. Next
to them was the persevering Daniel Dyer. In front was a red-faced
gentleman, with a bright blue tie and an eighteen-inch-wide green
ribbon. He addressed himself to Mr. Dyer.

"Two nice young ladies you've got there, sir."

Judging from what he looked like at the back, I should say that
Mr. Dyer grinned. Obviously Jane and Ellen tittered: they put their
heads together in charming confusion. The red-faced gentleman
continued—

"One more than your share, haven't you, sir? You couldn't spare one of them for another gentleman? meaning me."

"You might have Jane," replied the affable Mr. Dyer.

"And which might happen to be Jane?"

Mr. Dyer supplied the information. The red-faced gentleman raised his hat. "Pleased to make your acquaintance, miss; hope we shall be better friends before the day is over."

My aunt, in the compartment behind, rose in her wrath.

"Daniel Dyer! Jane! How dare you behave in such a manner!"

The red-faced gentleman twisted himself round in his seat.

"Beg pardon, miss—was you speaking to me? If you're alone, I dare say there's another gentleman present who'll be willing to oblige. Every young lady ought to have a gent to herself on a day like this. Do me the favour of putting this to your lips; you'll find it's the right stuff."

Taking out a flat bottle, wiping it upon the sleeve of his coat, he offered it to my aunt. She succumbed.

When I found myself a struggling unit in the struggling mass on the Crystal Palace platform, my aunt caught me by the arm.

"Thomas, where have you brought us to?"

"This is the Crystal Palace, aunt."

"The Crystal Palace! It's pandemonium! Where are the members of our party?"

That was the question. My aunt collared such of them as she could lay her hands on. Matthew Holman was missing. Personally, I was not sorry. He had been "putting his lips" to more than one friendly bottle in the compartment behind mine, and was on a fair way to having a "nice day" on lines of his own. I was quite willing that he should have it by himself. But my aunt was not. She was for going at once for the police and commissioning them to hunt for and produce him then and there.

"I'm responsible for the man," she kept repeating. "I have his ticket."

"Very well, aunt—that's all right. You'll find him, or he'll find you; don't you trouble."

But she did trouble. She kept on troubling. And her cause for troubling grew more and more as the day went on. Before we were in the main building—it's a journey from the low level station through endless passages, and up countless stairs, placed at the most inconvenient intervals—Mrs. Penna was *hors de combat*. As no seat was handy she insisted on sitting down upon the floor. Passers-by made the most disagreeable comments, but she either could not or would not move. My aunt seemed half beside herself. She said to me most unfairly,

"You ought not to have brought us here on a day like this. It is evident that there are some most dissipated creatures here. I have a horror of a crowd—and with all the members of our party on my hands—and such a crowd!"

"How was I to know? I had not the faintest notion that anything particular was on till we were in the train."

"But you ought to have known. You live in London."

"It is true that I live in London. But I do not, on that account, keep an eye on what is going on at the Palace. I have something else to occupy my time. Besides, there is an easy remedy—let us leave the place at once. We might find fewer people in the Tower of London—I was never there, so I can't say—or on the top of the Monument."

"Without Matthew Holman?"

"Personally, I should say 'Yes.' He, at any rate, is in congenial company."

"Thomas!"

I wish I could reproduce the tone in which my aunt uttered my name! it would cause the edges of the sheet of paper on which I am writing to curl.

Another source of annoyance was the manner in which the red-faced gentleman persisted in sticking to us, like a limpet—as if he were a member of the party. Jane and Ellen kept themselves glued together. On Ellen's right was Daniel Dyer, and on Jane's left was the red-faced gentleman. This was a condition of affairs of which my aunt strongly disapproved. She remonstrated with the stranger, but without the least effect. I tried my hand on him, and failed. He was the best-tempered and thickest-skinned individual I ever remember to have met.

"It's this way," I explained—he needed a deal of explanation. "This lady has brought these people for a little pleasure excursion to town, for the day only; and, as these young ladies are in her sole charge, she feels herself responsible for them. So would you just mind leaving us?"

It seemed that he did mind; though he showed no signs of having his feelings hurt by the suggestion, as some persons might have done.

"Don't you worry, governor; I'll help her look after 'em. I've looked after a few people in my time, so the young lady can trust me—can't you, miss?"

Jane giggled. My impression is that my aunt felt like shaking her. But just then I made a discovery.

"Hallo! Where's the youngster?"

My aunt twirled herself round.

"Stephen! Goodness! where has that boy gone to?"

Jane looked through the glass which ran all along one side of the corridor.

"Why, miss, there's Stephen Treen over in that crowd there."

"Go and fetch him back this instant."

I believe that my aunt spoke without thinking. It did seem to me that Jane showed an almost criminal eagerness to obey her. Off she flew into the grounds, through the great door which was wide open close at hand, with Ellen still glued to her arm, and Daniel Dyer at her heels, and the red-faced gentleman after him. Almost in a moment they became melted, as it were, into the crowd and were lost to view. My aunt peered after them through her glasses.

"I can't see Stephen Treen—can you?"

"No, aunt, I can't. I doubt if Jane could, either."

"Thomas! What do you mean? She said she did."

"Ah! there are people who'll say anything. I think you'll find that, for a time, at any rate, you've got three more members of the party off your hands."

"Thomas! How can you talk like that? After bringing us to this dreadful place! Go after those benighted girls at once, and bring them back, and that wretched Daniel Dyer, and that miserable child, and Matthew Holman, too."

It struck me, from her manner, that my aunt was hovering on the verge of hysterics. When I was endeavouring to explain how it was that I did not see my way to start off, then and there, in a sort of general hunt, an official, sauntering up, took a bird's-eye view of Mrs. Penna.

"Hallo, old lady what's the matter with you? Aren't you well?"

"No, I be not well—I be dying. Take me home and let me die upon my bed."

"So bad as that, is it? What's the trouble?"

"I've been up all night and all day, and little to eat and naught to drink, and I be lame."

"Lame, are you?" The official turned to my aunt. "You know you didn't ought to bring a lame old lady into a crowd like this."

"I didn't bring her. My nephew brought us all."

"Then the sooner, I should say, your nephew takes you all away again, the better."

The official took himself off. Mr. Poltifen made a remark. His tone was a trifle sour.

"I cannot say that I think we are spending a profitable and pleasurable day in London. I understood that the object which we had in view was to make researches into Dickens's London, or I should not have brought my books."

The "parish idiot" began to moan.

"I be that hungry—I be! I be!"

"Here," I cried: "here's half-a-crown for you. Go to that refreshment-stall and cram yourself with penny buns to bursting point."

Off started Sammy Trevenna; he had sense enough to catch my meaning. My aunt called after him.

"Sammy! You mustn't leave us. Wait until we come."

But Sammy declined. When, hurrying after him, catching him by the shoulder, she sought to detain him, he positively showed signs of fight.

Oh! it was a delightful day! Enjoyable from start to finish. Somehow I got Mrs. Penna, with my aunt and the remnant, into the main building and planted them on chairs, and provided them with buns and similar dainties, and instructed them not, on any pretext, to budge from where they were until I returned with the truants, of whom, straightway, I went in search. I do not mind admitting that I commenced by paying a visit to a refreshment-bar upon my own account—I needed something to support me. Nor, having comforted the inner man, did I press forward on my quest with undue haste. Exactly as I expected, I found Jane and Ellen in a sheltered alcove in the grounds, with Daniel Dyer on one side, the red-faced gentleman on the other, and Master Stephen Treen nowhere to be seen. The red-faced gentleman's friendship with Jane had advanced so rapidly that when I suggested her prompt return to my aunt, he considered himself entitled to object with such vehemence that he actually took his coat off and invited me to fight. But I was not to be browbeaten by him; and, having made it clear that if he attempted to follow I should call the police, I marched off in triumph with my prizes, only to discover that the young women had tongues of their own, with examples of whose capacity they favoured me as we proceeded. I believe that if I had been my aunt, I should, then and there, have boxed their ears.

My aunt received us with a countenance of such gloom that I immediately perceived that something frightful must have occurred.

"Thomas!" she exclaimed, "I have been robbed!"

"Robbed? My dear aunt! Of what—your umbrella?"

"Of everything!"

"Of everything? I hope it's not so bad as that."

"It is. I have been robbed of purse, money, tickets, everything, down to my pocket-handkerchief and bunch of keys."

It was the fact—she had. Her pocket, containing all she possessed—out of Cornwall—had been cut out of her dress and carried clean away. It was a very neat piece of work, as the police agreed when we laid the case before them. They observed that, of course, they would do their best, but they did not think there was much likelihood of any of the stolen property being regained; adding that, in a crowd like that, people ought to look after their pockets, which was cold comfort for my aunt, and rounded the day off nicely.

Ticketless, moneyless, returning to Cornwall that night was out of the question. I put "the party" up. My aunt had my bed, Mrs. Penna was accommodated in the same room, the others somewhere and somehow. I camped out. In the morning, the telegraph being put in motion, funds were forthcoming, and "the party" started on its homeward way. The railway authorities would listen to nothing about lost excursion tickets. My aunt had to pay full fare—twenty-one and twopence halfpenny—for each. I can still see her face as she paid.

Two days afterwards Master Stephen Treen and Mr. Matthew Holman were reported found by the police, Mr. Holman showing marked signs of a distinct relapse from grace. My aunt had to pay for their being sent home. The next day she received, through the post, in an unpaid envelope, the lost excursion tickets. No comment accompanied them. Her visiting-card was in the purse; evidently the thief, having no use for old excursion tickets, had availed himself of it to send them back to her. She has them to this day, and never looks at them without a qualm. That was her first excursion; she tells me that never, under any circumstances, will she try another.

The Irregularity of the Juryman

CHAPTER I

THE JURYMAN IS STARTLED

His first feeling was one of annoyance. All-round annoyance. Comprehensive disgust. He did not want to be a juryman. He flattered himself that he had something better to do with his time. Half-a-dozen matters required his attention. Instead of which, here he was obtruding himself into matters in which he did not take the faintest interest. Actually dragged into interference with other people's most intimate affairs. And in that stuffy court. And it had been a principle of his life never to concern himself with what was no business of his. Talk about the system of trial by jury being a bulwark of the Constitution! At that moment he had no opinion of the Constitution; or its bulwarks either.

Then there were his colleagues. He had never been associated with eleven persons with whom he felt himself to be less in sympathy. The fellow they had chosen to be foreman he felt convinced was a cheesemonger. He looked it. The others looked, if anything, worse. Not, he acknowledged, that there was anything inherently wrong in being a cheesemonger. Still, one did not want to sit cheek by jowl with persons of that sort for an indefinite length of time. And there were cases—particularly in the Probate Court—which lasted days; even weeks. If he were in for one of those! The perspiration nearly stood on his brow at the horror of the thought.

What was the case about? What was that inarticulate person saying? Philip Roland knew nothing about courts—and did not want to—but he took it for granted that the gentleman in a wig and gown, with his hands folded over his portly stomach, was counsel for one side or the other—though he had not the slightest notion which. He had no idea how they managed things in places of this sort. As he eyed him he felt that he was against him anyhow. If he were paid to speak, why did not the man speak up?

By degrees, for sheer want of something else, Mr. Roland found that he was listening. After all, the man was audible. He seemed capable, also, of making his meaning understood. So it was about a will, was it? He might have taken that for granted. He always had had the impression that the Probate Court was the place for wills. It seemed that somebody had left a will; and this will was in favour of the portly gentleman's client; and was as sound, as equitable, as admirable a legal instrument as ever yet was executed; and how, therefore, anyone could have anything to say against it surprised the portly gentleman to such a degree that he had to stop to wipe his forehead with a red silk pocket-handkerchief.

The day was warm. Mr. Roland was not fond of listening to speeches. And this one was—well, weighty. And about something for which he did not care two pins. His attention wandered. It strayed perilously near the verge of a dose. In fact, it must have strayed right over the verge. Because the next thing he understood was that one of his colleagues was digging his elbow into his side, and proffering the information that they were going to lunch. He felt a little bewildered. He could not think how it had happened. It was not his habit to go to sleep in the morning. As he trooped after his fellows he was visited by a hazy impression that that wretched jury system was at the bottom of it all.

They were shown into an ill-ventilated room. Someone asked him what he would have to eat. He told them to bring him what they had. They brought some hot boiled beef and carrots. The sight of it nearly made him ill. His was a dainty appetite. Hot boiled beef on such a day, in such a place, after such a morning, was almost the final straw. He could not touch it.

His companion attacked his plate with every appearance of relish. He made a hearty meal. Possibly he had kept awake. He commented on the fashion in which Mr. Roland had done his duty to his Queen and country.

"Shouldn't think you were able to pronounce much of an opinion on the case so far as it has gone, eh?"

"My good sir, the judge will instruct us as to our duty. If we follow his instructions we shan't go wrong."

"You think, then, that we are only so many automata, and that the judge has but to pull the strings."

Mr. Roland looked about him, contempt in his eye.

"It would be fortunate, perhaps, if we were automata."

"Then I can only say that we take diametrically opposite views of our office. I maintain that it is our duty to listen to the evidence, to weigh it carefully, and to record our honest convictions in the face of all the judges whoever sat upon the Bench."

Mr. Roland was silent. He was not disposed to enter into an academical discussion with an individual who evidently had a certain command of language. Others, however, showed themselves to be not so averse. The luncheon interval was enlivened by some observations on the jury system which lawyers—had any been present—would have found instructive. There were no actual quarrels. But some of the arguments were of the nature of repartees. Possibly it was owing to the beef and carrots.

They re-entered the court. The case recommenced. Mr. Roland had a headache. He was cross. His disposition was to return a verdict against everything and everyone, as his neighbour had put it, "in the face of all the judges who ever sat upon the Bench." But this time he did pay some attention to what was going on.

It appeared, in spite of the necessity which the portly gentleman had been under to use his red silk pocket-handkerchief, that there were objections to the will he represented. It was not easy at that stage to pick up the lost threads, but from what Mr. Roland could gather it seemed it was asserted that a later will had been made, which was still in existence. Evidence was given by persons who had been present at the execution of that will; by the actual witnesses to the testator's signature; by the lawyer who had drawn the will. And then—!

Then there stepped into the witness-box a person whose appearance entirely changed Mr. Roland's attitude towards the proceedings; so that, in the twinkling of an eye, he passed from bored indifference to the keenest and liveliest interest. It was a young woman. She gave her name as Delia Angel. Her address as Barkston Gardens, South Kensington. At sight of her things began to hum inside Mr. Roland's brain. Where had he seen her before? It all came back in a flash. How could he have forgotten her, even for a moment, when from that day to this she had been continually present to his mind's eye?

It was the girl of the train. She had travelled with him from Nice to Dijon in the same carriage, which most of the way they had had to themselves. What a journey it was! And what a girl! During those fast-fleeting hours—on that occasion they had fled fast—they had discussed all subjects from Alpha to Omega. He had approached closer to terms of friendship with a woman than he had ever done in the whole course of his life before—or since. He was so taken aback by the encounter, so wrapped in recollections of those pleasant hours, that for a time he neglected to listen to what she was saying. When he did begin to listen he pricked up his ears still higher.

It was in her favour the latest will had been made—at least, partly. She had just returned from laying the testator in the cemetery in Nice when he met her in the train—actually! He recalled her deep mourning. The impression she had given him was that she had lately lost a friend. She was even carrying the will in question with her at the time. Then she began to make a series of statements which brought Mr. Roland's heart up into his mouth.

"Tell us," suggested counsel, "what happened in the train."

She paused as if to collect her thoughts. Then told a little story which interested at least one of her hearers more than anything he had ever listened to.

"I had originally intended to stop in Paris. On the way, however, I decided not to do so but to go straight through."

Mr. Roland remembered he had told her he was going, and wondered; but he resolved to postpone his wonder till she had finished.

"When we were nearing Dijon I made up my mind to send a telegram to the concierge asking her to address all letters to me in town. When we reached the station I got out of the train to do so. In the compartment in which I had travelled was a gentleman. I asked him to keep an eye on my bag till I returned. He said he would. On the platform I met some friends. I stopped to talk to them. The time must have gone quicker than I supposed, because when I reached the telegraph office I found I had only a minute or two to spare. I scribbled the telegram. As I turned I slipped and fell—I take it because of the haste I was in. As I fell my head struck upon something; because the next thing I realized was that I was lying on a couch in a strange room, feeling very queer indeed. I did ask, I believe, what had become of the train. They told me it was gone. I understand that during the remainder of the day, and through the night, I continued more or less unconscious. When next day I came back to myself it was too late. I found my luggage awaiting me at Paris. But of the bag, or of the gentleman with whom I left it in charge, I have heard nothing since. I have advertised, tried every means my solicitor advised; but up to the present without result."

"And the will," observed counsel, "was in that bag?"

"It was."

Mr. Roland had listened to the lady's narrative with increasing amazement. He remembered her getting out at Dijon; that she had left a bag behind. That she had formally intrusted it to his charge he did not remember. He recalled the anxiety with which he watched for her return; his keen disappointment when he still saw nothing of her as the train steamed out of the station. So great was his chagrin that it almost amounted to dismay. He had had such a good time; had taken it for granted that it would continue for at least a few more hours, and perhaps—perhaps all sorts of things. Now, without notice, on the instant, she had gone out of his life as she had come into it. He had seen her talking to her friends. Possibly she had joined herself to them. Well, if she was that sort of person, let her go!

As for the bag, it had escaped his recollection that there was such a thing. And possibly would have continued to do so had it not persisted in staring at him mutely from the opposite seat. So she had left it behind? Serve her right. It was only a rubbishing hand-bag. Pretty old, too. It seemed that feather-headed young women could not be even depended upon to look after their own rubbish. She would come rushing up to the carriage window at one of the stations. Or he would see her at Paris. Then she could have the thing. But he did not see her. To be frank, as they neared Paris, half obliviously he crammed it with his travelling cap into his kit-bag, and to continue on the line of candour—ignored its existence till he found it there in town.

And in it was the will! The document on which so much hinged—especially for her! The bone of contention which all this pother was about. Among all that she said this was the statement which took him most aback. Because, without the slightest desire to impugn in any detail the lady's veracity, he had the best of reasons for knowing that she had—well—made a mistake.

If he had not good reason to know it, who had? He clearly called to mind the sensation, almost of horror, with which he had recognised that the thing was in his kit-bag. Half-a-dozen courses which he ought to have pursued occurred to him—too late. He ought to have handed it over to the guard of the train; to the station-master; to the lost property office. In short, he ought to have done anything except bring it with him in his bag to town. But since he had brought it, the best thing to do seemed to be to ascertain if it contained anything which would be a clue to its owner.

It was a small affair, perhaps eight inches long. Of stamped brown leather. Well worn. Original cost possibly six or seven shillings. Opened by pressing a spring lock. Contents: Four small keys on a piece of ribbon; two pocket-handkerchiefs, each with an embroidered D in the corner; the remains of a packet of chocolate; half a cedar lead-pencil; a pair of shoe-laces. And that was all. He had turned that bag upside down upon his bed, and was prepared to go into the witness-box and swear that there was nothing else left inside. At least he was almost prepared to swear. For since here was Miss Delia Angel—how well the name fitted the owner!— positively affirming that among its contents was the document on which for all he knew all her worldly wealth depended, what was he to think?

The bag had continued in his possession until a week or two ago. Then one afternoon his sister, Mrs. Tranmer, had come to his rooms, and having purchased a packet of hairpins, or something of the kind, had wanted something to put them in. Seeing the bag in the corner of one of his shelves, in spite of his protestations she had snatched it up, and insisted on annexing it to help her carry home her ridiculous purchase. Its contents—as described above—

he retained. But the bag! Surely Agatha was not such an idiot, such a dishonest creature, as to allow property which was not hers to pass for a moment out of her hands.

During the remainder of Miss Angel's evidence—so far as it went that day—one juryman, both mentally and physically, was in a state of dire distress. What was he to do? He was torn in a dozen different ways. Would it be etiquette for a person in his position to spring to his feet and volunteer to tell his story? He would probably astonish the Court. But—what would the Court say to him? Who had ever heard of a witness in the jury-box? He could not but suspect that, at the very least, such a situation would be in the highest degree irregular. And, in any case, what could he do? Give the lady the lie? It will have been perceived that his notions of the responsibilities of a juryman were his own, and it is quite within the range of possibility that he had already made up his mind which way his verdict should go; whether the will was in the bag or not—and "in the face of all the judges who ever sat upon the Bench."

The bag! the bag! Where was it? If, for once in a way, Agatha had shown herself to be possessed of a grain of the common sense with which he had never credited her!

At the conclusion of Miss Angel's examination in chief the portly gentleman asked to be allowed to postpone his cross-examination to the morning. On which, by way of showing its entire acquiescence, the Court at once adjourned.

And off pelted one of the jurymen in search of the bag.

CHAPTER II

MRS. TRANMER IS STARTLED

MRS. TRANMER was just going up to dress for dinner when in burst her brother. Mr. Roland was, as a rule, one of the least excitable of men. His obvious agitation therefore surprised her the more. Her feelings took a characteristic form of expression—to her, an attentive eye to the proprieties of costume was the whole duty of a Christian.

"Philip!—what have you done to your tie?"

Mr. Roland mechanically put up his hand towards the article referred to; returning question for question.

"Agatha, where's that bag?"

"Bag? My good man, you're making your tie crookeder!"

"Bother the tie!" Mrs. Tranmer started: Philip was so seldom interjectional. "Do you hear me ask where that bag is?"

"My dear brother, before you knock me down, will you permit me to suggest that your tie is still in a shocking condition?"

He gave her one look—such a look! Then he went to the looking-glass and arranged his tie. Then he turned to her.

"Will that do?"

"It is better."

"Now, will you give me that bag—at once?"

"Bag? What bag?"

"You know very well what bag I mean—the one you took from my room."

"The one I took from your room?"

"I told you not to take it. I warned you it wasn't mine. I informed you that I was its involuntary custodian. And yet, in spite of all I could say—of all I could urge, with a woman's lax sense of the difference between *meum* and *tuum*, you insisted on removing it from my custody. The sole reparation you can make is to return it at once—upon the instant."

She observed him with growing amazement—as well she might. She subsided into an armchair.

"May I ask you to inform me from what you're suffering now?"

He was a little disposed towards valetudinarianism, and was apt to imagine himself visited by divers diseases. He winced.

"Agatha, the only thing from which I am suffering at this moment is—is——"

"Yes; is what?"

"A feeling of irritation at my own weakness in allowing myself to be persuaded by you to act in opposition to my better judgment."

"Dear me! You must be ill. That you are ill is shown by the fact that your tie is crooked again. Don't consider my feelings, and pray present yourself in my drawing-room in any condition you choose. But perhaps you will be so good as to let me know if there is any sense in the stuff you have been talking about a bag."

"Agatha, you remember that bag you took from my room?"

"That old brown leather thing?"

"It was made of brown leather—a week or two ago?"

"A week or two? Why, it was months ago."

"My dear Agatha, I do assure you——"

"Please don't let us argue. I tell you it was months ago."

"I told you not to take it——"

"You told me not to take it? Why, you pressed it on me. I didn't care to be seen with such a rubbishing old thing; but you took it off your shelf and said it would do very well. So, to avoid argument, as I generally do, I let you have your way."

"I—I don't want to be rude, but a—a more outrageous series of statements I never heard. I told you distinctly that it wasn't mine."

"You did nothing of the sort. Of course I took it for granted that such a disreputable article, which evidently belonged to a woman, was not your property. But as I had no wish to pry into your private affairs I was careful not to inquire how such a curiosity found its way upon your shelves."

"Agatha, your—your insinuations——"

"I insinuate nothing. I only want to know what this fuss is about. As I wish to dress for dinner, perhaps you'll tell me in a couple of words."

"Agatha, where's that bag?"

"How should I know?"

"Haven't you got it?"

"Got it? Do you suppose I have a museum in which I preserve rubbish of the kind?"

"But—what have you done with it?"

"You might as well ask me what I've done with last year's gloves."

"Agatha—think! More hinges upon this than you have any conception. What did you do with that bag?"

"Since you are so insistent—and I must say, Philip, that your conduct is most peculiar—I will think, or I'll try to. I believe I gave the bag to Jane. Or else to Mrs. Pettigrew's little girl. Or to my needle-woman—to carry home some embroidery she was mending for me; I am most particular about embroidery, especially when it's good. Or to the curate's wife, for a jumble sale. Or I might have given it to someone else. Or I might have lost it. Or done something else with it."

"Did you look inside?"

"Of course I did. I must have done. Though I don't remember doing anything of the kind."

"Was there anything in it?"

"Do you mean when you gave it me? If there was I never saw it. Am I going to be accused of felony?"

"Agatha, I believe you have ruined me."

"Ruined you! Philip, what nonsense are you talking? I insist upon your telling me what you mean. What has that wretched old bag, which would have certainly been dear at twopence, to do with either you or me?"

"I will endeavour to explain. I believe that I stood towards that bag in what the law regards as a fiduciary relation. I was responsible for its safety. Its loss will fall on me."

"The loss of a twopenny-halfpenny bag?"

"It is not a question of the bag, but of its contents."

"What were its contents?"

"It contained a will."

"A will?—a real will? Do you mean to say that you gave me that bag without breathing a word about there being a will inside?"

"I didn't know myself until to-day."

By degrees the tale was told. Mrs. Tranmer's amazement grew and grew. She seemed to have forgotten all about its being time to dress for dinner.

"And you are a juryman?"

"I am."

"And you actually have the bag on which the whole case turns?"

"I wish I had."

"But was the will inside?"

"I never saw it."

"Nor I. It was quite an ordinary bag, and if it had been we must have seen it. A will isn't written on a scrappy piece of paper which could have been overlooked. Philip, the will wasn't in the bag. That young woman's an impostor."

"I don't believe it for a moment—not for a single instant. I am convinced that she supposes herself to be speaking the absolute truth. Even granting that she is mistaken, in what position do I stand? I cannot go and say, 'I have lost your bag, but it doesn't matter, for the will was not inside.' Would she not be entitled to reply, 'Return me the bag in the condition in which I intrusted it to your keeping, and I will show that you are wrong'? It will not be enough for me to repeat that I have not the bag; my sister threw it into her dust-hole."

"Philip!"

"May she not retort, 'Then, for all the misfortunes which the loss of the bag brings on me, you are responsible'? The letter of the law might acquit me. My conscience never would. Agatha, I fear you have done me a serious injury."

"Don't talk like that! Under the circumstances you had no right to give me the bag at all."

"You are wrong; I did not give it you. On the contrary, I implored you not to take it. But you insisted."

"Philip, how can you say such a wicked thing? I remember exactly what happened. I had been buying some veils. I was saying to you how I hated carrying parcels, even small ones——"

"Agatha, don't let us enter into this matter now. You may be called upon to make your statement in another place. I can only hope that our statements will not clash."

For the first time Mrs. Tranmer showed symptoms of genuine anxiety.

"You don't mean to say that I'm to be dragged into a court of law because of that twopenny-halfpenny bag?"

"I think it possible. What else can you expect? I must tell this unfortunate young lady how the matter stands. I apprehend that I shall have to repeat my statement in open court, and that you will be called upon to supplement it. I also take it that no stone will be left unturned to induce you to give a clear and satisfactory account of what became of the bag after it passed into your hands."

"My goodness! And I know no more what became of it than anything."

"I must go to Miss Angel at once."

"Philip!"

"I must. Consider my position. I cannot enter the court as a juryman again without explaining to someone how I am placed. The irregularity would transgress all limits. I must communicate with Miss Angel immediately; she will communicate with her advisers, who will no doubt communicate with you."

"My goodness!" repeated Mrs. Tranmer to herself after he had gone. Still she did not proceed upstairs to dress.

CHAPTER III

THE PLAINTIFF IS STARTLED

MISS ANGEL was dressed for dinner. She was in the drawing-room with other guests of the hotel, waiting for the gong to sound, when she was informed that a gentleman wished to see her. On the heels of the information entered the gentleman himself. It seemed that Mr. Roland had only eyes for her. As if oblivious of others he moved rapidly forward. She regarded him askance. He, perceiving her want of recognition, introduced himself in a fashion of his own.

"Miss Angel, I'm the man who travelled with you from Nice to Dijon."

At once her face lighted up. Her eyes became as if they were illumined.

"Of course! To think that we should have met again! At last!"

To judge from certain comments which were made by those around one could not but suspect that Miss Angel's story was a theme of general interest. As a matter of fact, they were being entertained by her account of the day's proceedings at the very moment of Mr. Roland's entry. People in these small "residential" hotels are sometimes so extremely friendly. Altogether unexpectedly Mr. Roland found himself an object of interest to quite a number of total strangers. He was not the sort of man to shine in such a position, particularly as it was only too plain that Miss Angel misunderstood the situation.

"Mr. Roland, you are like a messenger from Heaven. I have prayed for you to come, so you must be one. And at this time of all times—just when you are most wanted! Really your advent must be miraculous."

"Ye-es." The gentleman glanced around. "Might I speak to you for a moment in private?"

She regarded him a little quizzically.

"Everybody here knows my whole strange history; my hopes and fears; all about me. You needn't be afraid to add another chapter to the tale, especially since you have arrived at so opportune a moment."

"Precisely." His tone was expressive of something more than doubt. "Still, if you don't mind, I think I would rather say a few words to you alone."

The bystanders commenced to withdraw with some little show of awkwardness, as if, since the whole business had so far been public, they rather resented the element of secrecy. The gong sounding, Miss Angel was moved to proffer a suggestion.

"Come dine with me. We can talk when we are eating."

He shrank back with what was almost a gesture of horror.

"Excuse me—you are very kind—I really couldn't. If you prefer it, I will wait here until you have dined."

"Do you imagine that I could wait to hear what you have to say till after dinner? You don't know me if you do. The people are going. We shall have the room all to ourselves. My dinner can wait."

The people went. They did have the room to themselves. She began to overwhelm him with her thanks, which, conscience-stricken, he endeavoured to parry.

"I cannot tell you how grateful I am to you for coming in this spontaneous fashion—at this moment, too, of my utmost need."

"Just so."

"If you only knew how I have searched for you high and low, and now, after all, you appear in the very nick of time."

"Exactly."

"It would almost seem as if you had chosen the dramatic moment; for this is the time of all times when your presence on the scene was most desired."

"It's very good of you to say so;—but if you will allow me to interrupt you—I am afraid I am not entitled to your thanks. The fact is, I—I haven't the bag."

"You haven't the bag?"

Although he did not dare to look at her he was conscious that the fashion of her countenance had changed. At the knowledge a chill seemed to penetrate to the very marrow in his bones.

"I—I fear I haven't."

"You had it—I left it in your charge!"

"Unfortunately, that is the most unfortunate part of the whole affair."

"What do you mean?"

He explained. For the second time that night he told his tale. It had not rolled easily off his tongue at the first time of telling. He found the repetition a task of exquisite difficulty. In the presence of that young lady it seemed so poor a story. Especially in the mood in which she was. She continually interrupted him with question and comment—always of the most awkward kind. By the time he had made an end of telling he felt as if most of the vitality had gone out of him. She was silent for some seconds—dreadful seconds; then she drew a long breath, and she said:—

"So I am to understand, am I, that your sister has lost the bag— my bag?"

"I fear that it would seem so, for the present."

"For the present? What do you mean by for the present? Are you suggesting that she will be able to find it during the next few hours? Because after that it will be too late."

"I—I should hardly like to go so far as that, knowing my sister."

"Knowing your sister? I see. Of course I am perfectly aware that I had no right to intrust the bag to your charge even for a single instant: to you, an entire stranger; though I had no notion that you were the kind of stranger you seem to be. Nor had I any right to slip, and fall, and become unconscious and so allow that train to leave me behind. Still—it does seem a little hard. Don't you think it does?"

"I can only hope that the loss was not of such serious importance as you would seem to infer."

"It depends on what you call serious. It probably means the difference between affluence and beggary. That's all."

"On one point you must allow me to make an observation. The will was not in the bag."

"The will was not in the bag!"

There was a quality in the lady's voice which made Mr. Roland quail. He hastened to proceed.

"I have here all which it contained."

He produced a neat packet, in which were discovered four keys, two handkerchiefs, scraps of what might be chocolate, a piece of pencil, a pair of brown shoe-laces. She regarded the various objects with unsympathetic eyes.

"It also contained the will."

"I can only assure you that I saw nothing of it; nor my sister either. Surely a thing of that kind could hardly have escaped our observation."

"In that bag, Mr. Roland, is a secret pocket; intended to hold— secure from observation—bank-notes, letters, or private papers. The will was there. Did you or your sister, in the course of your investigations, light upon the secret of that pocket?"

Something of the sort he had feared. He rubbed his hands together, almost as if he were wringing them.

"Miss Angel, I can only hint at my sense of shame; at my consciousness of my own deficiencies; and can only reiterate my sincere hope that the consequences of your loss may still be less serious than you suppose."

"I imagine that nothing worse than my ruin will result."

"I will do my best to guard against that."

"You!—what can you do—now?"

"I am at least a juryman."

"A juryman?"

"I am one of the jury which is trying the case."

"You!" Her eyes opened wider. "Of course! I thought I had seen you somewhere before today! That's where it was! How stupid I am! Is it possible?" Exactly what she meant by her disjointed remarks was not clear. He did not suspect her of an intention to flatter. "And you propose to influence your colleagues to give a decision in my favour?"

"You may smile, but since unanimity is necessary I can, at any rate, make sure that it is not given against you."

"I see. Your idea is original. And perhaps a little daring. But before we repose our trust on such an eventuality I should like to do something. First of all, I should like to interview your sister."

"If you please."

"I do please. I think it possible that when I explain to her how the matter is with me her memory may be moved to the recollection of what she did with my poor bag. Do you think I could see her if I went to her at once?"

"Quite probably."

"Then you and I will go together. If you will wait for me to put a hat on, in two minutes I will return to you here."

CHAPTER IV

TWO CABMEN ARE STARTLED

HATS are uncertain quantities. Sometimes they represent ten minutes, sometimes twenty, sometimes sixty. It is hardly likely that any woman ever "put a hat on" in two. Miss Angel was quick. Still, before she reappeared Mr. Roland had arrived at something which resembled a mental resolution. He hurled it at her as soon as she was through the doorway.

"Miss Angel, before we start upon our errand I should like to make myself clear to you at least upon one point. I am aware that I am responsible for the destruction of your hopes—morally and actually. I should like you therefore to understand that, should the case go against you, you will find me personally prepared to make good your loss so far as in my power lies. I should, of course, regard it as my simple duty."

She smiled at him, really nicely.

"You are Quixotic, Mr. Roland. Though it is very good of you all the same. But before we talk about such things I should like to see your sister, if you don't mind."

At this hint he moved to the door. As they went towards the hall he said:—

"I hope you are building no high hopes upon your interview with my sister. I know my sister, you understand; and though she is the best woman in the world, I fear that she attached so little importance to the bag that she has allowed its fate to escape her memory altogether."

"One does allow unimportant matters to escape one's memory, doesn't one?"

Her words were ambiguous. He wondered what she meant. It was she who started the conversation when they were in the cab.

"Would it be very improper to ask what you think of the case so far as it has gone?"

He was sensible that it would be most improper. But, then, there had been so much impropriety about his proceedings already that perhaps he felt that a little more or less did not matter. He answered as if he had followed the proceedings with unflagging attention.

"I think your case is very strong."

"Really? Without the bag?"

It was a simple fact that he had but the vaguest notion of what had been stated upon the other side. Had he been called upon to give even a faint outline of what the case for the opposition really was he would have been unable to do so. But so trivial an accident did not prevent his expressing a confident opinion.

"Certainly; as it stands."

"But won't it look odd if I am unable to produce the will?"

Mr. Roland pondered; or pretended to.

"No doubt the introduction of the will would bring the matter to an immediate conclusion. But, as it is, your own statement is so clear that it seems to me to be incontrovertible."

"Truly? And do your colleagues think so also?"

He knew no more what his "colleagues" thought than the man in the moon. But that was of no consequence.

"I think you may take it for granted that they are not all idiots. I believe, indeed, that it is generally admitted that in most juries there is a preponderance of common sense."

She sighed, a little wistfully, as if the prospect presented by his words was not so alluring as she would have desired. She kept her eyes fixed on his face—a fact of which he was conscious.

"Oh, I wish I could find the will!"

While he was still echoing her wish with all his heart a strange thing happened.

The cabman turned a corner. It was dark. He did not think it necessary to slacken his pace. Nor, perhaps, to keep a keen look-out for what was advancing in an opposite direction. Tactics which a brother Jehu carefully followed. Another hansom was coming round that corner too. Both drivers, perceiving that their zeal was excessive, endeavoured to avoid disaster by dragging their steeds back upon their haunches. Too late! On the instant they were in collision. In that brief, exciting moment Mr. Roland saw that the sole occupant of the other hansom was a lady. He knew her. She knew him.

"It's Agatha!" he cried.

"Philip!" came in answer.

Before either had a chance to utter another word hansoms, riders, and drivers were on the ground. Fortunately the horses kept their heads, being possibly accustomed to little diversions of the kind. They merely continued still, as if waiting to see what would happen next. In consequence he was able to scramble out himself, and to assist Miss Angel in following him.

"Are you hurt?" he asked.

"I don't think so; not a bit."

"Excuse me, but my sister's in the other cab."

"Your sister!"

He did not wait to hear. He was off like a flash. From the ruins of the other vehicle—which seemed to have suffered most in the contact—he gradually extricated the dishevelled Mrs. Tranmer. She seemed to be in a sad state. He led her to a chemist's shop, which luckily stood open close at hand, accompanied by Miss Angel and a larger proportion of the crowd than the proprietor appeared disposed to welcome. He repeated the inquiry he had addressed to Miss Angel.

"Are you hurt?"

This time the response was different.

"Of course I'm hurt. I'm shaken all to pieces; every bone in my body's broken; there's not a scrap of life left in me. Do you suppose I'm the sort of creature who can be thrown about like a shuttlecock and not be hurt?"

Something, however, in her tone suggested that her troubles might after all be superficial.

"If you will calm yourself, Agatha, perhaps you may find that your injuries are not so serious as you imagine."

"They couldn't be, or I should be dead. The worst of it is that this all comes of my flying across London to take that twopenny-halfpenny bag to that ridiculous young woman of yours."

He started.

"The bag! Agatha! have you found it?"

"Of course I've found it. How do you suppose I could be tearing along with it in my hands if I hadn't?" The volubility of her utterance pointed to a rapid return to convalescence. "It seems that I gave it to Jane, or she says that I did, though I have no recollection of doing anything of the kind. As she had already plenty of better bags of her own, probably most of them mine, she didn't want it, so she gave it to her sister-in-law. Directly I heard that, I dragged her into a cab and tore off to the woman's house. The woman was out, and, of course, she'd taken the bag with her to do some shopping. I packed off her husband and half-a-dozen children to scour the neighbourhood for her in different directions, and I thought I should have a fit while I waited. The moment she appeared I snatched the bag from her hand, flung myself back into the cab—and now the cab has flung me out into the road, and heaven only knows if I shall ever be the same woman I was before I started."

"And the bag! Where is it?"

She looked about her with bewildered eyes.

"The bag? I haven't the faintest notion. I must have left it in the cab."

Mr. Roland rushed out into the street. He gained the vehicle in which Mrs. Tranmer had travelled. It seemed that one of the shafts had been wrenched right off, but they had raised it to what was as nearly an upright position as circumstances permitted.

"Where's the hand-bag which was in that cab?"

"Hand-bag?" returned the driver. "I ain't seen no hand-bag. So far I ain't hardly seen the bloomin' cab."

A voice was heard at Mr. Roland's elbows.

"This here bloke picked up a bag—I see him do it."

Mr. Roland's grip fastened on the shoulder of the "bloke" alluded to, an undersized youth apparently not yet in his teens. The young gentleman resented the attention.

" 'Old 'ard, guv'nor! I picked up the bag, that's all right; I was just a-wondering who it might belong to."

"It belongs to the lady who was riding in the cab. Kindly hand it over."

It was "handed over"; borne back into the chemist's shop; proffered to Miss Angel.

"I believe that this is the missing bag, apparently not much the worse for its various adventures."

"It is the bag." She opened it. Apparently it was empty. But on her manipulating an unseen fastening an inner pocket was disclosed. From it she took a folded paper. "And here is the will!"

CHAPTER V

THE COURT IS STARTLED

THEY dined together—it was still not too late to dine—in a private room at the Piccadilly Restaurant. Mrs. Tranmer found that she was, indeed, not irreparably damaged; and by the time she could be induced to look over the fact that she was not what she called "dressed" she began to enjoy herself uncommonly well. Delia Angel was in the highest spirits, which, on the whole, was not surprising. The recovery of the bag and the will had transformed the world into a rose-coloured Paradise. The evening was one continuous delight. As for Philip Roland—his mood was akin to Miss Angel's. Everything which had begun badly was ending well. He was the host. The meal did credit to his choice—and to the cook. The wine was worthy of the toasts they drank. There was one toast which was not formally proposed, and of which, even in his heart he did not dream, but whose presence was answerable for not a little of the rapture which crowned the feast—"The Birth of Romance." His life had been tolerably commonplace and grey. For the first time that night Romance had entered into it. It was just possible that, maintaining the place it had gained, it would continue to the end. So might it be; for sure, the Spirit is the best of company.

After dinner the three journeyed together to Miss Angel's solicitor. He lived in town, not far away from where they were, and though the hour was uncanonical it was not so very late. And though he was amazed at being required to do business at such a season, the tale they had to tell amazed him more. Nor was he indisposed to commend them for coming straight away to him with it at once.

He heard them to an end. Then he looked at the bag; then at the will. Then once more at the bag; then at the will again. Then he smoothed his chin.

"It seems to me—speaking without prejudice—that this ends the matter. In the face of this the other side is left without a leg to stand upon. With this in your hand"—he was tapping the will with his finger-tip—"I cannot but think, Miss Angel, that you must carry all before you."

"So I should imagine."

He contemplated Mr. Roland.

"So you, sir, are one of the jury. As at present advised, I cannot see how, in the course of action which you have pursued, blame can in any way be attached to you. But, at the same time, I am bound to observe that in the course of a somewhat lengthy experience I cannot recall a single instance of a juryman—an actual juryman—playing such a part as you have done. In fact, not to put too fine a point on it, the position you have taken up is—in a really superlative degree—irregular."

Such, also, seemed to be the opinion of counsel before whom, at a matutinal hour, he laid the facts of the case. When, in view of those facts, counsel on both sides conferred before the case was opened, the general feeling plainly pointed in the same direction. And, on its being stated in open court that, in face of the discovery of the vanished will, all opposition to Miss Delia Angel would, with permission, be at once withdrawn, it was incidentally mentioned how the discovery had been brought about. All eyes, turning to the jury-box, fastened on Philip Roland, whose agitated countenance pointed the allusion. The part which he had played having been made sufficiently plain, the judge himself joined in the general stare. His lordship went so far as to remark that while he was pleased to accede to the application which had been made to him to consider the case at an end, being of opinion that the matter had been brought to a very proper termination, still he could not conceal from himself that, so far as he could gather from what had been said, the conduct of one of the jurymen, even allowing some latitude—here his lordship's eyes seemed to twinkle—was marked by a considerable amount of irregularity.

Mitwaterstraand

THE STORY OF A SHOCK

CHAPTER I

THE DISEASE

ON the night before their daughter's Wedding Mr. and Mrs. Staunton gave a ball. As the festivities were drawing to a close, Mr. Staunton button-holed the bridegroom of the morrow.

"By the way, Burgoyne, there's one thing with reference to Minnie I wish to speak to you about. I—I'm not sure I oughtn't to have spoken to you before."

In the ball-room they were playing a waltz. Mr. Burgoyne's heart was with the dancers.

"About Minnie? What about Minnie? Don't you think that the little I don't know about her already, I shall find out soon enough upon my own account?"

"This is something—this is something that you ought to be told."

Mr. Staunton hesitated, and the opportunity was lost. The next morning Mr. Burgoyne was married.

During their honeymoon the newly-married pair spent a night at Mont St. Michel. In the course of that night an unpleasant incident took place. There was a bright moon, and the occupants of the bedrooms gathered on the balconies of the Maison Blanche to enjoy its radiance. The room next to theirs was tenanted by two sisters, Brooklyn girls. The costumes of these young ladies, although in that somewhat remote corner of the world, would have made an impression on the Boulevards, and still more emphatically in the Park. The married one—a Mrs. Homer Joy— wore some striking jewellery, in particular a diamond brooch, redolent of Tiffany, which would have attracted notice on a Shah

night at the opera. Mr. Burgoyne had noticed this brooch earlier
in the day, and had told himself that we must have returned to
the days of King Alfred—with several points in our favour—if a
woman could journey round the world with that advertisement in
diamond work flashing in the sun.

Someone proposed a midnight stroll about the rock.
They strolled. In the morning there was a terrible to-do. The
advertisement in diamond work had disappeared!—stolen!—
giving satisfactory proof that in those parts, at any rate, the days
of King Alfred were now no more.

Mrs. Joy stated that, previous to starting for the midnight
ramble about the Mount, she had placed it on her dressing-table,
apparently despising the precaution of placing it even in an ordinary
box. She was not even sure that she had closed her bedroom door,
so it had, of course, struck the eye of the first person who strolled
that way, and, in all probability, that person had, in the American
sense, "struck it." Mont St. Michel was still in a little tumult of
excitement when Mr. and Mrs. Burgoyne journeyed on their way.

Oddly enough, this discordant note, once struck, was struck
again—kept on striking, in fact. At almost every place where the
honeymooners stopped for an appreciable length of time there
something was lost. It seemed fatality. At Morlaix, a set of quaint,
old, hammered silver-spoons, which had accompanied their coffee,
vanished—not, according to the indignant innkeeper, into thin
air, but into somebody's pockets. It was most annoying. At Brest,
Quimper, Vannes, Nantes, and afterwards through Touraine and up
the Loire, it was the same tale, the loss of something of appreciable
value—somebody else's property, not their's—accompanied their
visitation. The coincidence was singular. However they did seem
to have shaken off the long arm of coincidence at last. There had
been no sort of unpleasantness at either of the last two or three
places at which they had stopped, and when they reached Paris at
last, they were so contented with all the world, that each seemed
to have forgotten everything in the existence of the other.

They stayed at the Grand Hotel—for privacy few places
can compete with a large hotel—and directly they stayed the
annoyances began again. It was indeed most singular. On the
very morning after their arrival a notice was posted in the *salle*

de lecture that the night before a lady had lost her fan—something historical in fans, and quite unique. She had been seated outside the reading-room—the Burgoynes must have been arriving at that very moment—preparatory to going to the opera. She laid this wonderful fan on a chair beside her, it was only for an instant, yet when she turned it was gone. The administration charitably suggested—in their notice—that someone of their lady guests had mistaken it for her own.

That same evening a really remarkable tale was whispered about the place. A certain lady and gentleman—not our pair, but another—happened to be honeymooning in the hotel. Monsieur had left Madame asleep in bed. When she got up and began to dress, she discovered that the larger and more valuable portion of the jewellery which had been given her as wedding presents, and which she, perhaps foolishly, had brought abroad, had gone— apparently vanished into air. The curious part of the tale was this. She had dreamed that she saw a woman—unmistakably a lady— trying on this identical jewellery before the looking-glass. Query, was it a dream? Or had she, lying in bed, in a half somnolent condition, been the unconscious witness of an actual occurrence?

"Upon my word," declared Mr. Burgoyne to his wife, "If the thing weren't actually impossible, I should be inclined to believe that we were the victims of some elaborate practical joke; that people were in a conspiracy to make us believe that ill luck dogged our steps!"

Mrs. Burgoyne smiled. She was putting on her bonnet before the glass. They were preparing to sally out for a quiet dinner on the boulevard.

"You silly Charlie! What queer ideas you get in your head. What does it matter to us if foolish people lose their things? We have not a mission to make folks wiser, or, what amounts to the same thing, to compel them to keep valuable things in secure places."

The lady, who had finished her performance at the glass, came and put her hands upon her lord's two shoulders,

"My dear child, don't look so black? I shall be much better prepared to discuss that, or any subject, when—we have dined."

The lady made a little *moue* and kissed him on the lips. Then they went downstairs. But when they had got so far upon their road, the gentleman discovered that he had brought no money in his pockets. Leaving his wife in the *salle de lecture,* he returned to his bedroom to supply the omission.

The desk in which he kept his loose cash was at that moment standing on the chest of drawers. On the top of it was a bag of his wife's—a bag on which she set much store. In it she kept her more particular belongings, and such care did she take of it that he never remembered to have seen it left out of her locked-up trunk before. Now, taking hold of it in his haste, he was rather surprised to find that it was unlocked—it was not only unlocked, but it flew wide open, and in flying open some of the contents fell upon the floor. He stooped to pick them up again.

The first thing he picked up was a silver spoon, the next was an ivory chessman, the next was a fan, and the next—was a diamond brooch.

He stared at these things in a sort of dream, and at the last especially. He had seen the thing before. But where?

Good God! it came upon him in a flash! It was the advertisement in diamond work which had been the property of Mrs. Homer Joy!

He was seized with a sort of momentary paralysis, continuing to stare at the brooch as though he had lost the power of volition. It was with an effort that he obtained sufficient mastery over himself to be able to turn his attention to the other articles he held. He knew two of them. The spoon was one of the spoons which had been lost at Morlaix; the chessman was one of a very curious set of chessmen which had disappeared at Vannes. From the notice which had been posted in the *salle de lecture* he had no difficulty in recognising the fan which had vanished from the chair.

It was some moments before he realised what the presence of those things must mean, and when he did realize it a metamorphosis had taken place—the Charles Burgoyne standing there was not the Charles Burgoyne who had entered the room. Without any outward display of emotion, in a cold, mechanical way he placed the articles he held upon one side, and turned the contents of the bag out upon the drawers.

They presented a curious variety at any rate. As he gazed at them he experienced that singular phenomenon—the inability to credit the evidence of his own eyes. There were the rest of the chessmen, the rest of the spoons, nick-nacks, a quaint, old silver cream-jug, jewellery—bracelets, rings, ear-rings, necklaces, pins, lockets, brooches, half the contents of a jeweller's shop. As he stood staring at this very miscellaneous collection, the door opened, and his wife came in.

She smiled as she entered.

"Charlie, have they taken your money too? Are you aware, sir, how hungry I am?"

He did not turn when he heard her voice. He continued motionless, looking at the contents of the bag. She advanced towards him and saw what he was looking at. Then he turned and they were face to face.

He never knew what was the fashion of his countenance. He could not have analysed his feelings to save his life. But, as he looked at her, his wife of yesterday, the woman whom he loved, she seemed to shrivel up before his eyes, and sank upon the floor. There was silence. Then she made a little gesture towards him with her two hands. She fell forward, hiding her face on the ground at his feet, prisoning his legs with her arms.

"How came these things into your bag?"

He did not know his own voice, it was so dry and harsh. She made no answer.

"Did you steal them?"

Still silence. He felt a sort of rage rising within him.

"There are one or two questions you must answer. I am sorry to have to put them; it is not my fault. You had better get up from the floor."

She never moved. For his life he could not have touched her.

"I suppose—." He was choked, and paused. "I suppose that woman's jewels are some of these?"

No answer. Recognising the hopelessness of putting questions to her now, he gathered the various articles together and put them back into the bag.

"I'm afraid you will have to dine alone."

That was all he said to her. With the bag in his hand he left the room, leaving her in a heap upon the floor. He sneaked rather than walked out of the hotel. Supposing they caught him red-handed, with that thing in his hand? He only began to breathe freely when he was out in the street.

Possibly no man in Paris spent the night of that twentieth of June more curiously than Mr. Burgoyne. When he returned it was four o'clock in the morning, and broad day. He was worn-out, haggard, the spectre of a man. In the bedroom he found his wife just as he had left her, in a heap upon the floor, but fast asleep. She had removed none of her clothes, not even her bonnet or her gloves. She had been crying—apparently had cried herself to sleep. As he stood looking down at her he realised how he loved her—the woman, the creature of flesh and blood, apart entirely from her moral qualities. He placed the bag within his trunk and locked it up. Then, kneeling beside his wife, he stooped and kissed her as she slept. The kiss aroused her. She woke as wakes a child, and, putting her arms about his neck, she kissed him back again. Not a word was spoken. Then she got up. He helped her to undress, and put her into a bed as though she were a child. Then he undressed himself, and joined her. And they fell fast asleep locked in each other's arms.

That night they returned to London. The bag went with them. On the morning after their arrival, Mr. Burgoyne took a cab into the city, the fatal bag beside him on the seat. He drove straight to Mr. Staunton's office. When he entered, unannounced, his father-in-law started as though he were a ghost.

"Burgoyne! What brings you here? I hope there's nothing wrong?"

Mr. Burgoyne did not reply at once. He placed the bag— Minnie's bag—upon the table. He kept his eyes fixed upon his father-in-law's countenance.

"Burgoyne! Why do you look at me like that?"

"I have something here I wish to show you." That was Mr. Burgoyne's greeting. He opened the bag, and turned its contents out upon the table.

"Not a bad haul from Breton peasants,—eh?"

Mr. Staunton stared at the heap of things thus suddenly disclosed.

"Burgoyne," he stammered, "what's the meaning of this?"

"Are you quite sure you don't know what it means?"

Looking up, Mr. Staunton caught the other's eyes. He seemed to read something there which carried dreadful significance to his brain. His glance fell and he covered his face with his hands. At last he found his voice.

"Minnie?"

The word was gasped rather than spoken. Mr. Burgoyne's reply was equally brief.

"Minnie!"

"Good God!"

There was silence for perhaps a minute. Then Mr. Burgoyne locked the door of the room and stood before the empty fire-place.

"It is by the merest chance that I am not at this moment booked for the *travaux forcés*. Some of those jewels were stolen from a woman's dressing case at the Grand Hotel, with the woman herself in bed and more than half awake at the time. She talked about having every guest in the place searched by the police. If she had done so, you would have heard from us as soon as the rules of the prison allowed us to communicate."

Mr. Burgoyne paused. Mr. Staunton kept his eyes fixed upon the table.

"That's what I wanted to tell you the night before the wedding, only you wouldn't stop. She's a kleptomaniac."

Mr. Burgoyne smiled, not gaily.

"Do you mean she's a habitual thief?"

"It's a disease."

"I've no doubt it's a disease. But perhaps you'll be so kind as to accurately define what in the present case you understand by disease."

"When she was a toddling child she took things, and secreted them—it's a literal fact. When she got into short frocks she continued to capture everything that caught her eye. When she exchanged them for long ones it was the same. It was not because she wanted the things, because she never attempted to use them when she had them. She just put them somewhere—as a magpie might—and forget their existence. You had only to find out where they were and take them away again, and she was never one whit the wiser. In that direction she's irresponsible—it's a disease in fact."

"If it is, as you say, a disease, have you ever had it medically treated?"

"She has been under medical treatment her whole life long. I suppose we have consulted half the specialists in England. Our own man, Muir, has given the case his continual attention. He has kept a regular journal, and can give you more light upon the subject than I can. You have no conception what a life-long torture it has been to me."

"I have a very clear conception indeed. But don't you think you might have enlightened me upon the matter before?"

Rising from his seat, Mr. Staunton began to pace the room.

"I do! I think so very strongly indeed. But—but—I was over persuaded. As you know, I tried at the very last moment; even then I failed. Besides, it was suggested to me that marriage might be the turning point, and that the woman might be different from the girl. Don't misunderstand me! She is not a bad girl; she is a good girl in the best possible sense, a girl in a million! No better daughter ever lived; you won't find a better wife if you search the whole world through; there is just this one point. Some people are somnambulists; in a sense she is a somnambulist too. I tell you I might put this watch upon the table"—Mr. Staunton produced his watch from his waistcoat pocket—"and she would take it from right underneath my nose, and never know what it was that she had done. I confess I can't explain it, but so it is!"

"I think," remarked Mr. Burgoyne, with a certain dryness, "that I had better see this doctor fellow—Muir."

"See him—by all means, see him. There is one point, Burgoyne. I realised from the first that if we kept you in the dark about this thing, and it forced itself upon you afterwards, you would be quite justified in feeling aggrieved."

"You realised that, did you? You did get so far?"

"And therefore I say this, that, although my child has only been your wife these few short days, although she loves you as truly as woman ever loved a man—and what strength of love she has I know—still, if you are minded to put her from you, I will not only not endeavour to change your purpose, but I will never ask you for a penny for her support—she shall be to you as though she had never lived."

Mr. Burgoyne looked his father-in-law in the face.

"No man shall part me from my wife, nor anything—but death." Mr. Burgoyne turned a little aside. "I believe I love her better because of this. God knows I loved her well enough before."

"I can understand that easily. Because of this she is dearer to us, too."

There was silence. Moving to the table, Mr. Burgoyne began to replace the things in the bag.

"I will go and see this man Muir."

Dr. Muir was at home. His appearance impressed Mr. Burgoyne favourably, and Mr. Burgoyne had a keen eye for the charlatan in medicine.

"Dr. Muir, I have come from Mr. Staunton. My name is Burgoyne. You are probably aware that I have married Mr. Staunton's daughter, Minnie. It is about my wife I wish to consult you." Dr. Muir simply nodded. "During our honeymoon in Brittany she has stolen all these things."

Mr. Burgoyne opened the bag sufficiently to disclose its contents. Dr. Muir scarcely glanced at them. He kept his eyes fixed on Mr. Burgoyne's face. There was a pause before he spoke.

"You were not informed of her—peculiarity?"

"I was not. I don't understand it now. It is because I wish to understand it that I have come to you."

"I don't understand it either."

"But I am told that you have always given the matter your attention."

"That is so, but I don't understand it any the more for that. I am not a specialist."

"Do you mean that she is mad?"

"I don't say that I mean anything at all; very shortly you will be quite as capable of judging of the case as I am. I've no doubt that if you wished to place her in an asylum, you would have no difficulty in doing so. So much I don't hesitate to say."

"Thank you. I have no intention of doing anything of the kind. Can you not suggest a cure?"

"I can suggest ten thousand, but they would all be experiments. In fact, I have tried several of them already, and the experiments have failed. For instance, I thought marriage might effect a cure. It is perhaps yet too early to judge, but it would appear that, so far, the thing has been a failure. Frankly, Mr. Burgoyne, I don't think you will find a man in Europe who, in this particular case, can give you help. You must trust to time. I have always thought myself that a shock might do it, though what sort of shock it will have to be is more than I can tell you. I thought the marriage shock might serve. Possibly the birth shock might prove of some avail. But we cannot experiment in shocks, you know. You must trust to time."

On that basis—*trust in time*—Mr. Burgoyne arranged his household. The bag with its contents was handed to his solicitor. The stolen property was restored to its several owners. It cost Mr. Burgoyne a pretty penny before the restoration was complete. A certain Mrs. Deal formed part of his establishment. She acted as companion and keeper to Mr. Burgoyne's wife. They never knew whether that lady realised what Mrs. Deal's presence really meant. And, in spite of their utmost vigilance, things were taken—from shops, from people's houses, from guests under her own roof. It was Mrs. Deal's business to discover where these things were, and to see that they were instantly restored. Her life was spent in a continual game of hide and seek.

It was a strange life they lived in that Brompton house, and yet—odd though it may sound—it was a happy one. He loved her, she loved him—there is a good deal in just that simple fact. There was one good thing—and that in spite of Dr. Muir's suggestion that a birth shock might effect a cure—there were no children.

CHAPTER II

THE CURE

THEY had been married five years. There came an invitation from one Arthur Watson, a friend of Mr. Burgoyne's boyhood. After long separation they had encountered each other by accident, and Mr. Watson had insisted upon Mr. Burgoyne's bringing his wife to spend the "week-end" with him in that Mecca of a certain section of modern Londoners—up the river. So the married couple went to see the single man.

After dinner conversation rather languished. But their host stirred it up again.

"I have something here to show you." Producing a leather case from the inner pocket of his coat, he addressed a question to Mr. Burgoyne. "Do much in mines?"

"How do you mean?"

"Because, if you do, here's a tip for you, and tips are things in which I don't deal as a rule—buy Mitwaterstraand. There is a boom coming along, and the foreshadowings of the boom are in this case. Mrs. Burgoyne, shut your eyes and you shall see."

Mrs. Burgoyne did not shut her eyes, but Mr. Watson opened the case, and she saw! More than a score of cut diamonds of the purest water, and of unusual size—lumps of light! With them, side by side, were about the same number of uncut stones, in curious contrast to their more radiant brethren.

"You see those?" He took out about a dozen of the cut stones, and held them loosely in his hand. "Are you a judge of diamonds? Well, I am. Hitherto there have been one or two defects about African diamonds—they cut badly, and the colour's wrong. But we have changed all that. I stake my reputation that you will find no finer diamonds than those in the world. Here is the stone in the rough. Here is exactly the same thing after it has been cut; judge for yourself, my boy! And those come from the district of Mitwaterstraand, Griqualand West. Take my tip, Burgoyne, and look out for Mitwaterstraand."

Mr. Burgoyne did take his tip, and looked out for Mitwaterstraand, though not in the sense he meant. He looked out for Mitwaterstraand all night, lying in bed with his eyes wide open, his thoughts fixed on his wife. Suppose they were stolen, those shining bits of crystal?

In the morning he was up while she still slept. He dressed himself and went downstairs. He felt that he must have just one whiff of tobacco, and then return—to watch. A little doze in which he had caught himself had frightened him. Suppose he fell into slumber as profound as hers, what might not happen in his dreams?

Early as was the hour, he was not the first downstairs. As he entered the room in which the diamonds had been exhibited, he found Mr. Watson standing at the table.

"Hullo, Watson! At this hour of the morning who'd have thought of seeing you?"

"I—I've had a shock." There was a perceptible tremor in Mr. Watson's voice, as though even yet he had not recovered from the shock of which he spoke.

"A shock? What kind of a shock?"

"When I woke this morning I found that I had left the case with the diamonds in downstairs. I can't think how I came to do it."

"It was a careless thing." Mr. Burgoyne's tones were even stern. He shuddered as he thought of the risk which had been run.

"It was. When I found that it was missing, I was out of bed like a flash. I put my things on anyhow, and when I found it was all right"—he at that moment was holding the case in his hands—"I felt like singing a Te Deum." He did not look like singing a Te Deum, by any means. "Let's have a look at you, my beauties." He pressed a spring and the case flew open. "My God!"

"What's the matter?"

"They're gone!"

"Gone!"

They were, sure enough. The case was empty. The shock was too much for Mr. Burgoyne.

"She's taken them after all," he gasped.

"Who?"

"My wife!"

"Your wife!—Burgoyne!—What do you mean?"

"Watson, my wife has stolen them."

"Burgoyne!"

The empty case fell to the ground with a crash. It almost seemed as though Mr. Watson would have fallen after it. He seemed even more distressed than his friend. His face was clammy, his hands were trembling.

"Burgoyne, what—whatever do you mean?"

"My wife's a kleptomaniac, that's what I mean."

"A kleptomaniac! You—you don't mean that she has taken the stones?"

"I do. Sounds like a joke doesn't it?"

"A joke! I don't know what you call a joke! It'll be no joke for me. There's to be a meeting, and those stones will have to be produced for experts to examine. If they are not forthcoming, I shall have to explain what has become of them, and those are not the men to listen to any talk of kleptomania. And it isn't the money they will want, it's the stones. At this crisis those stones are worth a hundred thousand pounds to us, and more! It'll be your ruin, and mine, if they are not found."

"They will be found. It is only a little game she plays. She hides, we seek and find. I think I may undertake to produce them for you in half-an-hour."

"I hope you will," said Mr. Watson, still with clammy face and trembling hands. "My God, I hope you will."

Mr. Burgoyne went upstairs. His wife was still asleep; and a prettier picture than she presented when asleep it would be hard to find. He put his hand upon her shoulder.

"Minnie!" No reply. "Minnie!" Still she slept.

When she did awake it was in the most natural and charming way conceivable. She stretched out her arms to her husband leaning over her.

"Charlie! Whatever is the time?"

"Where are those stones?"

"What?" With the back of her hands she began to rub her eyes. "Where are what?"

"Where are those stones?"

"I don't know what—" yawn—"you mean."

"Minnie!—Don't trifle with me!—Where have you put those diamonds?"

"Charlie! Whatever do you mean?"

Her eyes were wide open now. She lay looking at him in innocent surprise.

"What a consummate actress you are!"

The words came from his lips almost unawares. They seemed to startle her. "Charlie!"

He—loving her with all his heart—was unable to meet her glance, and began moving uneasily about the room, talking as he moved.

"Come, Minnie, tell me where they are?"

"Where what are?"

"The diamonds!"

"The diamonds! What diamonds? Whatever do you mean?"

"You know what I mean very well. I mean the Mitwaterstraand diamonds which Watson showed us last night, and which you have taken from the case."

"Which I have taken from the case!" She rose from the bed, and stood on the floor in her night-dress, the embodiment of surprise. "If you will leave the room I shall be able to dress."

"Minnie! Do you really think I am a fool? I can make every allowance—God knows I have done so often enough before—but you must tell me where those stones are before I leave this room."

"Do you mean to suggest that I—I have stolen them?"

"Call it what you please! I am only asking you to tell me where you have put them. That is all."

"On what evidence do you suspect me of this monstrous crime?"

"Evidence? What do I need with evidence? Minnie, for God's sake, don't let us argue. You know that you are dearer to me than life, but this time—even at the sacrifice of life!—I cannot save you from the consequence of your own act."

"The consequence of my own act. What do you mean?"

"I mean this, that unless those diamonds are immediately forthcoming, this night you will sleep in jail."

"In jail! I sleep in jail! Is this some hideous dream?"

"Oh, my darling, for both our sakes tell me where the diamonds are."

"Charlie, I know no more where they are than the man in the moon."

"Then God help us, for we are lost!"

He ransacked every article of furniture the room contained. Tore open the mattresses, ripped up the boards, looked up the chimney. But there were no diamonds. And that night she slept in jail. Mr. Watson started off to tell his story to the meeting as best he might. Mr. and Mrs. Burgoyne remained behind, searching for the missing stones. About one o'clock, Mr. Watson still being absent, a telegram was received at the local police station containing instructions to detain Mrs. Burgoyne on a charge of felony, "warrant coming down by train." Mr. Watson had evidently told his story to an unsympathetic audience. Mrs. Burgoyne was arrested and taken off to the local lock-up—all idea of bail being peremptorily pooh-poohed. Mr. Burgoyne tore up to town in a state of semi-madness. When Mr. Staunton heard the story, his affliction was at least, equal to his son-in-law's. Dr. Muir was telegraphed for, and a hurried conference was held in the office of a famous criminal lawyer. That gentleman told them plainly that at present nothing could be done.

"Even suppose the diamonds are immediately forthcoming, the case will have to go before a magistrate. You don't suppose the police will allow you to compound a felony. That is what it amounts to, you know."

As for the medical point of view, it must be urged, of course; but the lawyer made no secret of his belief that if the medical point of view was all they had to depend on, the case would, of a certainty, be sent to trial.

"But it seems to me that at present there is not a tittle of evidence. Your wife, Mr. Burgoyne, has been arrested, I won't say upon your information, but on the strength of words which you allowed to escape your lips. But they can't put you in the box; you could prove nothing if they did. When the case comes on they'll ask for a remand. Probably they'll get it, one remand at any rate. I shall offer bail, which they'll accept. When the case comes on again, unless they have something to go on, which they haven't now, it will be dismissed. Mrs. Burgoyne will leave the court without a stain upon her character. We shan't even have to hint at kleptomania, or klepto anything."

More than once that night Mr. Burgoyne meditated suicide. All was over. She—his beloved!—through his folly—slept in jail. And if, by the skin of her teeth, she escaped this time, how would it be the next? She was guilty now—they might prove it then! And when he thought of the numerous precautions he had hedged her round with heretofore, it seemed marvellous that she had gone scot free so long. And suppose she had been taken at the outset of her career—in the affair of the jewels at the Grand Hotel—what would have availed any plea he might have urged before a French tribunal? He shuddered as he thought of it.

He never attempted to go to bed. He paced to and fro in his study like a caged wild animal. If he might only have shared her cell! The study was on the ground floor. It opened on to the garden. Between two and three in the morning he thought he heard a tapping at the pane. With a trembling hand he unlatched the window. A man stood without.

"Watson!"

As the name broke from him Mr. Watson staggered, rather than walked, into the room.

"I—I saw the light outside. I thought I had better knock at the window than disturb the house."

He sank into a chair, putting his arms upon the table, pillowing his face upon his hands. There was silence. Mr. Burgoyne, in his surprise, was momentarily struck dumb. At last, finding his voice, and eyeing his friend, he said—

"This is a bad job for both of us."

Mr. Watson looked up. Mr. Burgoyne, in spite of his own burden which he had to bear, was startled by something which he saw written on his face.

"As you say, it is a bad job for both of us." Mr. Watson rose as he was speaking. "But it is worst for me. Why did you tell me all that stuff about your wife?"

"God knows I am not in the mood to talk of anything, but rather than that, talk of what you please."

"Why the devil did you put that thought into my head?"

"What thought? I do not understand. I don't think you understand much either."

"Why did you tell me she had taken the stones? Why, you damned fool, I had them in my pocket all the time."

Mr. Watson took his hand out of his pocket. It was full of what seemed little crystals. He dashed these down upon the table with such force that they were scattered all over the room. They were some of the Mitwaterstraand diamonds.

"Watson! Good God! What do you mean?"

"I was the thief! Not she!"

"You—hound!"

"Don't look as though you'd like to murder me! I tell you I feel like murdering you! I am a ruined man. The thought came into my head that if I could get off with those Mitwaterstraand diamonds, I should have something with which to start afresh. Like an idiot, I took them from the case last night, meaning to hatch some cock-and-bull story about having forgotten to bring the case upstairs, and their having been stolen from it in the night. But on reflection I perceived how extremely thin the tale would be. I went downstairs to put them back again. I was in the very act of doing it when you came in. I showed you the empty box. You immediately cried out that your wife had stolen them. It was a temptation straight from hell! I was too astounded at first to understand your meaning. When I did, I let you remain in possession of your belief. Now, Burgoyne, don't you be a fool."

But Mr. Burgoyne was a fool. He fell on to the floor in a fit; this last straw was one too many. When he recovered, Mr. Watson was gone, but the diamonds were there, piled in a neat little heap upon the table. He had been guilty of a really curious lapse into the paths of honesty, for, as he truly said, he was a ruined man. It was one of those resonant smashes which are the sensation of an hour.

Mrs. Burgoyne was released—without a stain upon her character. She never stole again! She had been guilty so many times, and never been accused of crime,—and the first time she was innocent they said she was a thief! Dr. Muir said the shock had done it,—he had said that a shock would do it, all along.

Exchange is Robbery

CHAPTER I

"IMPOSSIBLE!"

"Really, Mr. Ruby, I wish you wouldn't say a thing was impossible when I say that it is actually a fact."

Mr. Ruby looked at the Countess of Grinstead, and the Countess of Grinstead looked at him.

"But, Countess, if you will just consider for one moment. You are actually accusing us of selling to you diamonds which we know to be false."

"Whether you knew them to be false or not is more than I can say. All I know is that I bought a set of diamond ornaments from you, for which you charged me eight hundred pounds, and which Mr. Ahrens says are not worth eight hundred pence."

"Mr. Ahrens must be dreaming."

"Oh no, he's not. I don't believe that Mr. Ahrens ever dreams."

Mr. Golden, who was standing observantly by, addressed an inquiry to the excited lady.

"Where are the diamonds now?"

"The diamonds, as you call them, and which I don't believe are diamonds, since Mr. Ahrens says they're not, and I'm sure he ought to know, are in this case."

The Countess of Grinstead produced from her muff one of those flat leather cases in which jewellers love to enshrine their wares.

Mr. Golden held out his hand for it.

"Permit me for one moment, Countess."

The Countess handed him the case. Mr. Golden opened it. Mr. Ruby, leaning back in his chair, watched his partner examine the contents. The Countess watched him too. Mr. Golden took out one glittering ornament after another. Through a little microscope he peered into its inmost depths. He turned it over and over, and peered and peered, as though he would read its very heart. When he had concluded his examination he turned to the lady.

"How came you to submit these ornaments to Mr. Ahrens?"

"I don't mind telling you. Not in the least! I happened to want some money. I didn't care to ask the Earl for it. I thought of those things—you had charged me £800 for them, so I thought that he would let me have £200 upon them as a loan. When he told me that they were nothing but rubbish I thought I should have had a fit."

"Where have they been in the interval between your purchasing them from us and your taking them to Mr. Ahrens?"

"Where have they been? Where do you suppose they've been? They have been in my jewel case, of course."

Mr. Golden replaced the ornaments in their satin beds. He closed the case.

"Every inquiry shall be made into the matter, Countess, you may rest assured of that. We cannot afford to lose our money, any more than you can afford to lose your diamonds."

Directly the lady's back was turned Mr. Ruby put a question to his partner. "Well, are they false?"

"They are. It is a good imitation, one of the best imitations I remember to have seen. Still it is an imitation."

"Do you—do you think she did it?"

"That is more than I can say. Still, when a lady buys diamonds on Saturday, upon credit, and takes them to a pawnbroker on Tuesday, to raise money on them, one may be excused for having one's suspicions."

While the partners were still discussing the matter, the door was opened by an assistant. "Mr. Gray wishes to see Mr. Ruby."

Before Mr. Ruby had an opportunity of saying whether or not he wished to see Mr. Gray, rather unceremoniously Mr. Gray himself came in.

"I should think I do want to see Mr. Ruby, and while I'm about it, I may as well see Mr. Golden too." Mr. Gray turned to the assistant, who still was standing at the open door. "You can go."

The assistant looked at Mr. Ruby for instructions. "Yes Thompson, you can go."

When Thompson was gone, and the door was closed, Mr. Gray, who wore his hat slightly on the side of his head, turned and faced the partners. He was a very young man, and was dressed in the extreme of fashion. Taking from his coat tail pocket the familiar leather case, he flung it on to the table with a bang. "I don't know what you call that, but I tell you what I call it. I call it a damned swindle."

Mr. Ruby was shocked.

"Mr. Gray! May I ask of what you are complaining?"

"Complaining! I'm complaining of your selling me a thing for two thousand pounds which is not worth two thousand pence!"

"Indeed? Have we been guilty of such conduct as that?" Mr. Golden picked up the case which Mr. Gray had flung down upon the table. "Is this the diamond necklace which we had the pleasure of selling you the other day?"

Mr. Golden opened the case. He took out the necklace which it contained. He examined it as minutely as he had examined the Countess of Grinstead's ornaments. "This is—very remarkable."

"Remarkable! I should think it is remarkable! I bought that necklace for a lady. As some ladies have a way of doing, she had it valued. When she found that the thing was trumpery, she, of course, jumped to the conclusion that I'd been having her—trying to gain kudos for giving her something worth having at the cheapest possible rate. A pretty state of things, upon my word!"

"This appears to be a lady of acute commercial instincts, Mr. Gray."

"Never mind about that! If you deny that that is the necklace which you sold to me I will prove that it is—in the police court. I am quite prepared for it. Men who are capable of selling a necklace of glass beads as a necklace of diamonds are capable of denying that they ever sold the thing at all."

"Mr. Gray, there is no necessity to use such language to us. If a wrong has been done we are ready and willing to repair it."

"Then repair it!"

It took some time to get rid of Mr. Gray. He had a great deal to say, and a very strong and idiomatic way of saying it. Altogether it was a bad quarter of an hour for Messrs. Ruby and Golden. When, at last, they did get rid of him, Mr. Ruby turned to his partner.

"Golden, it's not possible that the stones in that necklace are false. Those are the stones which we got from Fungst—you remember?"

"I remember very well indeed. They were the stones which we got from Fungst. They are not now. The gems which are at present in this necklace are paste, covered with a thin veneer of real stones. It is an old trick, but I never saw it better done. The workmanship, both in Mr. Gray's necklace and in the Countess of Grinstead's ornaments, is, in its way, perfection."

While Mr. Ruby was still staring at his partner, the door opened and again Mr. Thompson entered. "The Duchess of Datchet."

"Let's hope," muttered Mr. Golden, "that she's not come to charge us with selling any more paste diamonds."

But the Duchess had come to do nothing of the kind. She had come on a much more agreeable errand, from Messrs. Ruby and Golden's point of view—she had come to buy. As it was Mr. Ruby's special *rôle* to act as salesman to the great—the very great—ladies who patronised that famed establishment, Mr. Golden left his partner to perform his duties.

Mr. Ruby found the Duchess, on that occasion, difficult to please. She wanted something in diamonds, to present to Lady Edith Linglithgow on the occasion of her approaching marriage. As Lady Edith is the Duke's first cousin, as all the world knows, almost, as it were, his sister, the Duchess wanted something very good indeed. Nothing which Messrs. Ruby and Golden had seemed to be quite good enough, except one or two things which were, perhaps, too good. The Duchess promised to return with the Duke himself to-morrow, or, perhaps, the day after. With that promise Mr. Ruby was forced to be content.

The instant the difficult very great lady had vanished, Mr. Golden came into the room. He placed upon the table some leather cases.

"Ruby what do you think of those?"

"Why, they're from stock, aren't they?" Mr. Ruby took up some of the cases which Mr. Golden had put down. There was quite a heap of them. They contained rings, bracelets, necklaces, odds and ends in diamond work. "Anything the matter with them, Golden?"

"There's this the matter with them—that they're all paste."

"Golden!"

"I've been glancing through the stock. I haven't got far, but I've come upon those already. Somebody appears to be having a little joke at our expense. It strikes me, Ruby, that we're about to be the victims of one of the greatest jewel robberies upon record."

"Golden!"

"Have you been showing this to the Duchess?" Mr. Golden picked up a necklace of diamonds from a case which lay open on the table, whose charms Mr. Ruby had been recently exhibiting to that difficult great lady. "Ruby!—Good Heavens!"

"Wha-what's the matter?"

"They're paste!"

Mr. Golden was staring at the necklace as though it were some hideous thing.

"Paste!—G-G-Golden!" Mr. Ruby positively trembled. "That's Kesteeven's necklace which he brought in this morning to see if we could find a customer for it."

"I'm quite aware that this was Kesteeven's necklace. Now it would be dear at a ten-pound note."

"A ten-pound note! He wants ten thousand guineas! It's not more than an hour since he brought it—no one can have touched it."

"Ruby, don't talk nonsense! I saw Kesteeven's necklace when he brought it, I see this thing now. This is not Kesteeven's necklace— it has been changed!"

"Golden!"

"To whom have you shown this necklace?"

"To the Duchess of Datchet."

"To whom else?"

"To no one."

"Who has been in this room?"

"You know who has been in the room as well as I do."

"Then—she did it"

"She?—Who?"

"The Duchess!"

"Golden! you are mad!"

"I shall be mad pretty soon. We shall be ruined! I've not the slightest doubt but that you've been selling people paste for diamonds for goodness knows how long."

"Golden!"

"You'll have to come with me to Datchet House. I'll see the

Duke—I'll have it out with him at once." Mr. Golden threw open the door. "Thompson, Mr. Ruby and I are going out. See that nobody comes near this room until we return."

To make sure that nobody did come near that room Mr. Golden turned the key in the lock, and pocketed the key.

CHAPTER II

WHEN Messrs. Ruby and Golden arrived at Datchet House they found the Duke at home. He received them in his own apartment. On their entrance he was standing behind a writing table.

"Well, gentlemen, to what am I indebted for the honour of this visit?"

Mr. Golden took on himself the office of spokesman.

"We have called, your Grace, upon a very delicate matter." The Duke inclined his head—he also took a seat. "The Duchess of Datchet has favoured us this morning with a visit."

"The Duchess!"

"The Duchess."

Mr. Golden paused. He was conscious that this was a delicate matter. "When her Grace quitted our establishment she *accidentally*"—Mr. Golden emphasised the adverb; he even repeated it—"*accidentally* left behind some of her property in exchange for ours."

"Mr. Golden!" The Duke stared. "I don't understand you."

Mr. Golden then and there resolved to make the thing quite plain.

"I will be frank with your Grace. When the Duchess left our establishment this morning she took with her some twenty thousand pounds worth of diamonds—it may be more, we have only been able to give a cursory glance at the state of things—and left behind her paste imitations of those diamonds instead."

The Duke stood up. He trembled—probably with anger.

"Mr. Golden, am I—am I to understand that you are mad?"

"The case, your Grace, is as I stated. Is not the case as I state it, Mr. Ruby?"

Mr. Ruby took out his handkerchief to relieve his brow. His

habit of showing excessive deference to the feelings and the whims of very great people was almost more than he could master.

"I—I'm afraid, Mr. Golden, that it is. Your—your Grace will understand that—that we should never have ventured to—to come here had we not been most—most unfortunately compelled."

"Pray make no apology, Mr. Ruby. Allow me to have a clear understanding with you, gentlemen. Do I understand that you charge the Duchess of Datchet—the Duchess of Datchet!"—the Duke echoed his own words, as though he were himself unable to believe in the enormity of such a thing—"with stealing jewels from your shop?"

"If your Grace will allow me to make a distinction without a difference—we charge no one with anything. If your Grace will give us your permission to credit the jewels to your account, there is an end of the matter."

"What is the value of the articles which you say have gone?"

"On that point we are not ourselves, as yet, accurately informed. I may as well state at once—it is better to be frank, your Grace—that this sort of thing appears to have been going on for some time. It is only an hour or so since we began to have even a suspicion of the extent of our losses."

"Then, in effect, you charge the Duchess of Datchet with robbing you wholesale?"

Mr. Golden paused. He felt that to such a question as this it would be advisable that he should frame his answer in a particular manner.

"Your Grace will understand that different persons have different ways of purchasing. Lady A. has her way. Lady B. has her way, and the Duchess of Datchet has hers."

"Are you suggesting that the Duchess of Datchet is a kleptomaniac?"

Mr. Golden was silent.

"Do you think that that is a comfortable suggestion to make to a husband, Mr. Golden?" Just then someone tapped at the door. "Who's there?"

A voice—a feminine voice—enquired without, "Can I come in?"

Before the Duke could deny the right of entry, the door opened and a woman entered. A tall woman, and a young and a lovely one. When she perceived Messrs. Ruby and Golden she cast an enquiring look in the direction of the Duke. "Are you engaged?"

The Duke was eyeing her with a somewhat curious expression of countenance. "I believe you know these gentlemen?"

"Do I? I ought to know them perhaps, but I'm afraid I don't."

Mr. Ruby was all affability and bows, and smiles and rubbings of hands.

"I have not had the honour of seeing the lady upon a previous occasion."

The Duke of Datchet stared. "You have not had the honour? Then what—what the dickens do you mean? This is the Duchess!"

"The Duchess!" cried Messrs. Ruby and Golden.

"Certainly—the Duchess of Datchet."

Messrs. Ruby and Golden looked blue. They looked more than blue—they looked several colours of the rainbow all at once. They stared as though they could not believe the evidence of their eyes and ears. The Duke turned to the Duchess. He opened the door for her.

"Duchess, will you excuse me for a moment? I have something which I particularly wish to say to these gentlemen."

The Duchess disappeared. When she had gone the Duke not only closed the door behind her, but he stood with his back against the door which he had closed. His manner, all at once, was scarcely genial.

"Now, what shall I do with you, gentlemen? You come to my house and charge the Duchess of Datchet with having been a constant visitor at your shop for the purpose of robbing you, and it turns out that you have actually never seen the Duchess of Datchet in your lives until this moment."

"But," gasped Mr. Ruby, "that—that is not the lady who came to our establishment, and—and called herself the Duchess of Datchet."

"Well, sir, and what has that to do with me? Am I responsible for the proceedings of every sharper who comes to your shop and chooses to call herself the Duchess of Datchet? I should advise you, in future, before advancing reckless charges, to make some enquiries into the *bona fides* of your customers, Mr. Ruby. Now, gentlemen, you may go."

The Duke held the door wide open, invitingly. Mr. Golden caught his partner by the sleeve, as though he feared that he would, with undue celerity, accept the invitation.

"Hardly, your Grace, there is still something which we wish to say to you." The Duke of Datchet shut the door again.

"Then say it. Only say it, if possible, in such a manner as not to compel me to—kick you, Mr. Golden."

"Your Grace will believe that in anything I have said, or in anything which I am to say, nothing is further from my wish than to cause your Grace annoyance. But, on the other hand, surely your Grace is too old, and too good a customer of our house, to wish to see us ruined."

"I had rather, Mr. Golden, see you ruined ten thousand times over than that you should ruin my wife's fair fame."

Mr. Golden hesitated; he seemed to perceive that the Duke's retort was not irrelevant. He turned to Mr. Ruby.

"Mr. Ruby, will you be so good as to explain what reasons we had for believing that this person was what she called herself—the Duchess of Datchet? Because your Grace must understand that we did not entertain that belief without having at least some grounds to go upon."

Mr. Ruby, thus appealed to, began to fidget. He did not seem to relish the office which his partner had imposed upon him. The tale which he told was rather lame—still, he told it.

"Your Grace will understand that I—I am acquainted, at least by sight, with most of the members of the British aristocracy, and—and, indeed, of other aristocracies. But it so happened that, at the period of your Grace's recent marriage, I happened to be abroad, and—and, not only so, but—but the lady your Grace married was—was a lady—from—from the country."

"I am perfectly aware, Mr. Ruby, whom I married."

"Quite so, your Grace, quite so. Only—only I was endeavouring to explain how it was that I—I did not happen to be acquainted with her Grace's personal appearance. So that when a carriage and pair drove up to our establishment with your Grace's crest upon the panel——"

"My crest upon the panel!"

"Your Grace's crest upon the panel"—as Mr. Ruby continued, the Duke of Datchet bit his lip—"and a lady stepped out of it and said, 'I am the Duchess of Datchet; my husband tells me that he is an old customer of yours,' I was only too glad to see her Grace, because, as your Grace is aware, we have the honour of having your Grace as an old customer of ours. 'My husband has given me this cheque to spend with you.' When she said that she took a cheque out of her purse, one of your Grace's own cheques drawn upon Messrs. Coutts, 'Pay Messrs. Ruby and Golden, or order, one thousand pounds,' with your Grace's signature attached. I have seen too many of your Grace's cheques not to know them well. She purchased goods to the value of a thousand pounds, and she gave us your Grace's cheque to pay for them."

"She gave you that cheque, did she?"

Mr. Golden interposed, "We presented the cheque, and it was duly honoured. On the face of such proof as that, what could we suppose?"

The Duke was moving about the room—it seemed, a little restlessly.

"It didn't necessarily follow, because a woman paid for her purchases with a cheque of mine that that woman was the Duchess of Datchet."

"I think, under the peculiar circumstances of the case, that it did. At least, the presumption was strong upon that side. May I ask to whom your Grace's cheque was given?"

"You may ask, but I don't see why I should tell you. It was honoured, and that is sufficient."

"I don't think it is sufficient, and I don't think that your Grace will think so either, if you consider for a moment. If it had not been for the strong presumptive evidence of your Grace's cheque, we should not have been robbed of many thousand pounds."

The Duke of Datchet paced restlessly to and fro. Messrs. Ruby and Golden watched him. At last he moved towards his writing table. He sat down on the chair behind it. He stretched out his legs in front of him. He thrust his hands into his trousers pockets.

"I'll make a clean breast of it. You fellows can keep a still tongue in your heads—keep a still tongue about what I am going to tell you." His hearers bowed. They were coming to the point—at last. "Eh"—in spite of his announced intention of making a clean breast of it, his Grace rather stumbled in his speech. "Before I was married I—I had some acquaintance with—with a certain lady. When I married, that acquaintance ceased. On the last occasion on which I saw her she informed me that she was indebted to you in the sum of a thousand pounds for jewellery. I gave her a cheque to discharge her liability to you, and to make sure that she did discharge the liability, I made the cheque payable to you, which, I now perceive, was perhaps not the wisest thing I could have done. But, at the same time, I wish you clearly to comprehend that I have every reason to believe that the lady referred to is, to put it mildly, a most unlikely person to—to rob any one."

"We must request you to furnish us with that lady's name and address. And I would advise your Grace to accompany us in an immediate visit to that lady."

"That is your advice is it, Mr. Golden? I am not sure that I appreciate it quite so much as it may possibly deserve."

"Otherwise, as you will yourself perceive, we shall be compelled to put the matter at once in the hands of the police, and, your Grace, there will be a scandal."

The Duke of Datchet reflected. He looked at Mr. Golden, he looked at Mr. Ruby, he looked at the ceiling, he looked at the floor, he looked at his boots—then he looked back again at Mr. Golden. At last he rose. He shook himself a little—as if to shake his clothes into their proper places. He seemed to have threshed the *pros* and *cons* of the matter well out, mentally, and to have finally decided.

"As I do not want a scandal, I think I will take your excellent advice, Mr. Golden—which I now really do appreciate at its proper value—and accompany you upon that little visit. Shall we go at once?"

"At once—if your Grace pleases."

CHAPTER III

THE Duke of Datchet's brougham, containing the Duke of Datchet himself upon one seat, and Messrs. Ruby and Golden cheek by jowl upon the other, drew up in front of a charming villa in the most charming part of charming St. John's Wood. The Duke's ring—for the Duke himself did ring, and there was no knocker—was answered by a most unimpeachable-looking man-servant in livery. The man-servant was not only unimpeachable-looking—which every servant ought to look—but good-looking, too, which, in a servant, is not regarded as quite so indispensable. He was, indeed, so good-looking as to be quite a "beauty man." So young, too! A mere youth!

When this man-servant opened the door, and saw to whom he had opened it, he started. And not only did he start, but Messrs. Ruby and Golden started too, particularly Mr. Golden. The Duke of Datchet, if he observed this little by-play, did not condescend to notice it.

"Is Mrs. Mansfield in?"

"I believe so. I will enquire. What name?"

"Never mind the name, and I will make my own enquiries. You needn't announce me, I know the way."

The Duke of Datchet seemed to know the way very well indeed. He led the way up the staircase; Messrs. Ruby and Golden followed. The man-servant remained at the foot of the stairs, as if doubtful whether or not he ought to follow. When they had reached the landing, and the man-servant, still remaining below, was out of sight, Mr. Golden turned to Mr. Ruby.

"Where on earth have I seen that man before?"

"I was just addressing to myself the same enquiry," said Mr. Ruby.

The Duke paused. He turned to the partners.

"What's that? The servant? Have you seen the man before? The plot is thickening. I am afraid 'the Duchess' is getting warm."

Apparently the Duke knew his way so well that he did not think it necessary to announce himself at the door of the room to which he led the partners. He simply turned the handle and went in, Messrs. Ruby and Golden close upon his heels. The room which he had entered was a pretty room, and contained a pretty occupant. A lady, young and fair, rose from a couch which was at the opposite side of the apartment, and, as was most justifiable under the circumstances, stared: "Hereward!"

"Mrs. Mansfield!"

"Whatever brings you here?"

"My dear Mrs. Mansfield, I have come to ask you what you think of Mr. Kesteeven's necklace."

"Hereward, what do you mean?"

The Duke's manner changed from jest to earnest.

"Rather, Gertrude, what do you mean? What have I done that deserved such a return from you? What have I done to you that you should have endeavoured to drag my wife's name in the mire?"

The lady stared. "I have no more idea what you are talking about than the man in the moon!"

"You dare to tell me so, in the presence of these men?"

"In the presence of what men?"

"In the presence of your victims—of Mr. Ruby and of Mr. Golden?"

Mr. Golden advanced a step or two.

"Excuse me, your Grace—this is not the lady."

"Eh?"

"This is not the lady."

"Not what lady?"

"This is not the lady who called herself the Duchess of Datchet."

"What the dickens do you mean? Really, Mr. Ruby and Mr. Golden, you seem to be leading me a pretty fine wild goose chase—a pretty fine wild goose chase! I know it will end in kicking—someone. You told me that the person to whom I had given that cheque was the person who had bestowed on you her patronage. This is the person to whom I gave that cheque."

"This is not the person who gave that cheque to us."

"Then—then who the devil did?"

"That, your Grace, is the point—will this lady allow me to ask her one or two questions?"

"Fire away—ask fifty!"

The lady thus referred to interposed, "This gentleman may ask fifty or five hundred questions, but unless you tell me what all this is about I very much doubt if I shall answer one."

"Let me manage it, Mr. Golden. Mrs. Mansfield, may I enquire what you did with that cheque for a thousand which I gave you?

You jade! To tell me that Ruby and Golden were dunning you out of your life, when you never owed them a stiver! Tell me what you did with that cheque!"

The Duke seemed at last to have said something which had reached the lady's understanding. She changed colour. She pressed her lips together. She looked at him with defiance in her eyes. A considerable pause ensued before she spoke.

"I don't know why I should tell you. What does it matter to you what I did with it—you gave it me."

"It does matter to me. As it happens, it matters also to you. If you will take my friendly advice, you will tell me what you did with that cheque."

The look of defiance about the lady's lips and in her eyes increased.

"I don't mind telling you. Why should I? It was my own. I gave it to Alfred."

The Duke emitted an ejaculation—which smacked of profanity.

"To Alfred? And, pray, who may Alfred be?"

The lady's crest rose higher. "Alfred is—is the man to whom I am engaged to be married."

The Duke of Datchet whistled. "And you got a cheque out of me for a thousand pounds to make a present of it to your intended? That beats everything; and pray to whom did Alfred give it?"

"He gave it to no one. He paid it into the bank. He told me so himself."

"Then I'm afraid that Alfred lied. Where is Alfred?"

"He's—he's here."

"Here? In this room? Where? Under the couch, or behind the screen?"

"I mean that he's in this house. He's downstairs."

"I won't ask how long he's been downstairs, but would it be too much to ask you to request Alfred to walk upstairs."

The lady burst into a sudden tempest of tears.

"I know you'll only laugh at me—I know you well enough to expect you to do that—but—I—I know I've not been a good woman, and—and I do love him—although—he's only—a—servant!"

"A servant! Gertrude! Was that the man who opened the door?"

Mr. Golden gave vent to an exclamation which positively amounted to a shout "By Jove!—I've got it!—I knew I'd seen the face before—I couldn't make out where—it was the man who opened the door. Your Grace, might I ask you to have that man who opened the door to us at once brought here?"

"Ring the bell, Mr. Golden."

The lady interposed. "You shan't—I won't have it! What do you want with him?"

"We wish to ask him one or two questions. If Alfred is an honest man it will be better for him that he should have an opportunity of answering them. If he is not an honest man, it will be better for you that you should know it."

Apparently this reasoning prevailed. Mr. Golden rang the bell; but his ring was not by any means immediately attended to. He rang a second and a third time, but still no answer came.

"It strikes me," suggested the Duke, "that we had better start on a voyage of discovery, and search for Alfred in the regions down below."

Before the Duke's suggestion could be acted on the door was opened—not by Alfred; not by a man at all, but by a maid.

"Send Alfred here."

"I can't find him anywhere. I think he must have gone."

"Gone!" gasped Mrs. Mansfield. "Where?"

"I don't know, ma'am. I've been up to his room to look for him, and it is all anyhow, and there's no one there. If you please, ma'am, I found this on the mat outside the door."

The maid held out an envelope. The Duke of Datchet took it from her hand. He glanced at its superscription.

"'Messrs. Ruby and Golden.' Gentlemen, this is for you."

He transferred it to Mr. Golden. It was a long blue envelope. The maid had picked it up from the mat which was outside the door of that very room in which they were standing. Mr. Golden opened it. It contained an oblong card of considerable size, on which were printed three photographs, in a sort of series. The first photograph was that of a young man—a beautiful young man— unmistakably "Alfred." The second was that of "Alfred" with his hair arranged in a fashion which was peculiarly feminine. The third was that of "Alfred" with a bonnet and a veil on, and a very nice-looking young woman he made. At the bottom of the card was written, in a fine, delicate, lady's hand-writing, "With the Duchess of Datchet's compliments."

"I knew," gasped Mrs. Mansfield, in the midst of her sorrow, "that he was very good at dressing up as a woman, but I never thought he would do this!"

★ ★ ★ ★ ★

The Duke of Datchet paid for the diamonds.

The Haunted Chair

CHAPTER I

"WELL, that's the most staggering thing I've ever known!"

As Mr. Philpotts entered the smoking-room, these were the words—with additions—which fell upon his, not unnaturally, startled ears. Since Mr. Bloxham was the only person in the room, it seemed only too probable that the extraordinary language had been uttered by him—and, indeed, his demeanour went far to confirm the probability. He was standing in front of his chair, staring about him in a manner which suggested considerable mental perturbation, apparently unconscious of the fact that his cigar had dropped either from his lips or his fingers and was smoking merrily away on the brand-new carpet which the committee had just laid down. He turned to Mr. Philpotts in a state of what seemed really curious agitation.

"I say, Philpotts, did you see him?"

Mr. Philpotts looked at him in silence for a moment, before he drily said, "I heard you."

But Mr. Bloxham was in no mood to be put off in this manner. He seemed, for some cause, to have lost the air of serene indifference for which he was famed—he was in a state of excitement, which, for him, was quite phenomenal.

"No nonsense, Philpotts—did you see him?"

"See whom?" Mr. Philpotts was selecting a paper from a side table. "I see your cigar is burning a hole in the carpet."

"Confound my cigar!" Mr. Bloxham stamped on it with an angry tread. "Did Geoff Fleming pass you as you came in?"

Mr. Philpotts looked round with an air of evident surprise.

"Geoff Fleming!—Why, surely he's in Ceylon by now."

"Not a bit of it. A minute ago he was in that chair talking to me."

"Bloxham!" Mr. Philpotts' air of surprise became distinctly

more pronounced, a fact which Mr. Bloxham apparently resented.

"What are you looking at me like that for pray? I tell you I was glancing through the *Field*, when I felt someone touch me on the shoulder. I looked round—there was Fleming standing just behind me. 'Geoff.' I cried, 'I thought you were on the other side of the world—what are you doing here?' 'I've come to have a peep at you,' he said. He drew a chair up close to mine—this chair—and sat in it. I turned round to reach for a match on the table, it scarcely took me a second, but when I looked his way again hanged if he weren't gone."

Mr. Philpotts continued his selection of a paper—in a manner which was rather marked.

"Which way did he go?"

"Didn't you meet him as you came in?"

"I did not—I met no one. What's the matter now?"

The question was inspired by the fact that a fresh volley of expletives came from Mr. Bloxham's lips. That gentleman was standing with his hands thrust deep into his trouser pockets, his legs wide open, and his eyes and mouth almost as wide open as his legs.

"Hang me," he exclaimed, when, as it appeared, he had temporarily come to the end of his stock of adjectives, "if I don't believe he's boned my purse."

"Boned your purse!" Mr. Philpotts laid a not altogether flattering emphasis upon the "boned!" "Bloxham! What do you mean?"

Mr. Bloxham did not immediately explain. He dropped into the chair behind him. His hands were still in his trouser pockets, his legs were stretched out in front of him, and on his face there was not only an expression of amazement, but also of the most unequivocal bewilderment. He was staring at the vacant air as if he were trying his hardest to read some riddle.

"This is a queer start, upon my word, Philpotts," he spoke in what, for him, were tones of unwonted earnestness. "When I was reaching for the matches on the table, what made me turn round so suddenly was because I thought I felt someone tugging at my purse—it was in the pocket next to Fleming. As I told you, when I did turn round Fleming was gone—and, by Jove, it looks as though my purse went with him."

"Have you lost your purse?—is that what you mean?"

"I'll swear that it was in my pocket five minutes ago, and that it's not there now; that's what I mean."

Mr. Philpotts looked at Mr. Bloxham as if, although he was too polite to say so, he could not make him out at all. He resumed his selection of a paper.

"One is liable to make mistakes about one's purse; perhaps you'll find it when you get home."

Mr. Bloxham sat in silence for some moments. Then, rising, he shook himself as a dog does when he quits the water.

"I say, Philpotts, don't ladle out this yarn of mine to the other fellows, there's a good chap. As you say, one is apt to get into a muddle about one's purse, and I dare say I shall come across it when I get home. And perhaps I'm not very well this afternoon; I am feeling out of sorts, and that's a fact. I think I'll just toddle home and take a seidlitz, or a pill, or something. Ta ta!"

When Mr. Philpotts was left alone he smiled to himself, that superior smile which we are apt to smile when conscious that a man has been making a conspicuous ass of himself on lines which may be his, but which, we thank Providence, are emphatically not ours. With not one, but half a dozen papers in his hand, he seated himself in the chair which Mr. Bloxham had recently relinquished. Retaining a single paper, he placed the rest on the small round table on his left—the table on which were the matches for which Mr. Bloxham declared he had reached. Taking out his case, he selected a cigar almost with the same care which he had shewn in selecting his literature, smiling to himself all the time that superior smile. Lighting the cigar he had chosen with a match from the table, he settled himself at his ease to read.

Scarcely had he done so than he was conscious of a hand laid gently on his shoulder from behind.

"What! back again?"

"Hullo, Phil!"

He had taken it for granted, without troubling to look round, that Mr. Bloxham had returned, and that it was he who touched him on the shoulder. But the voice which replied to him, so far from being Mr. Bloxham's was one the mere sound of which caused him not only to lose his bearing of indifference but to spring from his seat with the agility almost of a jack-in-the-box. When he saw who it was had touched him on the shoulder, he stared.

"Fleming! Then Bloxham was right, after all. May I ask what brings you here?"

The man at whom he was looking was tall and well-built, in age about five and thirty. There were black cavities beneath his eyes; the man's whole face was redolent, to a trained perception, of something which was, at least, slightly unsavoury. He was dressed from head to foot in white duck—a somewhat singular costume for Pall Mall, even on a summer afternoon.

Before Mr. Philpotts' gaze, his own eyes sank. Murmuring something which was almost inaudible, he moved to the chair next to the one which Mr. Philpotts had been occupying, the chair of which Mr. Bloxham had spoken.

As he seated himself, Mr. Philpotts eyed him in a fashion which was certainly not too friendly.

"What did you mean by disappearing just now in that extraordinary manner, frightening Bloxham half out of his wits? Where did you get to?"

The new comer was stroking his heavy moustache with a hand which, for a man of his size and build, was unusually small and white. He spoke in a lazy, almost inaudible, drawl.

"I just popped outside."

"Just popped outside! I must have been coming in just when you went out. I saw nothing of you; you've put Bloxham into a pretty state of mind."

Re-seating himself, Mr. Philpotts turned to put the paper he was holding on to the little table. "I don't want to make myself a brute, but it strikes me that your presence here at all requires explanation. When several fellows club together to give another fellow a fresh start on the other side of the world——"

Mr. Philpotts stopped short. Having settled the paper on the table to his perfect satisfaction, he turned round again towards the man he was addressing—and as he did so he ceased to address him, and that for the sufficiently simple reason that he was not there to address—the man had gone! The chair at Mr. Philpotts' side was empty; without a sign or a sound its occupant had vanished, it would almost seem, into space.

CHAPTER II

UNDER the really remarkable circumstances of the case, Mr. Philpotts preserved his composure to a singular degree. He looked round the room; there was no one there. He again fixedly regarded the chair at his side; there could be no doubt that it was empty. To make quite sure, he passed his hand two or three times over the seat; it met with not the slightest opposition. Where could the man have got to? Mr. Philpotts had not, consciously, heard the slightest sound; there had not been time for him to have reached the door. Mr. Philpotts knocked the ash off his cigar. He stood up. He paced leisurely two or three times up and down the room.

"If Bloxham is ill, I am not. I was never better in my life. And the man who tells me that I have been the victim of an optical delusion is talking of what he knows nothing. I am prepared to swear that it was Geoffrey Fleming who touched me on the shoulder; that he spoke to me; and that he seated himself upon that chair. Where he came from, or where he has gone to, are other questions entirely." He critically examined his finger nails.

"If those Psychical Research people have an address in town, I think I'll have a talk with them. I suppose it's three or four minutes since the man vanished. What's the time now? Whatever has become of my watch?"

He might well ask—it had gone, both watch and chain—vanished, with Mr. Fleming, into air. Mr. Philpotts stared at his waistcoat, too astonished for speech. Then he gave a little gasp.

"This comes of playing Didymus! The brute has stolen it! I must apologise to Bloxham. As he himself said, this is a queer start, upon my honour! Now, if you like, I do feel a little out of sorts; this sort of thing is enough to make one. Before I go, I think I'll have a drop of brandy."

As he was hesitating, the smoking-room door opened to admit Frank Osborne. Mr. Osborne nodded to Mr. Philpotts as he crossed the room.

"You're not looking quite yourself, Philpotts."

Mr. Philpotts seemed to regard the observation almost in the light of an impertinence.

"Am I not? I was not aware that there was anything in my appearance to call for remark." Smiling, Mr. Osborne seated himself in the chair which the other had not long ago vacated. Mr. Philpotts regarded him attentively. "You're not looking quite yourself, either."

The smile vanished from Mr. Osborne's face.

"I'm not feeling myself!—I'm not! I'm worried about Geoff Fleming."

Mr. Philpotts slightly started.

"About Geoff Fleming?—what about Fleming?"

"I'm afraid—well, Phil, the truth is that I'm afraid that Geoff's a hopeless case."

Mr. Philpotts was once more busying himself with the papers which were on the side table.

"What do you mean?"

"As you know, he and I have been very thick in our time, and when he came a cropper it was I who suggested that we who were at school with him might have a whip round among ourselves to get the old chap a fresh start elsewhere. You all of you behaved like bricks, and when I told him what you had done, poor Geoff was quite knocked over. He promised voluntarily that he would never touch a card again, or make another bet, until he had paid you fellows off with thumping interest. Well, he doesn't seem to have kept his promise long."

"How do you know he hasn't?"

"I've heard from Deecie."

"From Deecie?—where's Fleming?"

"In Ceylon—they'd both got there before Deecie's letter left."

"In Ceylon!" exclaimed Mr. Philpotts excitedly, staring hard at Mr. Osborne. "You are sure he isn't back in town?"

In his turn, Mr. Osborne was staring at Mr. Philpotts.

"Not unless he came back by the same boat which brought Deecie's letter. What made you ask?"

"I only wondered."

"Mr. Philpotts turned again to the paper. The other went on.

"It seems that a lot of Australian sporting men were on the boat on which they went out. Fleming got in with them. They played—he played too. Deecie remonstrated—but he says that it only seemed to make bad worse. At first Geoff won—you know the usual sort of thing; he wound up by losing all he had, and about four hundred pounds beside. He had the cheek to ask Deecie for the money." Mr. Osborne paused. Mr. Philpotts uttered a sound which might have been indicative of contempt—or anything. "Deecie says that when the winners found out that he couldn't pay, there was a regular row. Geoff swore, in that wild way of his, that if he couldn't pay them before he died, he would rise from the dead to get the money."

Mr. Philpotts looked round with a show of added interest.

"What was that he said?"

"Oh, it was only his wild way of speaking—you know that way of his. If they don't get their money before he dies, and I fancy that it's rather more than even betting that they won't, I don't think that there's much chance of his rising from his grave to get it for them. He'll break that promise, as he has broken so many more. Poor Geoff! It seems that we might as well have kept our money in our pockets; it doesn't seem to have done him much good. His prospects don't look very rosy—without money, and with a bad name to start with."

"As I fancy you have more than once suspected, Frank, I never have had a high opinion of Mr. Geoffrey Fleming. I am not in the least surprised at what you tell me, any more than I was surprised when he came his cropper. I have always felt that, at a pinch, he would do anything to save his own skin." Mr. Osborne said nothing, but he shook his head. "Did you see anything of Bloxham when you came in?"

"I saw him going along the street in a cab."

"I want to speak to him! I think I'll just go and see if I can find him in his rooms."

CHAPTER III

MR. FRANK OSBORNE scarcely seemed to be enjoying his own

society when Mr. Philpotts had left him. As all the world knows, he is a man of sentiment—of the true sort, not the false. He has had one great passion in his life—Geoffrey Fleming. They began when they were at Chilchester together, when he was big, and Fleming still little. He did his work for him, fought for him, took his scrapes upon himself, believed in him, almost worshipped him. The thing continued when Fleming joined him at the University. Perhaps the fact that they both were orphans had something to do with it; neither of them had kith nor kin. The odd part of the business was that Osborne was not only a clear-sighted, he was a hard-headed man. It could not have been long before it dawned upon him that the man with whom he fraternised was a naturally bad egg. Fleming was continually coming to grief; he would have come to eternal grief at the very commencement of his career if it had not been for Osborne at his back. He went through his own money; he went through as much of his friend's as his friend would let him. Then came the final smash. There were features about the thing which made it clear, even to Frank Osborne, that in England, at least, for some years to come, Geoffrey Fleming had run his course right out. He strained all his already strained resources in his efforts to extricate the man from the mire. When he found that he himself was insufficient, going to his old schoolfellows, he begged them, for his sake—if not for Fleming's—to join hands with him in giving the scapegrace still another start. As a result, interest was made for him in a Ceylon plantation, and Mr. Fleming with, under the circumstances, well-lined pockets, was despatched over the seas to turn over a new leaf in a sunnier clime.

How he had vowed that he would turn over a new leaf, actually with tears upon his knees! And this was how he had done it; before he had reached his journey's end, he had gambled away the money which was not his, and was in debt besides. Frank Osborne must have been fashioned something like the dog which loves its master the more, the more he illtreats it. His heart went out in pity to the scamp across the seas. He had no delusions; he had long been conscious that the man was hopeless. And yet he knew very well that if he could have had his way he would have gone at once to comfort him. Poor Geoff! What an all-round mess he seemed to have made of things—and he had had the ball at his feet when he started—poor, dear old Geoff! With his knuckles Mr. Osborne wiped a suspicious moisture from his eyes. Geoff was all right—if he had only been able to prevent money from slipping from between his fingers, had been gifted with a sense of *meum et tuum*—not a nicer fellow in the world!

Mr. Osborne sat trying to persuade himself into the belief that the man was an injured paragon though he knew very well that he was an irredeemable scamp. He endeavoured to see only his good qualities, which was a task of exceeding difficulty—they were hidden in such a cloud of blackness. At least, whatever might be said against Geoff—and Mr. Osborne admitted to himself that there might be something—it was certain that Geoff loved him almost as much as he loved Geoff. Mr. Osborne declared to himself—putting pressure on himself to prevent his making a single mental reservation—that Geoff Fleming, in spite of all his faults, was the only person in the wide, wide world who did love him. And he was a stranger in a strange land, and in trouble again—poor dear old Geoff! Once more Mr. Osborne's knuckles went up to wipe that auspicious moisture from his eyes.

While he was engaged in doing this, a hand was laid gently on his shoulder from behind. It was, perhaps, because he was unwilling to be detected in such an act that, at the touch, he rose from his seat with a start—which became so to speak, a start of petrified amazement when he perceived who it was who had touched him. It was the man of whom he had been thinking, the friend of his boyhood—Geoffrey Fleming.

"Geoff!" he gasped. "Dear old Geoff!" He paused, seemingly in doubt whether to laugh or cry. "I thought you were in Ceylon!"

Mr. Fleming did exactly what he had done when he came so unexpectedly on Mr. Philpotts—he moved to the chair at Mr. Osborne's side. His manner was in contrast to his friend's—it was emphatically not emotional.

"I've just dropped in," he drawled.

"My dear old boy!" Mr. Osborne, as he surveyed his friend, seemed to become more and more torn by conflicting emotions. "Of course I'm very glad to see you Geoff, but how did you get in here? I thought that they had taken your name off the books of the club." He was perfectly aware that Mr. Fleming's name had been taken off the books of the club, and in a manner the reverse of complimentary. Mr. Fleming offered no remark. He sat looking down at the carpet stroking his moustache. Mr. Osborne went stammeringly on—"As I say, Geoff—and as, of course you know,—I am very glad to see you, anywhere; but—we don't want any unpleasantness, do we? If some of the fellows came in and found you here, they might make themselves nasty. Come round to my rooms; we shall be a lot more comfortable there, old man."

Mr. Fleming raised his eyes. He looked his friend full in the face. As he met his glance, Mr. Osborne was conscious of a curious sort of shiver. It was not only because the man's glance was, to say the least, less friendly than it might have been—it was because of something else, something which Mr. Osborne could scarcely have defined.

"I want some money."

Mr. Osborne smiled, rather fatuously.

"Ah, Geoff, the same old tale! Deecie has told me all about it. I won't reproach you; you know, if I had some, you should have it; but I'm not sure that it isn't just as well for both ourselves that I haven't, Geoff."

"You have some money in your pocket now."

Mr. Osborne's amazement grew apace—his friend's manner was so very strange.

"What a nose you always have for money; however did you find that out? But it isn't mine. You know Jim Baker left me guardian to that boy of his, and I've been drawing the youngster's dividends—it's only seventy pounds, Geoff."

Mr. Fleming stretched out his hand—his reply was brief and to the point.

"Give it to me!"

"Give it to you!—Geoff!—young Baker's money!"

Mr. Fleming reiterated his demand.

"Give it to me!"

His manner was not only distinctly threatening, it had a peculiar effect upon his friend. Although Mr. Osborne had never before shewn fear of any living man, and had, in that respect, proved his superiority over Fleming many a time, there was something at that moment in the speaker's voice, or words, or bearing, or in all three together, which set him shivering, as if with fear, from head to foot.

"Geoff!—you are mad! I'll see what I can find for you, but I can't give you young Baker's dividends."

Mr. Osborne was not quite clear as to exactly what it was that happened. He only knew that the friend of his boyhood—the man for whom he had done so much—the only person in the world who loved him—rose and took him by the throat, and, forcing him backwards, began to rifle the pocket which contained the seventy pounds. He was so taken by surprise, so overwhelmed by a feeling of utter horror, against which he was unable even to struggle, that it was only when he felt the money being actually withdrawn from his pocket that he made an attempt at self-defence. Then, when he made a frantic clutch at his assailant's felonious arm, all he succeeded in grasping was the empty air. The pressure was removed from his throat. He was able to look about him. Mr. Fleming was gone. He thrust a trembling hand into his pocket— the seventy pounds had vanished too.

"Geoff! Geoff!" he cried, the tears streaming from his eyes. "Don't play tricks with me! Give me back young Baker's dividends!"

When no one answered and there seemed no one to hear, he began to searching round and round the room with his eyes, as if he suspected Mr. Fleming of concealing himself behind some article of furniture.

"Geoff! Geoff!" he continued crying. "Dear old boy!—give me back young Baker's dividends!"

"Hullo!" exclaimed a voice—which certainly was not Mr. Fleming's. Mr. Osborne turned. Colonel Lanyon was standing with the handle of the open door in his hand. "Frank, are you rehearsing for a five-act tragedy?"

Mr. Osborne replied to the Colonel's question with another.

"Lanyon, did Geoffrey Fleming pass you as you came in?"

"Geoffrey Fleming!" The Colonel wheeled round on his heels like a teetotum. He glanced behind him. "What the deuce do you mean, Frank? If I catch that thief under the roof which covers me, I'll make a case for the police of him."

Then Mr. Osborne remembered what, in his agitation, he had momentarily forgotten, that Geoffrey Fleming had had no bitterer, more out-spoken, and, it may be added, more well-merited an opponent than Colonel Lanyon in the Climax Club. The Colonel advanced towards Mr. Osborne.

"Do you know that that's the blackguard's chair you're standing by?"

"His chair!"

Mr. Osborne was leaning with one hand on the chair on which Mr. Fleming had, not long ago, been sitting.

"That's what he used to call it himself,—with his usual impudence. He used to sit in it whenever he took a hand. The men would give it up to him—you know how you gave everything up to him, all the lot of you. If he couldn't get it he'd turn nasty— wouldn't play. It seems that he had the cheek to cut his initials on the chair—I only heard of it the other day, or there'd have been a clearance of him long ago. Look here—what do you think of that for a piece of rowdiness?"

The Colonel turned the chair upside down. Sure enough in the woodwork underneath the seat were the letters, cut in good-sized characters—"G.F."

"You know that rubbishing way in which he used to talk. When men questioned his exclusive right to the chair, I've heard him say he'd prove his right by coming and sitting in it after he was dead and buried—he swore he'd haunt the chair. Idiot!—What is the matter with you Frank? You look as if you'd been in a rough and tumble—your necktie's all anyhow."

"I think I must have dropped asleep, and dreamed—yes, I fancy I've been dreaming."

Mr. Osborne staggered, rather than walked, to the door, keeping one hand in the inside pocket of his coat. The Colonel followed him with his eyes.

"Frank's ageing fast," was his mental comment as Mr. Osborne disappeared. "He'll be an old man yet before I am."

He seated himself in Geoffrey Fleming's chair.

It was, perhaps, ten minutes afterwards that Edward Jackson went into the smoking room—"Scientific" Jackson, as they call him, because of the sort of catch phrase he is always using—"Give me science!" He had scarcely been in the room a minute before he came rushing to the door shouting—

"Help, help!"

Men came hurrying from all parts of the building. Mr. Griffin came from the billiard-room, where he is always to be found. He had a cue in one hand, and a piece of chalk in the other. He was the first to address the vociferous gentleman standing at the smoking-room door.

"Jackson!—What's the matter?"

Mr. Jackson was in such a condition of fluster and excitement that it was a little difficult to make out, from his own statement, what was the matter.

"Lanyon's dead! Have any of you seen Geoff Fleming? Stop him if you do—he's stolen my pocket-book!" He began mopping his brow with his bandanna handkerchief, "God bless my soul! an awful thing!—I've been robbed—and old Lanyon's dead!"

One thing was quickly made clear—as they saw for themselves when they went crowding into the smoking-room—Lanyon was dead. He was kneeling in front of Geoffrey Fleming's chair, clutching at either side of it with a tenacity which suggested some sort of convulsion. His head was thrown back, his eyes were still staring wide open, his face was distorted by a something which was half fear, half horror—as if, as those who saw him afterwards agreed, he had seen sudden, certain death approaching him, in a form which even he, a seasoned soldier, had found too horrible for contemplation.

Mr. Jackson's story, in one sense, was plain enough, though it was odd enough in another. He told it to an audience which evinced unmistakable interest in every word uttered.

"I often come in for a smoke about this time, because generally the place is empty, so that you get it all to yourself."

He cast a somewhat aggressive look upon his hearers—a look which could hardly be said to convey a flattering suggestion.

"When I first came in I thought that the room was empty. It was only when I was half-way across that something caused me to look round. I saw that someone was kneeling on the floor. I looked to see who it was. It was Lanyon. 'Lanyon!' I cried. 'Whatever are you doing there?' He didn't answer. Wondering what was up with him and why he didn't speak, I went closer to where he was. When I got there I didn't like the look of him at all. I thought he was in some sort of a fit. I was hesitating whether to pick him up, or at once to summon assistance, when—"

Mr. Jackson paused. He looked about him with an obvious shiver.

"By George! when I think of it now, it makes me go quite creepy. Cathcart, would you mind ringing for another drop of brandy?"

The brandy was rung for. Mr. Jackson went on.

"All of a sudden, as I was stooping over Lanyon, someone touched me on the shoulder. You know, there hadn't been a sound—I hadn't heard the door open, not a thing which could suggest that anyone was approaching. Finding Lanyon like that had make me go quite queer, and when I felt that touch on my shoulder it so startled me that I fairly screeched. I jumped up to see who it was, and when I saw"—Mr. Jackson's bandanna came into play—"who it was, I thought my eyes would have started out of my head. It was Geoff Fleming."

"Who?" came in chorus from his auditors.

"It was Geoffrey Fleming. 'Good God!—Fleming!' I cried. 'Where did you come from? I never heard you. Anyhow, you're just in the nick of time. Lanyon's come to grief—lend me a hand with him.' I bent down, to take hold of one side of poor old Lanyon, meaning Fleming to take hold of the other. Before I had a chance of touching Lanyon, Fleming, catching me by the shoulder, whirled me round—I had had no idea the fellow was so strong, he gripped me like a vice. I was just going to ask what the dickens he meant by handling me like that, when, before I could say Jack Robinson, or even had time to get my mouth open, Fleming, darting his hand into my coat pocket, snatched my pocket-book clean out of it."

He stopped, apparently to gasp for breath. "And, pray, what were you doing while Mr. Fleming behaved in this exceedingly peculiar way—even for Mr. Fleming?" inquired Mr. Cathcart.

"Doing!" Mr. Jackson was indignant. "Don't I tell you I was doing nothing? There was no time to do anything—it all happened in a flash. I had just come from my bankers—there were a hundred and thirty pounds in that pocket-book. When I realised that the fellow had taken it, I made a grab at him. And"—again Mr. Jackson looked furtively about him, and once more the bandanna came into active play—"directly I did so, I don't know where he went to, but it seemed to me that he vanished into air—he was gone, like a flash of lightning. I told myself I was mad—stark mad! but when I felt for my pocket-book, and found that that was also gone, I ran yelling to the door."

CHAPTER IV

IT was, as the old-time novelists used to phrase it, about three weeks after the events transpired which we have recorded in the previous chapter. Evening—after dinner. There was a goodly company assembled in the smoking room at the Climax Club. Conversation was general. They were talking of some of the curious circumstances which had attended the death of Colonel Lanyon. The medical evidence at the inquest had gone to shew that the Colonel had died of one of the numerous, and, indeed, almost innumerable, varieties of heart disease. The finding had been in accordance with the medical evidence. It seemed to be felt, by some of the speakers, that such a finding scarcely met the case.

"It's all very well," observed Mr. Cathcart, who seemed disposed to side with the coroner's jury, "for you fellows to talk, but in such a case, you must bring in some sort of verdict—and what other verdict could they bring? There was not a trace of any mark of violence to be found upon the man."

"It's my belief that he saw Fleming, and that Fleming frightened him to death."

It was Mr. Jackson who said this. Mr. Cathcart smiled a rather provoking smile.

"So far as I observed, you did not drop any hint of your belief when you were before the coroner."

"No, because I didn't want to be treated as a laughing-stock by a lot of idiots."

"Quite so; I can understand your natural objection to that, but still I don't see your line of argument. I should not have cared to question Lanyon's courage to Lanyon's face while he was living. Why should you suppose that such a man as Geoffrey Fleming was capable of such a thing as, as you put it, actually frightening him to death? I should say it was rather the other way about. I have seen Fleming turn green, with what looked very much like funk, at the sight of Lanyon."

Mr. Jackson for some moments smoked in silence.

"If you had seen Geoffrey Fleming under the circumstances in which I did, you would understand better what it is I mean."

"But, my dear Jackson, if you will forgive my saying so, it seems to me that you don't shew to great advantage in your own story. Have you communicated the fact of your having been robbed to the police?"

"I have."

"And have you furnished them with the numbers of the notes which were taken?"

"I have."

"Then, in that case, I shouldn't be surprised if Mr. Fleming were brought to book any hour of any day. You'll find he has been lying close in London all the time—he soon had enough of Ceylon."

A new comer joined the group of talkers—Frank Osborne. They noticed, as he seated himself, how much he seemed to have aged of late and how particularly shabby he seemed just then. The first remark which he made took them all aback.

"Geoff Fleming's dead."

"Dead!" cried Mr. Philpotts, who was sitting next to Mr. Osborne.

"Yes—dead. I've heard from Deecie. He died three weeks ago."

"Three weeks ago!"

"On the day on which Lanyon died."

Mr. Cathcart turned to Mr. Jackson, with a smile.

"Then that knocks on the head your theory about his having frightened Lanyon to death; and how about your interview with him—eh Jackson?"

Mr. Jackson did not answer. He suddenly went white. An intervention came from an unexpected quarter—from Mr. Philpotts.

"It seems to me that you are rather taking things for granted, Cathcart. I take leave to inform you that I saw Geoffrey Fleming, perhaps less than half-an-hour before Jackson did."

Mr. Cathcart stared.

"You saw him!—Philpotts!"

Then Mr. Bloxham arose and spoke.

"Yes, and I saw him, too—didn't I, Philpotts?"

Any tendency on the part of the auditors to smile was checked by the tone of exceeding bitterness in which Frank Osborne was also moved to testify.

"And I—I saw him, too!—Geoff!—dear old boy!"

"Deecie says that there were two strange things about Geoff's death. He was struck by a fit of apoplexy. He was dead within the hour. Soon after he died, the servant came running to say that the bed was empty on which the body had been lying. Deecie went to see. He says that, when he got into the room, Geoff was back again upon the bed, but it was plain enough that he had moved. His clothes and hair were in disorder, his fists were clenched, and there was a look upon his face which had not been there at the moment of his death, and which, Deecie says, seemed a look partly of rage and partly of triumph.

"I have been calculating the difference between Cingalese and Greenwich time. It must have been between three and four o'clock when the servant went running to say that Geoff's body was not upon the bed—it was about that time that Lanyon died."

He paused—and then continued—

"The other strange thing that happened was this. Deecie says that the day after Geoff died a telegram came for him, which, of course, he opened. It was an Australian wire, and purported to come from the Melbourne sporting man of whom I told you." He turned to Mr. Philpotts. "It ran, 'Remittance to hand. It comes in rather a miscellaneous form. Thanks all the same.' Deecie can only suppose that Geoff had managed, in some way, to procure the four hundred pounds which he had lost and couldn't pay, and had also managed, in some way, to send it on to Melbourne."

There was silence when Frank Osborne ceased to speak—silence which was broken in a somewhat startling fashion.

"Who's that touched me?" suddenly exclaimed Mr. Cathcart, springing from his seat.

They stared.

"Touched you!" said someone. "No one's within half a mile of you. You're dreaming, my dear fellow."

Considering the provocation was so slight, Mr. Cathcart seemed strangely moved.

"Don't tell me that I'm dreaming—someone touched me on the shoulder!—What's that?"

"That" was the sound of laughter proceeding from the, apparently, vacant seat. As if inspired by a common impulse, the listeners simultaneously moved back.

"That's Fleming's chair," said Mr. Philpotts, beneath his breath.

Nelly

CHAPTER I

"WHY!" Mr. Gibbs paused. He gave a little gasp. He bent still closer. Then the words came with a rush: "It's Nelly!"

He glanced at the catalogue. "No. 259—'Stitch! Stitch! Stitch!'— Philip Bodenham." It was a small canvas, representing the interior of an ill-furnished apartment in which a woman sat, on a rickety chair, at a rickety table, sewing. The picture was an illustration of "The Song of the Shirt."

Mr. Gibbs gazed at the woman's face depicted on the canvas, with gaping eyes.

"It's Nelly!" he repeated. There was a catch in his voice. "Nelly!"

He tore himself away as if he were loth to leave the woman who sat there sewing. He went to the price list which the Academicians keep in the lobby. He turned the leaves. The picture was unsold. The artist had appraised it at a modest figure. Mr. Gibbs bought it there and then. Then he turned to his catalogue to discover the artist's address. Mr. Bodenham lived in Manresa Road, Chelsea.

Not many minutes after a cab drove up to the Manresa Studios. Mr. Gibbs knocked at a door on the panels of which was inscribed Mr. Bodenham's name.

"Come in!" cried a voice.

Mr. Gibbs entered. An artist stood at his easel.

"Mr. Bodenham?"

"I am Mr. Bodenham."

"I am Mr. Gibbs. I have just purchased your picture at the Academy, 'Stitch! Stitch! Stitch!'" Mr. Bodenham bowed. "I—I wish to make a—a few inquiries about—about the picture."

Mr. Gibbs was as nervous as a schoolboy. He stammered and he blushed. The artist seemed to be amused. He smiled.

"You wish to make a few inquiries about the picture—yes?"

"About the—about the subject of the picture. That is, about—about the model."

Mr. Gibbs became a peony red. The artist's smile grew more pronounced.

"About the model?"

"Yes, about the model. Where does she live?"

Although the day was comparatively cool, Mr. Gibbs was so hot that it became necessary for him to take out his handkerchief to wipe his brow. Mr. Bodenham was a sunny-faced young man. He looked at his visitor with laughter in his eyes.

"You are aware, Mr. Gibbs, that yours is rather an unusual question. I have not the pleasure of your acquaintance, and we artists are not in the habit of giving information about our models to perfect strangers. It would not do. Moreover, how do you know that I painted from a model? The faces in pictures are sometimes creations of the artist's imagination. Perhaps oftener than the public think."

"I know the model in 'Stitch! Stitch! Stitch!'"

"You know her? Then why do you come to me for information?"

"I should have said that I knew her years ago."

Mr. Gibbs looked round the room a little doubtfully. Then he laid his hand on the back of a chair, as if for the support, moral and physical, which it afforded him. He looked at the artist with his big, grave eyes.

"As I say, Mr. Bodenham, I knew her years ago—and I loved her."

There was a catch in his voice. The artist seemed to be growing more and more amused. Mr. Gibbs went on:

"I was a younger man then. She was but a girl. We both of us were poor. We loved each other dearly. We agreed that I should go abroad and make my fortune. When I had made it, I was to come back to her."

The big man paused. His listener was surprised to find how much his visitor's curious earnestness impressed him. "I had hard times of it at first. Now and then I heard from her. At last her letters ceased. About the time her letters ceased, my prospects bettered. Now I'm doing pretty well. So I've come to take her back with me to the other side. Mr. Bodenham, I've looked for her everywhere. As they say, high and low. I've been to her old home, and to mine—I've been just everywhere. But no one seems to know anything about her. She has just clean gone, vanished out of sight. I was thinking that I should have to go back, after all, without her, when I saw your picture in the Academy, and I knew the girl you had painted was Nelly. So I bought your picture—her picture. And now I want you to tell me where she lives."

There was a momentary silence when the big man finished.

"Yours is a very romantic story, Mr. Gibbs. Since you have done me the honour to make of me your confidant, I shall have pleasure in giving you the address of the original of my little picture—the address, that is, at which I last heard of her. I have reason to believe that her address is not infrequently changed. When I last heard of her, she was—what shall I say?—hard up."

"Hard up, was she? Was she very hard up, Mr. Bodenham?"

"I'm afraid, Mr. Gibbs, that she was as hard up as she could be—and live."

Mr. Gibbs cleared his throat:

"Thank you. Will you give me her address, Mr. Bodenham?"

Mr. Bodenham wrote something on a slip of paper.

"There it is. It is a street behind Chelsea Hospital—about as unsavoury a neighbourhood as you will easily find."

Mr. Gibbs found that the artist's words were justified by facts—it was an unsavoury neighbourhood into which the cabman found his way. No. 20 was the number which Mr. Bodenham had given him. The door of No. 20 stood wide open. Mr. Gibbs knocked with his stick. A dirty woman appeared from a room on the left.

"Does Miss Brock live here?"

"Never heard tell of no such name. Unless it's the young woman what lives at the top of the 'ouse—third floor back. Perhaps it's her you want. Is it a model that you're after? Because, that's what she is—leastways I've heard 'em saying so. Top o' the stairs, first door to your left."

Mr. Gibbs started to ascend.

"Take care of them stairs," cried the woman after him. "They wants knowing."

Mr. Gibbs found that what the woman said was true—they did want knowing. Better light, too would have been an assistant to a better knowledge. He had to strike a match to enable him to ascertain if he had reached the top. A squalid top it was—it smelt!

By the light of the flickering match he perceived that there was a door upon his left. He knocked. A voice cried to him, for the second time that day:

"Come in!"

But this voice was a woman's. At the sound of it, the heart in the man's great chest beat, in a sledge-hammer fashion, against his ribs. His hand trembled as he turned the handle, and when he had opened the door, and stood within the room, his heart, which had been beating so tumultuously a moment before, stood still.

The room, which was nothing but a bare attic with raftered ceiling, was imperfectly lighted by a small skylight—a skylight which seemed as though it had not been cleaned for ages, so obscured was the glass by the accumulations of the years. By the light of this skylight Mr. Gibbs could see that a woman was standing in the centre of the room.

"Nelly!" he cried.

The woman shrank back with, as it were, a gesture of repulsion. Mr. Gibbs moved forward.

"Nelly! Don't you know me? I am Tom."

"Tom?"

The woman's voice was but an echo.

"Tom! Yes, my own, own darling, I am Tom."

Mr. Gibbs advanced. He held out his arms. He was just in time to catch the woman, or she would have fallen to the floor.

CHAPTER II

"NELLY, don't you know me?" The woman was coming to.

"Haven't you a light?" The woman faintly shook her head.

"See, I have your portrait where you placed it; it has never left me all the time. But when I saw your picture I did not need your portrait to tell me it was you."

"When you saw my picture?"

"Your portrait in Mr. Bodenham's picture at Academy 'Stitch! Stitch! Stitch!'"

"Mr. Bodenham's—I see."

The woman's tone was curiously cold.

"Nelly, you don't seem to be very glad to see me."

"Have you got any money?"

"Any money, Nelly?"

"I am hungry."

"Hungry!"

The woman's words seemed to come to him with the force of revelation.

"Hungry!" She turned her head away. "Oh, my God, Nelly." His voice trembled. "Wa-wait here, I—I sha'n't be a moment. I've a cab at the door."

He was back almost as soon as he went. He brought with him half the contents of a shop—among other things, a packet of candles. These he lighted, standing them, on their own ends, here and there about the room. The woman ate shyly, as if, in spite of her confession of hunger, she had little taste for food. She was fingering the faded photograph of a girl which Mr. Gibbs had taken from his pocket-book.

"Is this my portrait?"

"Nelly! Don't you remember it?"

"How long is it since it was taken?"

"Why, it's more than seven years, isn't it?"

"Do you think I've altered much?"

Mr. Gibbs went to her. He studied her by the light of the candles.

"Well, you might be plumper, and you might look happier, perhaps, but all that we'll quickly alter. For the rest, thank God, you're my old Nelly." He took her in his arms. As he did so she drew a long, deep breath. Holding her at arms-length, he studied her again. "Nelly, I'm afraid you haven't been having the best of times."

She broke from him with sudden passion.

"Don't speak of it! Don't speak of it! The life I've lived——" She paused. All at once her voice became curiously hard. "But through it all I've been good. I swear it. No one knows what the temptation is, to a woman who has lived the life I have, to go wrong. But I never went. Tom"—she laid her hand upon Mr. Gibbs' arm as, with marked awkwardness, his name issued from her lips—"say that you believe that I've been good."

His only answer was to take her in his arms again, and to kiss her.

Mr. Gibbs provided his new-found lost love with money. With that money she renewed her wardrobe. He found her other lodgings in a more savoury neighbourhood at Putney. In those lodgings he once more courted her.

He told himself during those courtship days, that, after all, the years had changed her. She was a little hard. He did not remember the Nelly of the old time as being hard. But, then, what had happened during the years which had come between! Father and mother both had died. She had been thrown out into the world without a friend, without a penny! His letters had gone astray. In those early days he had been continually wandering hither and thither. Her letters had strayed as well as his. Struggling for existence, when she saw that no letters reached her, she told herself either that he too had died, or that he had forgotten her. Her heart hardened. It was with her a bitter striving for daily bread. She had tried everything. Teaching, domestic service, chorus singing, needlework, acting as an artist's model—she had failed in everything alike. At the best she had only been able to keep body and soul together. It had come to the worst at last. On the morning on which he found her, she had been two days without food. She had decided that, that night, if things did not mend during the intervening hours—of which she had no hope—that she would seek for better fortune—in the Thames.

She told her story, not all at once, but at different times, and in answer to her lover's urgent solicitations. She herself at first evinced a desire for reticence. The theme seemed too painful a theme for her to dwell upon. But the man's hungry heart poured forth such copious stores of uncritical sympathy that, after a while, it seemed to do her good to pour into his listening ears a particular record of her woes. She certainly had suffered. But now that the days of suffering were ended, it began almost to be a pleasure to recall the sorrows which were past.

In the sunshine of prosperity the woman's heart became young again, and softer. It was not only that she became plumper—which she certainly did—but she became, inwardly and outwardly, more beautiful. Her lover told himself, and her, that she was more beautiful even than she had been as a girl. He declared that she was far prettier than she appeared in the old-time photograph. She smiled, and she charmed him with an infinite charm.

The days drew near to the wedding. Had he had his way he would have married her, off-hand, when he found her in the top attic in that Chelsea slum. But she said no. Then she would not even talk of marriage. To hear her, one would have thought that the trials she had undergone had unfitted her for wedded life. He laughed her out of that—a day was fixed. She postponed it once, and then again. She had it that she needed time to recuperate— that she would not marry with the shadow of that grisly past still haunting her at night. He argued that the royal road to recuperation was in his arms. He declared that she would be troubled by no haunting shadows as his dear wife. And, at last, she yielded. A final date was fixed. That day drew near.

As the day drew near, she grew more tender. On the night before the wedding-day her tenderness reached, as it were, its culminating point. Never before had she been so sweet—so softly caressing. They were but to part for a few short hours. In the morning they were to meet, never, perhaps, to part again. But it seemed as if he could not tear himself away, and as if she could not let him go.

Just before he left her a little dialogue took place between them, which if lover-like, none the less was curious.

"Tom" she said, "suppose, after we are married, you should find out that I have not been so good as you thought, what would you say?"

"Say?—nothing."

"Oh yes, you would, else you would be less than man. Suppose, for instance, that you found out I had deceived you."

"I decline to suppose impossibilities."

She had been circled by his arms. Now she drew herself away from him. She stood where the gaslight fell right on her.

"Tom, look at me carefully! Are you sure you know me?"

"Nelly!"

"Are you quite sure you are not mistaking me for some one else? Are you quite sure, Tom?"

"My own!"

He took her in his arms again. As he did so, she looked him steadfastly in the face.

"Tom, I think it possible that, some day, you may think less of me than you do now. But"—she put her hand over his mouth to stop his speaking—"whatever you may think of me, I shall always love you"—there was an appreciable pause, and an appreciable catching of her breath—"better than my life."

She kissed him, with unusual abandonment, long and fervently, upon the lips.

The morning of the following day came with the promise of fine weather. Theirs had been an unfashionable courtship—it was to be an unfashionable wedding. Mr. Gibbs was to call for his bride, at her lodgings. They were to drive together, in a single hired brougham, to the church.

Even before the appointed hour, the expectant bridegroom drew up to the door of the house in which his lady-love resided. His knock was answered with an instant readiness which showed that his arrival had been watched and waited for. The landlady herself opened the door, her countenance big with tidings.

"Miss Brock has gone, sir."

"Gone!" Mr. Gibbs was puzzled by the woman's tone. "Gone where? For a walk?"

"No, sir, she's gone away. She's left this letter, sir, for you."

The landlady thrust an envelope into his hand. It was addressed simply, "Thomas Gibbs, Esq." With the envelope in his hand, and an odd something clutching at his heart, he went into the empty sitting-room. He took the letter out of its enclosure, and this is what he read:

"My own, own Tom,—You never were mine, and it is the last time I shall ever call you so. I am going back, I have only too good reason to fear, to the life from which you took me, because—*I am not your Nelly*."

The words were doubly underlined, they were unmistakable, yet he had to read them over and over again before he was able to grasp their meaning. What did they mean? Had his darling suddenly gone mad? The written sheet swam before his eyes. It was with an effort he read on.

"How you ever came to mistake me for her I cannot understand.

The more I have thought of it, the stranger it has seemed. I suppose there must be a resemblance between us—between your Nelly and me. Though I expect the resemblance is more to the face in Mr. Bodenham's picture than it is to mine. I never did think the woman in Mr. Bodenham's picture was like me—though I was his model. I never could have been the original of your photograph of Nelly—it is not in the least like me. I think that you came to England with your heart and mind and eyes so full of Nelly, and so eager for a sight of her, that, in your great hunger of love, you grasped at the first chance resemblance you encountered. That is the only explanation I can think of, Tom, of how you can have mistaken me for her.

"My part is easier to explain. It is quite true, as I told you, that I was starving when you came to me. I was so weak and faint, and sick at heart, that your sudden appearance and strange behaviour—in a perfect stranger, for you were a perfect stranger, Tom—drove from me the few senses I had left. When I recovered I found myself in the arms of a man who seemed to know me, and who spoke to me words of love—words which I had never heard from the lips of a man before. I sent you to buy me food. While you were gone I told myself—wickedly! I know, Tom it was wickedly!—what a chance had come at last, which would save me from the river, at least for a time, and I should be a fool to let it slip. I perceived that you were mistaking me for some one else. I resolved to allow you to continue under your misapprehension. I did not doubt that you would soon discover your mistake. What would happen then I did not pause to think. But events marched quicker than I, in that first moment of mad impulse, had bargained for. You never did discover your mistake. How that was, even now I do not understand. But you began to talk of marriage. That was a prospect I dared not face.

"For one thing—forgive me for writing it, but I must write it, now that I am writing to you for the first and for the last time—I began to love you. Not for the man I supposed you to be, but for the man I knew you were. I loved you—and I love you! I shall never cease to love you, with a love of which I did not think I was capable. As I told you, Tom, last night—when I kissed you!—I love you better than my own life. Better, far better, for my life is worthless, and you—you are not worthless, Tom! And I would not—even had I dared!—allow you to marry me; not for myself, but for another; not for the present, but for the past; not for the thing I was, but for the thing which you supposed I had been, once. I would have married you for your own sake; you would not have married me for mine. And so, since I dared not undeceive you—I feared to see the look which would come in your face and your eyes—I am going to steal back, like a thief, to the life from which you took me. I have had a greater happiness than ever I expected. I have enjoyed those stolen kisses which they say are sweetest. Your happiness is still to come. You will find Nelly. Such love as yours will not go unrewarded. I have been but an incident, a chapter in your life, which now is closed. God bless you, Tom! I am yours, although you are not mine—not yours, Nelly Brock—but yours, Helen Reeves."

Mr. Gibbs read this letter once, then twice, and then again. Then he rang the bell. The landlady appeared with a suspicious promptitude which suggested the possibility of her having been a spectator of his proceedings through the keyhole.

"When did Miss Brock go out?"

"Quite early, sir. I'm sure, sir, I was quite taken aback when she said that she was going—on her wedding-day and all."

"Did she say where she was going?"

"Not a word, sir. She said: 'Mrs. Horner, I am going away. Give this letter to Mr. Gibbs when he comes.' That was every word she says, sir; then she goes right out of the front door."

"Did she take any luggage?"

"Just the merest mite of a bag, sir—not another thing."

Mr. Gibbs asked no other questions. He left the room and went out into the street. The driver of the brougham was instructed to drive, not to church, but—to his evident and unconcealed surprise—to that slum in Chelsea. She had written that she was returning to the old life. The old life was connected with that top attic. He thought it might be worth his while to inquire if anything had been seen or heard of her. Nothing had. He left his card, with instructions to write him should any tidings come that way. Then, since it was unadvisable to drive about all day under the ægis of a

Jehu, whose button-hole was adorned with a monstrous wedding favour, he dismissed the carriage and sent it home.

He turned into the King's Road. He was walking in the direction of Sloane Square, when a voice addressed him from behind.

"Tom!"

It was a woman's voice. He turned. A woman was standing close behind him, looking and smiling at him—a stout and a dowdy woman. Cheaply and flashily dressed in faded finery—not the sort of woman whose recognition one would be over-anxious to compel. Mr. Gibbs looked at her. There was something in her face and in her voice which struck faintly some forgotten chord in his memory.

"Tom! don't you know me? I am Nelly."

He looked at her intently for some instants. Then it all flashed over him. This was Nelly, the real Nelly, the Nelly of his younger days, the Nelly he had come to find. This dandy sloven, whose shrill voice proclaimed her little vulgar soul—so different from that other Nelly, whose soft, musical tones had not been among the least of her charms. The recognition came on him with the force of a sudden shock. He reeled, so that he had to clutch at a railing to help him stand.

"Tom! what's the matter? Aren't you well? Or is it the joy of seeing me has sent you silly?"

She laughed, the dissonant laughter of the female Cockney of a certain class. Mr. Gibbs recovered his balance and his civility.

"Thank you, I am very well. And you?"

"Oh, I'm all right. There's never much the matter with me. I can't afford the time to be ill." She laughed again. "Well, this is a start my meeting you. Come and have a bit o' dinner along with us."

"Who is us? Your father and your mother?"

"Why, father, he's been dead these five years, and mother, she's been dead these three. I don't want you to have a bit of dinner along with them—not hardly." Again she laughed. "It's my old man I mean. Why, you don't mean to say you don't know I'm married! Why, I'm the mother of five."

He had fallen in at her side. They were walking on together—he like a man in a dream.

"We're doing pretty well considering, we manage to live, you know." She laughed again. She seemed filled with laughter, which was more than Mr. Gibbs was then. "We're fishmongers, that's what we are. William he's got a very tidy trade, as good as any in the road. There, here's our shop!" She paused in front of a fishmonger's shop. "And there's our name"—she pointed up at it. "Nelly Brock I used to be, and now I'm Mrs. William Morgan."

She laughed again. She led the way through the shop to a little room beyond. A man was seated on the table, reading a newspaper, a man without a coat on, and with a blue apron tied about his waist.

"William, who do you think I've brought to see you? You'll never guess in a month of Sundays. This is Tom Gibbs, of whom you've heard me speak dozens of times."

Mr. Morgan wiped his hand upon his apron. Then he held it out to Mr. Gibbs. Mr. Gibbs was conscious, as he grasped it, that it reeked of fish.

"How are you, Gibbs? Glad to see you!" Mr. Morgan turned to his wife. "Where's that George? There's a pair of soles got to be sent up to Sydney Street, and there's not a soul about the place to take 'em."

"That George is a dratted nuisance, that's what he is. He never is anywhere to be found when you want him. You remember, William, me telling you about Tom Gibbs? My old sweetheart, you know, he was. He went away to make his fortune, and I was to wait for him till he came back, and I daresay I should have waited if you hadn't just happened to come along."

"I wish I hadn't just happened, then. I wish she'd waited for you, Gibbs. It'd have been better for me, and worse for you, old man."

"That's what they all say, you know, after a time."

Mrs. Morgan laughed. But Mr. Morgan did not seem to be in a particularly jovial frame of mind.

"It's all very well for you to talk, you know, but I don't like the way things are managed in this house, and so I tell you. There's your new lodger come while you've been out, and her room's like a regular pig-sty, and I had to show her upstairs myself, with the shop chock-full of customers." Mr. Morgan drew his hand across his nose. "See you directly, Gibbs; some one must attend to business."

Mr. Morgan withdrew to the shop. Mr. Gibbs and his old love were left alone.

"Never you mind, William. He's all right; but he's a bit huffy—men will get huffy when things don't go just as they want 'em. I'll just run upstairs and send the lodger down here, while I tidy up her room. The children slept in it last night. I never expected her till this afternoon; she's took me unawares. You wait here; I shan't be half a minute. Then we'll have a bit of dinner."

Mr. Gibbs, left alone, sat in a sort of waking dream. Could this be Nelly—the Nelly of whom he had dreamed, for whom he had striven, whom he had come to find—this mother of five? Why, she must have begun to play him false almost as soon as his back was turned. She must have already been almost standing at the altar steps with William Morgan while writing the last of her letters to him. And had his imagination, or his memory, tricked him? Had youth, or distance, lent enchantment to the view? Had she gone back, or had he advanced? Could she have been the vulgar drab which she now appeared to be, in the days of long ago?

As he sat there, endeavouring to resolve these riddles which had been so suddenly presented for solution, the door opened and some one entered.

"I beg your pardon," said the voice of the intruder, on perceiving that the room was already provided with an occupant.

Mr. Gibbs glanced up. The voice fell like the voice of a magician on his ear. He rose to his feet, all trembling. In the doorway was standing the other Nelly—the false, and yet the true one. The Nelly of his imagination. The Nelly to whom he was to have been married that day. He went to her with a sudden cry.

"Nelly!"

"Tom!" She shrank away. But in spite of her shrinking, he took her in his arms.

"My own, own darling."

"Tom," she moaned, "don't you understand—I'm not Nelly!"

"I know it, and I thank God, my darling, you are not."

"Tom! What do you mean?"

"I mean that I have found Nelly, and I mean that, thank Heaven!

I have found you too—never, my darling, please Heaven! to lose sight of you again."

They had only just time to withdraw from a too suspicious neighbourhood, before the door opened again to admit Mrs. Morgan.

"Tom, this is our new lodger. I just asked her if she'd mind stepping downstairs while I tidied up her room a bit. Miss Reeves, this is an old sweetheart of mine—Mr. Gibbs."

Mr. Gibbs turned to the "new lodger."

"Miss Reeves and I are already acquainted. Miss Reeves, you have heard me speak of Mrs. Morgan, though not by that name. This is Nelly."

Miss Reeves turned and looked at Mrs. Morgan, and as she looked—she gasped.

La Haute Finance

A TALE OF THE BIGGEST COUP ON RECORD

CHAPTER I

"By Jove! I believe it could be done!"

Mr. Rodney Railton took the cigarette out of his mouth and sent a puff of smoke into the air.

"I believe it could, by Jove!"

Another puff of smoke.

"I'll write to Mac."

He drew a sheet of paper towards him and penned the following:—

"DEAR ALEC,—Can you give me some dinner to-night? Wire me if you have a crowd. I shall be in the House till four. Have something to propose which will make your hair stand up.

"Yours, R.R."

This he addressed "Alexander Macmathers, Esq., 27, Campden Hill Mansions." As he went downstairs he gave the note to the commissionaire, with instructions that it should be delivered at once by hand.

That night Mr. Railton dined with Mr. Macmathers. The party consisted of three, the two gentlemen and a lady—Mrs. Macmathers, in fact. Mr. Macmathers was an American—a Southerner—rather tall and weedy, with a heavy, drooping moustache, like his hair, raven black. He was not talkative. His demeanour gave a wrong impression of the man—the impression that he was not a man of action. As a matter of fact, he was a man of action before all things else. He was not rich, as riches go, but certainly he was not poor. His temperament was cosmopolitan, and his profession Jack-of-all-trades. Wherever there was money to be made, he was there. Sometimes, it must be confessed, he was there, too, when there was money to be lost. His wife was

English—keen and clever. Her chief weakness was that she would persist in looking on existence as a gigantic lark. When she was most serious she regarded life least *au sérieux*.

Mr. Railton, who had invited himself to dinner, was a hybrid—German mother, English father. He was quite a young man—say thirty. His host was perhaps ten, his hostess five years older than himself. He was a stockjobber—ostensibly in the Erie market. All that he had he had made, for he had, as a boy, found himself the situation of a clerk. But his clerkly days were long since gone. No one anything like his age had a better reputation in the House; it was stated by those who had best reason to know that he had never once been left, and few had a larger credit. Lately he had wandered outside his markets to indulge in little operations in what he called *La Haute Finance*. In these Mr. Macmathers had been his partner more than once, and in him he had found just the man he wished to find.

When they had finished dinner, the lady withdrew, and the gentlemen were left alone.

"Well," observed Mr. Macmathers, "what's going to make my hair stand up?"

Mr. Railton stroked his chin as he leaned both his elbows on the board.

"Of course, Mac, I can depend on you. I'm just giving myself away. It's no good my asking you to observe strict confidence, for, if you won't come in, from the mere fact of your knowing it the thing's just busted up, that's all."

"Sounds like a mystery-of-blood-to-thee-I'll-now-unfold sort of thing."

"I don't know about mystery, but there'll be plenty of blood."

Mr. Railton stopped short and looked at his friend.

"Blood, eh? I say, Rodney, think before you speak."

"I have thought. I thought I'd play the game alone. But it's too big a game for one."

"Well, if you have thought, out with it, or be silent evermore."

"You know Plumline, the dramatist?"

"I know he's an ass."

"Ass or no ass, it's from him I got the idea."

"Good Heavens! No wonder it smells of blood."

"He's got an idea for a new play, and he came to me to get some local colouring. I'll just tell you the plot—he was obliged to tell it me, or I couldn't have given him the help he wanted."

"Is it essential? I have enough of Plumline's plots when I see them on the stage."

"It is essential. You will see."

Mr. Railton got up, lighted a cigar, and stood before the fireplace. When he had brought the cigar into good going order he unfolded Mr. Plumline's plot.

"I'm not going to bore you. I'm just going to touch upon that part which gave me my idea. There's a girl who dreams of boundless wealth—a clever girl, you understand."

"Girls who dream of boundless wealth sometimes are clever," murmured his friend. Perhaps he had his wife in his mind's eye.

"She is wooed and won by a financier. Not wooed and won by a tale of love, but by the exposition of an idea."

"That's rather new—for Plumline."

"The financier has an idea for obtaining the boundless wealth of which she only dreams."

"And the idea?"

"Is the bringing about of a war between France and Germany."

"Great snakes!" The cigarette dropped from between Mr. Macmather's lips. He carefully picked it up again. "That's not a bad idea—for Plumline."

"It's my idea as well. In the play it fails. The financier comes to grief. I shouldn't fail. There's just that difference."

Mr. Macmathers regarded his friend in silence before he spoke again.

"Railton, might I ask you to enlarge upon your meaning? I want to see which of us two is drunk."

"In the play the man has a big bear account—the biggest upon record. I need hardly tell you that a war between France and Germany would mean falling markets. Supposing we were able to calculate with certainty the exact moment of the outbreak— arrange it, in fact—we might realise wealth beyond the dreams of avarice—hundreds of thousands of millions, if we chose."

"I suppose you're joking?"

"How?"

"That's what I want to know—how."

"It does sound, at first hearing, like a joke, to suppose that a couple of mere outsiders can, at their own sweet will and pleasure, stir up a war between two Great Powers."

"A joke is a mild way of describing it, my friend."

"Alec, would you mind asking Mrs. Macmathers to form a third on this occasion?"

Mr. Macmathers eyed his friend for a moment, then got up and left the room. When he returned his wife was with him. It was to the lady Mr. Railton addressed himself.

"Mrs. Macmathers, would you like to be possessed of wealth compared to which the wealth of the Vanderbilts, the Rothschilds, the Mackays, the Goulds, would shrink into insignificance?"

"Why, certainly."

It was a peculiarity of the lady's that, while she was English, she affected what she supposed to be American idioms.

"Would you stick at a little to obtain it?"

"Certainly not."

"It would be worth one's while to run a considerable risk."

"I guess."

"Mrs. Macmathers, I want to go a bear, a large bear, to win, say—I want to put it modestly—a hundred millions."

"Pounds?"

"Pounds."

It is to be feared that Mrs. Macmathers whistled.

"Figures large," she said.

"All the world knows that war is inevitable between France and Germany."

"Proceed."

"I want to arrange that it shall break out at the moment when it best suits me."

"I guess you're a modest man," she said.

Her husband smiled.

"If you consider for a moment, it would not be so difficult as it first appears. It requires but a spark to set the fire burning. There is at least one party in France to whom war would mean the achievement of all their most cherished dreams. It is long odds that a war would bring some M. Quelquechose to the front with a

rush. He will be at least untried. And, of late years, it is the untried
men who have the people's confidence in France. A few resolute
men, my dear Mrs. Macmathers, have only to kick up a shindy on
the Alsatian borders—Europe will be roused, in the middle of the
night, by the roaring of the flames of war."

There was a pause. Mrs. Macmathers got up and began to pace
the room.

"It's a big order," she said.

"Allowing the feasibility of your proposition, I conclude that
you have some observations to make upon it from a moral point
of view. It requires them, my friend."

Mr. Macmathers said this with a certain dryness.

"Moral point of view be hanged! It could be argued, mind, and
defended; but I prefer to say candidly, the moral point of view be
hanged!"

"Has it not occurred to you to think that the next Franco-German
war may mean the annihilation of one of the parties concerned?"

"You mistake the position. I should have nothing to do with
the war. I should merely arrange the date for its commencement.
With or without me they would fight."

"You would merely consign two or three hundred thousand
men to die at the moment which would best suit your pocket."

"There is that way of looking at it, no doubt. But you will allow
me to remind you that you considered the possibility of creating
a corner in corn without making unpleasant allusions to the fact
that it might have meant starvation to thousands."

The lady interposed.

"Mr. Railton, leaving all that sort of thing alone, what is it that
you propose?"

"The details have still to be filled in. Broadly I propose to
arrange a series of collisions with the German frontier authorities.
I propose to get them boomed by the Parisian Press. I propose to
give some M. Quelquechose his chance."

"It's the biggest order ever I heard."

"Not so big as it sounds. Start to-morrow, and I believe that we
should be within measureable distance of war next week. Properly
managed, I will at least guarantee that all the Stock Exchanges of
Europe go down with a run."

"If the thing hangs fire, how about carrying over?"

"Settle. No carrying over for me. I will undertake that there is a sufficient margin of profit. Every account we will do a fresh bear until the trick is made. Unless I am mistaken, the trick will be made with a rapidity of which you appear to have no conception."

"It is like a dream of the Arabian nights," the lady said.

"Before the actual reality the Arabian nights pale their ineffectual fires. It is a chance which no man ever had before, which no man may ever have again. I don't think, Macmathers, we ought to let it slip."

They did not let it slip.

CHAPTER II

MR. RAILTON was acquainted with a certain French gentleman who rejoiced in the name—according to his own account—of M. Hippolyte de Vrai-Castille. The name did not sound exactly French—M. de Vrai-Castille threw light on this by explaining that his family came originally from Spain. But, on the other hand, it must be allowed that the name did not sound exactly Spanish, either. London appeared to be this gentleman's permanent place of residence. Political reasons—so he stated—rendered it advisable that he should not appear too prominently upon his— theoretically—beloved *boulevards*. Journalism—always following this gentleman's account of himself—was the profession to which he devoted the flood-tide of his powers. The particular journal or journals which were rendered famous by the productions of his pen were rather difficult to discover—there appeared to be political reasons, too, for that.

"The man is an all-round bad lot." This was what Mr. Railton said when speaking of this gentleman to Mr. and Mrs. Macmathers. "A type of scoundrel only produced by France. Just the man we want."

"Flattering," observed his friend. "You are going to introduce us to high company."

Mr. Railton entertained this gentleman to dinner in a private room at the Hôtel Continental. M. de Vrai-Castille did not seem to know exactly what to make of it. Nothing in his chance acquaintance with Mr. Railton had given him cause to suppose that the Englishman regarded him as a respectable man, and this sudden invitation to fraternise took him a little aback. Possibly he was taken still more aback before the evening closed. Conversation languished during the meal; but when it was over—and the waiters gone—Mr. Railton became very conversational indeed.

"Look here, What's-your-name"—this was how Mr. Railton addressed M. de Vrai-Castille—"I know very little about you, but I know enough to suspect that you have nothing in the world excepting what you steal."

"M. Railton is pleased to have his little jest."

If it was a jest, it was not one, judging from the expression of M. de Vrai-Castille's countenance which he entirely relished.

"What would you say if I presented you with ten thousand pounds?"

"I should say——"

What he said need not be recorded, but M. de Vrai-Castille used some very bad language indeed, expressive of the satisfaction with which the gift would be received.

"And suppose I should hint at your becoming possessed of another hundred thousand pounds to back it?"

"Pardon me, M. Railton, but is it murder? If so, I would say frankly at once that I have always resolved that in those sort of transactions I would take no hand."

"Stuff and nonsense! It is nothing of the kind! You say you are a politician. Well, I want you to pose as a patriot—a French patriot, you understand."

Mr. Railton's eyes twinkled. M. de Vrai-Castille grinned in reply.

"The profession is overcrowded," he murmured, with a deprecatory movement of his hands.

"Not on the lines I mean to work it. Did you lose any relatives in the war?"

"It depends."

"I feel sure you did. And at this moment the bodies of those patriots are sepultured in Alsatian soil. I want you to dig them up again."

"Mon Dieu! Ce charmant homme!"

"I want you to form a league for the recovery of the remains of those noble spirits who died for their native land, and whose bones now lie interred in what was France, but which now, alas! is France no more. I want you to go in for this bone recovery business as far as possible on a wholesale scale."

"Ciel! Maintenant j'ai trouvé un homme extraordinaire!"

"You will find no difficulty in obtaining the permission of the necessary authorities sanctioning your schemes; but at the very last moment, owing to some stated informality, the German brigands will interfere even at the edge of the already open grave; patriot bones will be dishonoured, France will be shamed in the face of all the world."

"And then?"

"The great heart of France is a patient heart, my friend, but even France will not stand that. There will be war."

"And then?"

"On the day on which war is declared, one hundred thousand pounds will be paid to you in cash."

"And supposing there is no war?"

"Should France prefer to cower beneath her shame, you shall still receive ten thousand pounds."

CHAPTER III

THE following extract is from the *Times'* Parisian correspondence—

"The party of La Revanche is taking a new departure. I am in a position to state that certain gentlemen are putting their heads together. A league is being formed for the recovery of the bodies of various patriots who are at present asleep in Alsace. I have my own reasons for asserting that some remarkable proceedings may be expected soon. No man knows better than myself that there is nothing some Frenchmen will not do."

On the same day there appeared in *La Patrie* a really touching article. It was the story of two brothers—one was, the other was not; in life they had been together, but in death they were divided. Both alike had fought for their native land. One returned—

désolé!—to Paris. The other stayed behind. He still stayed behind. It appeared that he was buried in Alsace, in a nameless grave! But they had vowed, these two, that they would share all things— among the rest, that sleep which even patriots must know, the unending sleep of death. "It is said," said the article in conclusion, "that that nameless grave, in what was France, will soon know none—or two!" It appeared that the surviving brother was going for that "nameless grave" on the principle of double or quits.

The story appeared, with variations, in a considerable number of journals. The *Daily Telegraph* had an amusing allusion to the fondness displayed by certain Frenchmen for their relatives—dead, for the "bones" of their fathers. But no one was at all prepared for the events which followed.

One morning the various money articles alluded to heavy sales which had been effected the day before, "apparently by a party of outside speculators." In particular heavy bear operations were reported from Berlin. Later in the day the evening papers came out with telegrams referring to "disturbances" at a place called Pont-sur-Leaune. Pont-sur-Leaune is a little Alsatian hamlet. The next day the tale was in everybody's mouth. Certain misguided but well-meaning Frenchmen had been "shot down" by the German authorities. Particulars had not yet come to hand, but it appeared, according to the information from Paris, that a party of Frenchmen had journeyed to Alsace with the intention of recovering the bodies of relatives who had been killed in the war; on the very edge of the open graves German soldiers had shot them down. Telegrams from Berlin stated that a party of body-snatchers had been caught in the very act of plying their nefarious trade; no mention of shooting came from there. Although the story was doubted in the City, it had its effect on the markets—prices fell. It was soon seen, too, that the bears were at it again. Foreign telegrams showed that their influence was being felt all round; very heavy bear raids were again reported from Berlin. Markets became unsettled, with a downward tendency, and closing prices were the worst of the day.

Matters were not improved by the news of the morrow. A Frenchman had been shot—his name was Hippolyte de Vrai-Castille, and a manifesto from his friends had already appeared in Paris. According to this, they had been betrayed by the German authorities. They had received permission from those authorities to take the bodies of certain of their relatives and lay them in French soil. While they were acting on this permission they were suddenly attacked by German soldiers, and he, their leader, that patriot soul, Hippolyte de Vrai-Castille, was dead. But there was worse than that. They had prepared flags in which to wrap the bodies of the dead. Those flags—emblems of France—had been seized by the rude German soldiers, torn into fragments, trampled in the dust. The excitement in Paris appeared to be intense. All that day there was a falling market.

The next day's papers were full of contradictory telegrams. From Berlin the affair was pooh-poohed. The story of permission having been accorded by the authorities was pure fiction—there had been a scuffle in which a man had been killed, probably by his own friends—the tale of the dishonoured flags was the invention of an imaginative brain. But these contradictions were for the most part frantically contradicted by the Parisian Press. There was a man in Paris who had actually figured on the scene. He had caught M. de Vrai-Castille in his arms as he fell, he had been stained by his heart's blood, his cheek had been torn open by the bullet which killed his friend. Next his heart he at that moment carried portions of the flags—emblems of France!—which had been subjected to such shame.

But it was on the following day that the situation first took a definitely serious shape. Placards appeared on every dead wall in Paris, small bills were thrust under every citizen's door—on the bills and placards were printed the same words. They were signed "Quelquechose." They pointed out that France owed her present degradation—like all her other degradations—to her Government. The nation was once more insulted; the Army was once more betrayed; the national flag had been trampled on again, as it had been trampled on before. Under a strong Government these things could not be, but under a Government of cowards——! Let France but breathe the word, "La Grande Nation" would exist once more. Let the Army but make a sign, there would be "La Grande Armée" as of yore.

That night there was a scene in the Chamber. M. de Caragnac—à propos des botte—made a truly remarkable speech.

He declared that permission had been given to these men. He produced documentary evidence to that effect. He protested that these men—true citizens of France!—had been the victims of a "Prussian" plot. As to the outrage to the national flag, had it been perpetrated, say, in Tonkin, "cannons would be belching forth their thunders now." But in Alsace—"this brave Government dare only turn to the smiters the other cheek." In the galleries they cheered him to the echo. On the tribune there was something like a free fight. When the last telegrams were despatched to London, Paris appeared to be approaching a state of riot.

The next day there burst a thunderbolt. Five men had been detained by the German authorities. They had escaped—had been detected in the act of flight—had been shot at while running. Two of them had been killed. A third had been fatally wounded. The news—flavoured to taste—was shouted from the roofs of the houses. Paris indulged in one of its periodical fits of madness. The condition of the troops bore a strong family likeness to mutiny. And in the morning Europe was electrified by the news that a revolution had been effected in the small hours of the morning, that the Chambers had been dissolved, and that with the Army were the issues of peace and war.

★   ★   ★   ★   ★

On the day of the declaration of the war between France and Germany—that heavy-laden day—an individual called on Mr. Rodney Railton whose appearance caused that gentleman to experience a slight sensation of surprise.

"De Vrai-Castille! I was wondering if you had left any instructions as to whom I was to pay that hundred thousand pounds. I thought that you were dead."

"Monsieur mistakes. My name is Henri Kerchrist, a name not unknown in my native Finistère. M. Hippolyte de Vrai-Castille is dead. I saw him die. It was to me he directed that you should pay that hundred thousand pounds."

As he made these observations, possibly owing to some local weakness, "Henri Kerchrist" winked the other eye.

Mrs. Riddle's Daughter

WHEN they asked me to spend the Long with them, or as much of it as I could manage, I felt more than half disposed to write and say that I could not manage any of it at all. Of course a man's uncle and aunt are his uncle and aunt, and as such I do not mean to say that I ever thought of suggesting anything against Mr. and Mrs. Plaskett. But then Plaskett is fifty-five if he's a day, and not agile, and Mrs. Plaskett always struck me as being about ten years older. They have no children, and the idea was that, as Mrs. Plaskett's niece—Plaskett is my mother's brother, so that Mrs. Plaskett is only my aunt by marriage—as I was saying, the idea was that, as Mrs. Plaskett's niece was going to spend her Long with them, I, as it were, might take pity on the girl, and see her through it.

I am not saying that there are not worse things than seeing a girl, single-handed, through a thing like that, but then it depends upon the girl. In this case, the mischief was her mother. The girl was Mrs. Plaskett's brother's child; his name was Riddle. Riddle was dead. The misfortune was, his wife was still alive. I had never seen her, but I had heard of her ever since I was breeched. She is one of those awful Anti-Everythingites. She won't allow you to smoke, or drink, or breathe comfortably, so far as I understand. I dare say you've heard of her. Whenever there is any new craze about, her name always figures in the bills.

So far as I know, I am not possessed of all the vices. At the same time, I did not look forward to being shut up all alone in a country house with the daughter of a "woman Crusader." On the other hand, Uncle Plaskett has behaved, more than once, like a trump to me, and as I felt that this might be an occasion on which he expected me to behave like a trump to him, I made up my mind that, at any rate, I would sample the girl and see what she was like.

I had not been in the house half an hour before I began to wish I hadn't come. Miss Riddle had not arrived, and if she was anything like the picture which my aunt painted of her, I hoped that she never would arrive—at least, while I was there. Neither of the Plasketts had seen her since she was the merest child. Mrs. Riddle never had approved of them. They were not Anti-Everythingite enough for her. Ever since the death of her husband she had practically ignored them. It was only when, after all these years, she found herself in a bit of a hole, that she seemed to have remembered their existence. It appeared that Miss Riddle was at some Anti-Everythingite college or other. The term was at an end. Her mother was in America, "Crusading" against one of her aversions. Some hitch had unexpectedly occurred as to where Miss Riddle was to spend her holidays. Mrs. Riddle had amazed the Plasketts by telegraphing to them from the States to ask if they could give her house-room. And that forgiving, tender-hearted uncle and aunt of mine had said they would.

I assure you, Dave, that when first I saw her you might have knocked me over with a feather. I had spent the night seeing her in nightmares—a lively time I had had of it. In the morning I went out for a stroll, so that the fresh air might have a chance of clearing my head at least of some of them. And when I came back there was a little thing sitting in the morning-room talking to aunt—I give you my word that she did not come within two inches of my shoulder. I do not want to go into raptures. I flatter myself I am beyond the age for that. But a sweeter-looking little thing I never saw! I was wondering who she might be, she seemed to be perfectly at home, when my aunt introduced us.

"Charlie, this is your cousin, May Riddle. May, this is your cousin, Charles Kempster."

She stood up—such a dot of a thing! She held out her hand—she found fours in gloves a trifle loose. She looked at me with her eyes all laughter—you never saw such eyes, never! Her smile, when she spoke, was so contagious, that I would have defied the surliest man alive to have maintained his surliness when he found himself in front of it.

"I am very glad to see you—cousin."

Her voice! And the way in which she said it! As I have written, you might have knocked me down with a feather.

I found myself in clover. And no man ever deserved good fortune better. It was a case of virtue rewarded. I had come to do my duty, expecting to find it bitter, and, lo, it was very sweet.

How such a mother came to have such a child was a mystery to all of us. There was not a trace of humbug about her. So far from being an Anti-Everythingite, she went in for everything, strong. That hypocrite of an uncle of mine had arranged to revolutionise the habits of his house for her. There were to be family prayers morning and evening, and a sermon, and three-quarters of an hour's grace before meat, and all that kind of thing. I even suspected him of an intention of locking up the billiard-room, and the smoke-room, and all the books worth reading, and all the music that wasn't "sacred," and, in fact, of turning the place into a regular mausoleum. But he had not been in her company five minutes when bang went all ideas of that sort. Talk about locking the billiard-room against her! You should have seen the game she played. Though she was such a dot, you should have seen her use the jigger. And sing! She sang everything. When she had made our hearts go pit-a-pat, and brought the tears into our eyes, she would give us comic songs—the very latest. Where she got them from was more than we could understand; but she made us laugh till we cried—aunt and all. She was an Admirable Crichton—honestly. I never saw a girl play a better game of tennis. She could ride like an Amazon. And walk—when I think of the walks we had together through the woods, I doing my duty towards her to the best of my ability, it all seems to have been too good a time to have happened in anything but a dream.

Do not think she was a rowdy girl, one of these "up-to-daters," or fast. Quite the other way. She had read more books than I had—I am not hinting that that is saying much, but still she had. She loved books, too; and, you know, speaking quite frankly, I never was a bookish man. Talking about books, one day when we were out in the woods alone together—we nearly always were alone together!—I took it into my head to read to her. She listened for a page or two; then she interrupted me.

"Do you call that reading?" I looked at her surprised. She held out her hand. "Now, let me read to you. Give me the book."

I gave it to her. Dave, you never heard such reading. It was not only a question of elocution; it was not only a question of the music that was in her voice. She made the dry bones live. The words, as they proceeded from between her lips, became living things. I never read to her again. After that, she always read to me. Many an hour have I spent, lying at her side, with my head pillowed in the mosses, while she materialised for me "the very Jew, which Shakespeare drew." She read to me all sorts of things. I believe she could even have vivified a leading article.

One day she had been reading to me a pen picture of a famous dancer. The writer had seen the woman in some Spanish theatre. He gave an impassioned description—at least, it sounded impassioned as she read it—of how the people had followed the performer's movements, with enraptured eyes and throbbing pulses, unwilling to lose the slightest gesture. When she had done reading, putting down the book, she stood up in front of me. I sat up to ask what she was going to do.

"I wonder," she said, "if it was anything like this—the dance which that Spanish woman danced."

She danced to me. Dave, you are my "fidus Achates," my other self, my chum, or I would not say a word to you of this. I never shall forget that day. She set my veins on fire. The witch! Without music, under the greenwood tree, all in a moment, for my particular edification, she danced a dance which would have set a crowded theatre in a frenzy. While she danced, I watched her as if mesmerised; I give you my word I did not lose a gesture. When she ceased—with such a curtsy!—I sprang up and ran to her. I would have caught her in my arms; but she sprang back. She held me from her with her outstretched hand.

"Mr. Kempster!" she exclaimed. She looked up at me as demurely as you please.

"I was only going to take a kiss," I cried. "Surely a cousin may take a kiss."

"Not every cousin—if you please."

With that she walked right off, there and then, leaving me standing speechless, and as stupid as an owl.

The next morning as I was in the hall, lighting up for an after breakfast smoke, Aunt Plaskett came up to me. The good soul had trouble written all over her face. She had an open letter in her hand. She looked up at me in a way which reminded me oddly of my mother.

"Charlie," she said, "I'm so sorry."

"Aunt, if you're sorry, so am I. But what's the sorrow?"

"Mrs. Riddle's coming."

"Coming? When?"

"To-day—this morning. I am expecting her every minute."

"But I thought she was a fixture in America for the next three months."

"So I thought. But it seems that something has happened which has induced her to change her mind. She arrived in England yesterday. She writes to me to say that she will come on to us as early as possible to-day. Here is the letter. Charlie, will you tell May?"

She put the question a trifle timidly, as though she were asking me to do something from which she herself would rather be excused. The fact is, we had found that Miss Riddle would talk of everything and anything, with the one exception of her mother. Speak of Mrs. Riddle, and the young lady either immediately changed the conversation, or she held her peace. Within my hearing, her mother's name had never escaped her lips. Whether consciously or unconsciously, she had conveyed to our minds a very clear impression that, to put it mildly, between her and her mother there was no love lost. I, myself, was persuaded that, to her, the news of her mother's imminent presence would not be pleasant news. It seemed that my aunt was of the same opinion.

"Dear May ought to be told, she ought not to be taken unawares. You will find her in the morning-room, I think."

I rather fancy that Aunt and Uncle Plaskett have a tendency to shift the little disagreeables of life off their own shoulders on to other people's. Anyhow, before I could point out to her that the part which she suggested I should play was one which belonged more properly to her, Aunt Plaskett had taken advantage of my momentary hesitation to effect a strategic movement which removed her out of my sight.

I found Miss Riddle in the morning-room. She was lying on a couch, reading. Directly I entered she saw that I had something on my mind.

"What's the matter? You don't look happy."

"It may seem selfishness on my part, but I'm not quite happy. I have just heard news which, if you will excuse my saying so, has rather given me a facer."

"If I will excuse you saying so! Dear me, how ceremonious we are! Is the news public, or private property?"

"Who do you think is coming?"

"Coming? Where? Here?" I nodded. "I have not the most remote idea. How should I have?"

"It is some one who has something to do with you."

Until then she had taken it uncommonly easily on the couch. When I said that, she sat up with quite a start.

"Something to do with me? Mr. Kempster! What do you mean? Who can possibly be coming here who has anything to do with me?"

"May, can't you guess?"

"Guess! How can I guess? What do you mean?"

"It's your mother."

"My—mother!"

I had expected that the thing would be rather a blow to her, but I had never expected that it would be anything like the blow it seemed. She sprang to her feet. The book fell from her hands, unnoticed, on to the floor. She stood facing me, with clenched fists and staring eyes.

"My—mother!" she repeated, "Mr. Kempster, tell me what you mean."

I told myself that Mrs. Riddle must be more, or less, of a mother even than my fancy painted her, if the mere suggestion of her coming could send her daughter into such a state of mind as this. Miss Riddle had always struck me as being about as cool a hand as you would be likely to meet. Now all at once, she seemed to be half beside herself with agitation. As she glared at me, she made me almost feel as if I had been behaving to her like a brute.

"My aunt has only just now told me."

"Told you what?"

"That Mrs. Riddle arrived——"

She interrupted me.

"Mrs. Riddle? My mother? Well, go on?"

She stamped on the floor. I almost felt as if she had stamped on me. I went on, disposed to feel that my back was beginning to rise.

"My aunt has just told me that Mrs. Riddle arrived in England yesterday. She has written this morning to say that she is coming on at once."

"But I don't understand!" She really looked as if she did not understand. "I thought—I was told that—she was going to remain abroad for months."

"It seems that she has changed her mind."

"Changed her mind!" Miss Riddle stared at me as if she thought that such a thing was inconceivable. "When did you say that she was coming?"

"Aunt tells me that she is expecting her every moment."

"Mr. Kempster, what am I to do?"

She appealed to me, with outstretched hands, actually trembling, as it seemed to me with passion, as if I knew—or understood her either.

"I am afraid, May, that Mrs. Riddle has not been to you all that a mother ought to be. I have heard something of this before. But I did not think that it was so bad as it seems."

"You have heard? You have heard! My good sir, you don't know what you're talking about in the very least. There is one thing very certain, that I must go at once."

"Go? May!"

She moved forward. I believe she would have gone if I had not stepped between her and the door. I was beginning to feel slightly bewildered. It struck me that, perhaps, I had not broken the news so delicately as I might have done. I had blundered somehow, somewhere. Something must be wrong, if, after having been parted from her, for all I knew, for years, immediately on hearing of her mother's return, her first impulse was towards flight.

"Well?" she cried, looking up at me like a small, wild thing.

"My dear May, what do you mean? Where are you going? To your room?"

"To my room? No! I am going away! away! Right out of this, as quickly as I can!"

"But, after all, your mother is your mother. Surely she cannot have made herself so objectionable that, at the mere thought of her arrival, you should wish to run away from her, goodness alone knows where. So far as I understand she has disarranged her plans, and hurried across the Atlantic, for the sole purpose of seeing you."

She looked at me in silence for a moment. As she looked, outwardly, she froze.

"Mr. Kempster, I am at a loss to understand your connection with my affairs. Still less do I understand the grounds on which you would endeavour to regulate my movements. It is true that you are a man, and I am a woman; that you are big and I am little; but—are those the only grounds?"

"Of course, if you look at it like that——"

Shrugging my shoulders, I moved aside. As I did so, some one entered the room. Turning, I saw it was my aunt. She was closely followed by another woman.

"My dear May," said my aunt, and unless I am mistaken, her voice was trembling, "here is your mother."

The woman who was with my aunt was a tall, loosely-built person, with iron-grey hair, a square determined jaw, and eyes which looked as if they could have stared the Sphinx right out of countenance. She was holding a pair of pince-nez in position on the bridge of her nose. Through them she was fixedly regarding May. But she made no forward movement. The rigidity of her countenance, of the cold sternness which was in her eyes, of the hard lines which were about her mouth, did not relax in the least degree. Nor did she accord her any sign of greeting. I thought that this was a comfortable way in which to meet one's daughter, and such a daughter, after a lengthened separation. With a feeling of the pity of it, I turned again to May. As I did so, a sort of creepy-crawly sensation went all up my back. The little girl really struck me as being frightened half out of her life. Her face was white and drawn; her lips were quivering; her big eyes were dilated in a manner which uncomfortably recalled a wild creature which has suddenly gone stark mad with fear.

It was a painful silence. I have no doubt that my aunt was as conscious of it as any one. I expect that she felt May's position as keenly as if it had been her own. She probably could not understand the woman's cold-bloodedness, the girl's too obvious shrinking from her mother. In what, I am afraid, was awkward, blundering fashion, she tried to smooth things over.

"May, dear, don't you see it is your mother?"

Then Mrs. Riddle spoke. She turned to my aunt.

"I don't understand you. Who is this person?"

I distinctly saw my aunt give a gasp. I knew she was trembling.

"Don't you see that it is May?"

"May? Who? This girl?"

Again Mrs. Riddle looked at the girl who was standing close beside me. Such a look! And again there was silence. I do not know what my aunt felt. But from what I felt, I can guess. I felt as if a stroke of lightning, as it were, had suddenly laid bare an act of mine, the discovery of which would cover me with undying shame. The discovery had come with such blinding suddenness, "a bolt out of the blue," that, as yet, I was unable to realise all that it meant. As I looked at the girl, who seemed all at once to have become smaller even than she usually was, I was conscious that, if I did not keep myself well in hand, I was in danger of collapsing at the knees. Rather than have suffered what I suffered then, I would sooner have had a good sound thrashing any day, and half my bones well broken.

I saw the little girl's body swaying in the air. For a moment I thought that she was going to faint. But she caught herself at it just in time. As she pulled herself together, a shudder went all over her face. With her fists clenched at her side, she stood quite still. Then she turned to my aunt.

"I am not May Riddle," she said, in a voice which was at one and the same time strained, eager, and defiant, and as unlike her ordinary voice as chalk is different from cheese. Raising her hands, she covered her face. "Oh, I wish I had never said I was!"

She burst out crying; into such wild grief that one might have been excused for fearing that she would hurt herself by the violence of her own emotion. Aunt and I were dumb. As for Mrs. Riddle—and, if you come to think of it, it was only natural—she did not seem to understand the situation in the least. Turning to my aunt, she caught her by the arm.

"Will you be so good as to tell me what is the meaning of these extraordinary proceedings?"

"My dear!" seemed to be all that my aunt could stammer in reply.

"Answer me!" I really believe that Mrs. Riddle shook my aunt "Where is my daughter—May?"

"We thought—we were told that this was May." My aunt addressed herself to the girl, who was still sobbing as if her heart would break. "My dear, I am very sorry, but you know you gave us to understand that you were—May."

Then some glimmering of the meaning of the situation did seem to dawn on Mrs. Riddle's mind. She turned to the crying girl; and a look came on her face which conveyed the impression that one had suddenly lighted on the key-note of her character. It was a look of uncompromising resolution. A woman who could summon up such an expression at will ought to be a leader. She never could be led. I sincerely trust that my wife—if I ever have one—when we differ, will never look like that. If she does, I am afraid it will have to be a case of her way, not mine. As I watched Mrs. Riddle, I was uncommonly glad she was not my mother. She went and planted herself right in front of the crying girl. And she said, quietly, but in a tone of voice the hard frigidity of which suggested the nether millstone:

"Cease that noise. Take your hands from before your face. Are you one of that class of persons who, with the will to do evil, lack the courage to face the consequences of their own misdeeds? I can assure you that, so far as I am concerned, noise is thrown away. Candour is your only hope with me. Do you hear what I say? Take your hands from before your face."

I should fancy that Mrs. Riddle's words, and still more her manner, must have cut the girl like a whip. Anyhow, she did as she was told. She took her hands from before her face. Her eyes were blurred with weeping. She still was sobbing. Big tears were rolling down her cheeks. I am bound to admit that her crying had by no means improved her personal appearance. You could see she was doing her utmost to regain her self-control. And she faced Mrs. Riddle with a degree of assurance, which, whether she was in the right or in the wrong, I was glad to see. That stalwart representative of the modern Women Crusaders continued to address her in the same unflattering way.

"Who are you? How comes it that I find you passing yourself off as my daughter in Mrs. Plaskett's house?"

The girl's answer took me by surprise.

"I owe you no explanation, and I shall give you none."

"You are mistaken. You owe me a very frank explanation. I promise you you shall give me one before I've done with you."

"I wish and intend to have nothing whatever to say to you. Be so good as to let me pass."

The girl's defiant attitude took Mrs. Riddle slightly aback. I was delighted. Whatever she had been crying for, it had evidently not been for want of pluck. It was plain that she had pluck enough for fifty. It did me good to see her.

"Take my advice, young woman, and do not attempt that sort of thing with me—unless, that is, you wish me to give you a short shrift, and send at once for the police."

"The police? For me? You are mad!"

For a moment Mrs. Riddle looked a trifle mad. She went quite green. She took the girl by the shoulder roughly. I saw that the little thing was wincing beneath the pressure of her hand. That was more than I could stand.

"Excuse me, Mrs. Riddle, but—if you would not mind!"

Whether she did or did not mind, I did not wait for her to tell me. I removed her hand, with as much politeness as was possible, from where she had placed it. She looked at me, not nicely.

"Pray, sir, who are you?"

"I am Mrs. Plaskett's nephew, Charles Kempster, and very much at your service, Mrs. Riddle."

"So you are Charles Kempster? I have heard of you." I was on the point of remarking that I also had heard of her. But I refrained. "Be so good, young man, as not to interfere."

I bowed. The girl spoke to me.

"I am very much obliged to you, Mr. Kempster." She turned to my aunt. One could see that every moment she was becoming more her cool collected self again. "Mrs. Plaskett, it is to you I owe an explanation. I am ready to give you one when and where you please. Now, if it is your pleasure."

My aunt was rubbing her hands together in a feeble, purposeless, undecided sort of way. Unless I err, she was crying, for a change. With the exception of my uncle, I should say that my aunt was the most peace-loving soul on earth. I believe that the pair of them would flee from anything in the shape of dissension as from the wrath to come.

"Well, my dear, I don't wish to say anything to pain you—as you must know!—but if you can explain, I wish you would. We have grown very fond of you, your uncle and I."

It was not a very bright speech of my aunt's, but it seemed to please the person for whom it was intended immensely. She ran to her, she took hold of both her hands, she kissed her on either cheek.

"You dear darling! I've been a perfect wretch to you, but not such a villain as your fancy paints me. I'll tell you all about it—now." Clasping her hands behind her back, she looked my aunt demurely in the face. But in spite of her demureness, I could see that she was full of mischief to the finger tips. "You must know that I am Daisy Hardy. I am the daughter of Francis Hardy, of the Corinthian Theatre."

Directly the words had passed her lips, I knew her. You remember how often we saw her in "The Penniless Pilgrim?" And how good she was? And how we fell in love with her, the pair of us? All along, something about her, now and then, had filled me with a sort of overwhelming conviction that I must have seen her somewhere before. What an ass I had been! But then to think of her—well, modesty—in passing herself off as Mrs. Riddle's daughter. As for Mrs. Riddle, she received the young lady's confession with what she possibly intended for an air of crushing disdain.

"An actress!" she exclaimed.

She switched her skirts on one side, with the apparent intention of preventing their coming into contact with iniquity. Miss Hardy paid no heed.

"May Riddle is a very dear friend of mine."

"I don't believe it," cried Mrs. Riddle, with what, to say the least of it, was perfect frankness. Still Miss Hardy paid no heed.

"It is the dearest wish of her life to become an actress."

"It's a lie!"

This time Miss Hardy did pay heed. She faced the frankly speaking lady.

"It is no lie, as you are quite aware. You know very well that, ever since she was a teeny weeny child, it has been her continual dream."

"It was nothing but a childish craze."

Miss Hardy shrugged her shoulders.

"Mrs. Riddle uses her own phraseology; I use mine. I can only say that May has often told me that, when she was but a tiny thing, her mother used to whip her for playing at being an actress. She used to try and make her promise that she would never go inside a theatre, and when she refused, she used to beat her cruelly. As she grew older, her mother used to lock her in her bedroom, and keep her without food for days and days——"

"Hold your tongue, girl! Who are you that you should comment on my dealings with my child? A young girl, who, by her own confession, has already become a painted thing, and who seems to glory in her shame, is a creature with whom I can own no common womanhood. Again I insist upon your telling me, without any attempt at rhodomontade, how it is that I find a creature such as you posing as my child."

The girl vouchsafed her no direct reply. She looked at her with a curious scorn, which I fancy Mrs. Riddle did not altogether relish. Then she turned again to my aunt.

"Mrs. Plaskett, it is as I tell you. All her life May has wished to be an actress. As she has grown older her wish has strengthened. You see all my people have been actors and actresses. I, myself, love acting. You could hardly expect me, in such a matter, to be against my friend. And then—there was my brother."

She paused. Her face became more mischievous; and, unless I am mistaken, Mrs. Riddle's face grew blacker. But she let the girl go on.

"Claud believed in her. He was even more upon her side than I was. He saw her act in some private theatricals——"

Then Mrs. Riddle did strike in.

"My daughter never acted, either in public or in private, in her life. Girl, how dare you pile lie upon lie?"

Miss Hardy gave her look for look. One felt that the woman knew that the girl was speaking the truth, although she might not choose to own it.

"May did many things of which her mother had no knowledge. How could it be otherwise? When a mother makes it her business to repress at any cost the reasonable desires which are bound up in her daughter's very being, she must expect to be deceived. As I say, my brother Claud saw her act in some private theatricals. And he was persuaded that, for once in a way, hers was not a case of a person mistaking the desire to be, for the power to be, because she was an actress born. Then things came to a climax. May wrote to me to say that she was leaving college, that her mother was in America, and that so far as her ever becoming an actress was concerned, so far as she could judge, it was a case of now or never. I showed her letter to Claud. He at once declared that it should be a case of now. A new play was coming out, in which he was to act, and in which, he said, there was a part which would fit May like a glove. It was not a large part; still, there it was. If she chose, he would see she had it. I wrote and told her what Claud said. She jumped for joy—through the post, you understand. Then they began to draw me in. Until her mother's return, May was to have gone, for safe keeping, to one of her mother's particular friends. If she had gone, the thing would have been hopeless. But, at the last moment, the plan fell through. It was arranged, instead, that she should go to her aunt—to you, Mrs. Plaskett. You had not seen her since her childhood; you had no notion of what she looked like. I really do not know from whom the suggestion came, but it was suggested that I should come to you, pretending to be her. And I was to keep on pretending till the rubicon was passed and the play produced. If she once succeeded in gaining a footing on the stage, though it might be never so slight a one, May declared that wild horses should not drag her back again. And I knew her well enough to be aware that, when she said a thing, she meant exactly what she said. Mrs. Plaskett, I should have made you this confession of my own initiative next week. Indeed, May would have come and told you the tale herself, if Mrs. Riddle had not returned all these months before any one expected her. Because, as it happens, the play was produced last night——"

Mrs. Riddle had been listening, with a face as black as a thundercloud. Here she again laid her hand upon Miss Hardy's shoulder.

"Where? Tell me! I will still save her, though, to do so, I have to drag her through the streets."

Miss Hardy turned to her with a smile.

"May does not need saving, she already has attained salvation.

I hear, not only that the play was a great success, but that May's part, as she acted it, was the success of the play. As for dragging her through the streets, you know that you are talking nonsense. She is of an age to do as she pleases. You have no more power to put constraint upon her, than you have to put constraint upon me."

All at once Miss Hardy let herself go, as it were.

"Mrs. Riddle, you have spent a large part of your life in libelling all that I hold dearest; you will now be taught of how great a libel you have been guilty. You will learn from the example of your daughter's own life, that women can, and do, live as pure and as decent lives upon one sort of stage, as are lived, upon another sort of stage, by 'Women Crusaders.'"

She swept the infuriated Mrs. Riddle such a curtsy. . . . Well, there's the story for you, Dave. There was, I believe, a lot more talking. And some of it, I dare say, approached to high faluting. But I had had enough of it, and went outside. Miss Hardy insisted on leaving the house that very day. As I felt that I might not be wanted, I also left. We went up to town together in the same carriage. We had it to ourselves. And that night I saw May Riddle, the real May Riddle. I don't mind telling you in private, that she is acting in that new thing of Pettigrewe's, "The Flying Folly," under the name of Miss Lyndhurst. She only has a small part; but, as Miss Hardy declares her brother said of her, she plays it like an actress born. I should not be surprised if she becomes all the rage before long.

One could not help feeling sorry for Mrs. Riddle, in a kind of a way. I dare say she feels pretty bad about it all. But then she only has herself to blame. When a mother and her daughter pull different ways, it is apt to become a question of pull butcher, pull baker. The odds are that, in the end, you will prevail. Especially when the daughter has as much resolution as the mother.

As for Daisy Hardy, whatever else one may say of her proceedings, one cannot help thinking of her—at least, I can't—as, as they had it in the coster ballad, "such a pal." I believe she is going to the Plasketts again next week. If she does I have half a mind—— though I know she will only laugh at me, if I do go. I don't care. Between you and me, I don't believe she's half so wedded to the stage as she pretends she is.

Miss Donne's Great Gamble

You cannot keep on meeting the same man by accident—not in that way. To suggest such a possibility would be to carry the doctrine of probabilities too far. Miss Donne began herself to think that such might be the case. She had first encountered him at Geneva—at the Pension Dupont. There his bearing had not only been extremely deferential, but absolutely distant. Possibly this was in some measure owing to Miss Donne herself, who, at that stage of her travels, was the most unapproachable of human beings. During the last few days of her stay he had sat next to her at table, in which position it had seemed to her that a certain amount of conversation was not to be avoided. He had informed her, in the course of the remarks which the situation necessitated, that he was an American and a bachelor, and also that his name was Huhn.

So far as Miss Donne was concerned the encounter would merely have been pigeon-holed among the other noticeable incidents of that memorable journey had it not been that two days after her arrival at Lausanne she met him in the open street—to be exact, in the Place de la Gare. Not only did he bow, but he stopped to talk with the air of quite an old acquaintance.

But it was at Lucerne that the situation began to assume a really curious phase. Miss Donne left Lausanne on a Thursday. On the day before she told Mr. Huhn she was going, and where she intended to stop. Mr. Huhn made no comment on the information, which was given casually while they waited among a crowd of other persons for the steamer. No one could have inferred from his manner that it was not his intention to end his days at Lausanne. When, therefore, on the morning after her arrival, she found him seated by her side at lunch she was thrown into a flurry of surprise. As he seemed, however, to conclude that she would take his appearance for granted—not attempting to offer the slightest explanation of how it was that he was where he was—she presently found herself talking to him as if his presence there was quite in accordance with the order of Nature. But when, afterwards, she went upstairs to put her hat on, she—well, she found herself disposed to try her best not to ask herself a question.

Those four weeks at Lucerne were the happiest she had known. A sociable set was staying in the house just then. Everyone behaved to her with surprising kindness. Scarcely an excursion was got up without her being attached to it. Another invariable pendant was Mr. Huhn. It was impossible to conceal from herself the fact that when the parties were once started it was Mr. Huhn who personally conducted her. A better conductor she could not have wished. Without being obtrusive, when he was wanted he was always there. Unostentatiously he studied her little idiosyncrasies, making it his especial business to see that nothing was lacking which made for her own particular enjoyment. As a conversationalist she had never met his equal. But then, as she admitted with that honesty which was her ruling passion, she never had had experience of masculine discourse. Nor, perhaps, was the position rendered less enjoyable by the fact that she was haunted by misgivings as to whether her relations with Mr. Huhn were altogether in accordance with strict propriety. She was a lady travelling alone. He was a stranger; self introduced. Whether, under any circumstances, a lady in her position ought to allow herself to be on terms of vague familiarity with a gentleman in his, was a point on which she could hardly be said to have doubts. She was convinced that she ought not. Theoretically, that was a principle for which she would have been almost willing to have died. When she reflected on what she had preached to others, metaphorically she shivered in her shoes. She was half alarmed by the necessity she was under to acknowledge that it was a kind of shivering which could not be correctly described as disagreeable.

The domain of the extraordinary was entered on after her departure from Lucerne. At the Pension Emeritus her plans were public property. It was generally known that she proposed to return to England by way of Paris and Dieppe. In Paris she was to spend a few days, and in Dieppe a week or two. Practically the whole pension was at the station to see her off. She was overwhelmed with confectionery and flowers. Mr. Huhn, in particular, gave her a gorgeous bouquet, and a box of what purported to be

chocolates. It was only after she had started that she discovered
the chocolates were a sham; and that, hidden in the very midst
of them, was another package. The very sight of it filled her with
singular qualms. Other people were in the carriage. She deemed
it prudent to ignore its existence in the presence of what quite
possibly were observant eyes. But directly she had a moment of
comparative privacy she removed it from its hiding-place with
what—positively!—were trembling fingers. It was secured by
pink baby-ribbon tied in a true-lover's knot. Within was a leather
case. In the case was a flexible gold bracelet, with on one side a
circular ornament which was incrusted with diamonds. As she was
fingering this she must have touched a hidden spring, because all at
once the glittering toy sprang open, revealing inside—of all things
in the world—a portrait of Mr. Huhn!

She gazed at it in bewildered amazement. All the way to Paris
she was rent by conflicting emotions. That a perfect stranger
should have dared to take such a liberty! Because, after all, she
knew nothing of him—absolutely nothing, except that he was
an American; which one piece of knowledge was, perhaps, a
sufficient explanation. For all she knew, the Americans might have
ideas of their own upon such subjects. This sort of behaviour
might be in complete accord with their standard of propriety. The
contemplation of such a possibility made her sigh. She actually
nearly regretted that her standard was the English one, so strongly
did she feel that there was something to be said for the American
point of view, if, that is, it truly was the American point of view;
which, of course, had still to be determined.

Had the bracelet been trumpery trash, costing say, fifteen or
twenty francs, the case would have been altered. Of that there
could be no doubt. But this triumph of the jeweller's art, with
its costly diamond ornaments! She herself had never owned a
decent trinket. Her personal knowledge of values was nil. Yet
her instincts told her that this cost money. Then there was the
name of "Tiffany" on the case. She had a dim consciousness of
having heard of Tiffany. It might have cost one hundred—even
two hundred—pounds! At the thought she burned. Who was she,
and what had she done, that wandering males—the merest casual
acquaintances—should feel themselves at liberty to throw bank

notes into her lap? As if she were a beggar—or worse. There was a moment in which she was inclined to throw the bracelet out of the carriage window.

The mischief was that she did not know where to return it. She had Mr. Huhn's own assurance that he also was leaving Lucerne on that same day. Where he was going she had not the faintest notion. At least, she assured herself that she had not the faintest notion. To return it, by post, to Ezra G. Huhn, America, would be absurd. She might send it back to the person whose name was on the case—to Tiffany. She would.

Then there was the portrait—hidden in the bracelet—which he had had the capital audacity to palm off on to her under cover of a box of chocolates. It was excellent—that was certain.

The shrewd face, with the kindly eyes in which there always seemed to be a twinkle, looked up at her out of the little gold frame like an old familiar friend. How pleasant he had been to her; how good. How she always felt at ease with him; never once afraid. Although he had never by so much as a single question sought to gain her confidence, what a curious feeling she had had that he knew all about her, that he understood her. How she had been impressed by his way of doing things; his quick resource; his capacity of getting—without any fuss—the best that was obtainable. How she had come to rely upon him—in an altogether indescribable sort of way—when he was at hand; she saw it now. How, in spite of herself, she had grown to feel at peace with all the world when he was near. How curious it seemed. As she thought of its exceeding curiousness, fancying that she perceived in the portrayed glance the twinkle which she had begun to know so well, her eyes filled with tears, so that she had to use her handkerchief to prevent them trickling down her cheeks. During the remainder of her journey to Paris that bracelet was about her wrist, covered by her jacket-sleeve. More than once she caught herself in the act of crying.

She found it impossible to remain in Paris. The weather was hot. In the brilliant sunshine the streets were one continuous glare. They seemed difficult to breathe in. They made her head ache. She longed for the sea. Within three days of her arrival she was hurrying towards Dieppe. In Dieppe she alighted at the Hotel de

Paris. The first person she saw as she crossed the threshold was Annie Moriarty—at least, she used to be Annie Moriarty until she became Mrs. Palmer. The two rushed into each other's arms— Mrs. Palmer going upstairs with Miss Donne to assist in the unpacking. When they descended Miss Donne was introduced to Mr. Palmer, who had been Annie's one topic in the epistolary communications with which Miss Donne was regularly favoured. Mr. Palmer, who was a husband of twelve months' standing, proved to be a sort of under-study for a giant, towering above Miss Donne's head in a manner which inspired her with awe. While she was wondering whether, when he desired to kiss his wife and retain his perpendicular position, he always lifted her upon a chair—for Annie was a mere pigmy in petticoats—who should come down the staircase into the hall but Mr. Huhn!

At that sight not only did Miss Donne's cheeks flame, but she was overwhelmed with confusion to such an extent that it was impossible to conceal the fact from the sharp-eyed person who was in front of her. Although Mr. Huhn merely raised his hat as he passed into the street, her distress continued after he was gone. She accompanied the Palmers—in an only partial state of consciousness—into the Etablissement grounds. While her husband continued with them Annie was discretion itself; but when Mr. Palmer, going into the building—it is within the range of possibility on a hint from her—left the two women seated on the terrace, she assailed Miss Donne in a fashion which in a moment laid all her defences low.

The whole story was told before its narrator was conscious of an intention to do anything of the kind. It plunged the hearer into raptures. Although, with a delicacy which well became her, she concealed the larger half of them, she revealed enough to throw Miss Donne into a state of agitation which was half pathetic and altogether delightful. As she sat there, listening to Annie's innuendoes, conscious of her delighted scrutiny, the heroine of all these strange adventures discovered herself hazily wondering whether this was the same world in which she had been living all these years, and whether she was awake in it or dreaming. After all the miracles which had lately changed the whole fashion of her life, was the greatest still upon the way?

Eva Donne was thirty-eight and three-quarters, as the children say. For over twenty years she had been a governess—without kith or kin. All the time she was haunted by a fear that the fat season was with her now, and that the lean one was coming soon. She was not a scholar; she was just the sweetest woman in the world. But while of the second fact she had no notion, of the first she was hideously sure. She had strained every nerve to improve her mental equipment; to keep herself abreast of the educational requirements of the day; to pass examinations; to win those certificates which teachers ought to have. Always and ever in vain. The dullest of her scholars was not more dull than she. How, under these circumstances, she found employment was beyond her comprehension. Why, for instance, Miss Law should have kept her upon her teaching staff for nearly thirteen consecutive years was to her, indeed a mystery. That Miss Law should consider it well worth her while to retain in her establishment a well-mannered, dainty lady; possessed of infinite patience, kindliness, and tact; the soul of honour; considering her employer's interests before her own; willing to work late and early: who was liked by every pupil with whom she came into contact, and so was able to smooth the head mistress's path in a hundred different ways; that the shrewd proprietress of St. Cecilia's College should esteem these qualifications as a sufficient set-off for certain scholastic deficiencies never entered into Miss Donne's philosophy. Therefore, though she said not a word of it to anyone, she was tortured by a continual fear that each term would be her last. Dismissed for inefficiency at her age, what should she do? For she was growing old; she knew she was. She was grey—almost!—behind the ears; her hair was thinner than it used to be; there were telltale wrinkles about her eyes; she was conscious of a certain stiffness in her joints. A governess so soon grows old, especially if she is not clever. Many a time she lay awake all through the night thinking, with horror, of the future which was in store for her. What should she do? She had saved so little. Out of such a salary how could she save?—with her soft, generous heart which could not resist a temptation to give. She sometimes wondered, when the morning dawned, how it was that she had not turned quite grey, after the racking anxieties of the sleepless night.

And then the miracle came—the god out of the machine. A cousin of her mother, of whom she had only heard, died in America, in Pittsburg—a bachelor, as alone in the world as she was—and left everything he had to his far-off kinswoman. Eight hundred sterling pounds a year it came to, actually, when everything was realized, and everything had been left in an easy realizable form. What a difference it made when she understood that the incredible had come to pass, and what it meant. She was rich, independent, secure from want and from the fear of it, thank God. And she thanked Him—how she thanked Him!—pouring out her heart before Him like some simple child. And she ceased to grow old; nay, she all at once grew young again. She was nearly persuaded that the greyness had vanished from behind her ears; her hair certainly did seem thicker. The wrinkles were so faint as to be not worth mentioning, while, as for the stiffness of her joints, she was suddenly conscious of an absurd and even improper inclination to run up the stairs and down them.

Then there came the wonderful journey. She, a solitary spinster, who had never been out of England in her life, made up her mind, after not more than six month's consideration, to go all by herself to Switzerland. And she went. After the strange happenings which, in such a journey, were naturally to be expected, to crown everything, here, on the terrace at Dieppe, sat Annie Moriarty that was—and a troublesome child she used to be—telling her—her!—the young woman's former and ought-to-be-revered preceptress—that a certain person—to wit, an American gentleman—was in love with her—with her! Miss Eva Donne. Not the least extraordinary part of it was that, instead of correcting the presumptuous Annie, Miss Donne beamed and blushed, and blushed and beamed, and was conscious of the most singular sensations.

A remark, however, which Mrs. Palmer apparently inadvertently made, brought her back to earth with a sudden jolt.

"I suppose that whoever does become Mrs. Huhn will become an American."

It was just a second or so before she comprehended. When she did it was with a quick sinking of the heart. Something, all at once, seemed to have gone out of the world. Perhaps because a cloud had crept over the sun.

Was it possible? A thing not to be avoided? An inevitable consequence? Of course, Mr. Huhn was an American; she did know so much. And although—as she had gathered—this was by no means his first visit to Europe, it might reasonably be imagined that he spent most of his time in his native country. It was equally fair to assume that his wife would be expected to stop there with him. Would she, therefore, perforce lose her nationality, her birthright, her title to call herself an Englishwoman? To say the least of it, that would be an extraordinary position for—for an Englishwoman to find herself in. Mischievous Annie could not have succeeded better had it been her deliberate intention to make Miss Donne's confusion worse confounded.

She dined with the Palmers at a little table by themselves. Mr. Huhn was at the long table round the corner, hidden from her sight by the peculiar construction of the room. Mrs. Palmer announced that he had gone there before she entered. Miss Donne took care that she went before he reappeared. She spent the evening in her bedroom, in spite of Mrs. Palmer's vigorous protestations, writing letters, so she said. It is true that she did write some letters. She began half-a-dozen to Mr. Huhn. Among a thousand and one other things, that bracelet was on her mind. Her wish was to return it, accompanied by a note which would exactly meet the occasion. But the construction of the note she wanted proved to be beyond her powers. It was far from her desire to wound his feelings; she was only too conscious how easy it is for the written word to do that. At the same time it was necessary that she should make her meaning plain, on which account it was a misfortune that she herself was not altogether clear as to what she did precisely mean. She did not want the bracelet; certainly not. Yet, while she did not wish to throw it at him, or lead him to suppose that she despised his gift, or was unconscious of his kindness in having made it, or liked him less because of his kindness, it was not her intention to allow him to suspect that she liked him at all, or appreciated his kindness to anything like the extent she actually did do, or indeed, leave him an excuse of any sort or kind on to which he might fasten to ask her to reconsider her refusal. How to combine these opposite desires and intentions within the four corners of one short note was a puzzle.

It was a nice bracelet—a beauty. No one could call it unbecoming on her wrist. She had had no idea that a single ornament could have made such a difference. She was convinced that it made her hand seem much smaller than it really was. She wondered if he had sent for it specially to New York, or if he had been carrying it about with him in his pocket. But that was not the point. The point was that, since she could not frame a note which, in all respects, met her views, she would herself see Mr. Huhn to-morrow and return him his gift with her own hands. Then the incident would be closed. Having arrived at which decision she slept like a top all night, with the bracelet under her pillow.

In the morning she dressed herself with unusual care—with so much care, indeed, that Mrs. Palmer greeted her with a torrent of ejaculations.

"You look lovelier than ever, my dear. Just like What's-his-name's picture, only ever so much sweeter. Doesn't she look a darling, Dick?"

"Dick" was Mr. Palmer. As this was said not only in the presence of that gentleman, but in the hearing of several others, Miss Donne was so distressed that she found herself physically incapable of telling the speaker that, as she was perfectly aware, she intensely disliked personal remarks, which were always in the very worst possible taste.

Nothing was seen of Mr. Huhn. She went with the Palmers to the market; to the man who carved grotesque heads out of what he called vegetable ivory; to watch the people bathe, while listening to the band upon the terrace; then to lunch. All the time she had that bracelet on her person. After lunch she accompanied her friends on a queer sort of vehicle, which was not exactly a brake or quite anything else, on what its proud proprietor called a "fashionable excursion" to the forest of Arques. It was nearly five when they returned. The Palmers went upstairs. She sat down on one of the chairs which were on the pavement in front of the hotel. She had been there for some minutes in a sort of waking dream when someone occupied the chair beside her.

It was Mr. Huhn. His appearance was so unexpected that it found her speechless. The foolish tremors to which she seemed to have been so liable of late seemed to paralyze her. She gazed at the shabby theatre on the other side of the square, trying to think of what she ought to say—but failed. No greetings were exchanged.

Presently he said, in his ordinary tone of voice:—

"Come with me into the Casino."

That was his way; a fair example of his habit of taking things for granted. She felt that if, after a prolonged absence, she met him on the other side of the world, he would just ask if she liked sugar in her tea, and discuss the sugar question generally, and take it for granted that that was all the situation demanded. That was not her standpoint. She considered that when explanations were required they ought to be given, and was distinctly of opinion that an explanation was required here. She intended that the remark she made should be regarded as a suggestion to that effect.

"I didn't expect to see you at Dieppe."

He looked at her—just looked—and she was a conscience-stricken wretch. Had he accused her, at the top of his voice, of deliberate falsehood, he could not have shamed her more.

"I meant to come to Dieppe. I thought you knew it."

She had known it; all pretence to the contrary was brushed away like so much cobweb. And she knew that he knew she knew it. It was dreadful. What could she say to this extraordinary man? She blundered from bad to worse. Fumbling with the buttons of her little jacket she took out from some inner receptacle a small flat leather case.

"I think this got into that box of chocolates by mistake."

He glanced at it out of the corner of his eye, then continued to draw figures on the pavement with the ferrule of his stick.

"No mistake. I put it there. I thought you'd understand."

Thought she would understand! What did he think she would understand? Did the man suppose that everyone took things for granted?

"I think it was a mistake."

"How? When I sent to New York for it specially for you?" So that question was solved. She was conscious of a small flutter of satisfaction. "Don't you think it's pretty?"

"It's beautiful." She gathered her courage. "But you must take it back."

"'Take it back! Take it back! I didn't think you were the kind of woman that would want to make a man unhappy."

Nothing was further from her desire.

"I am not in the habit of accepting presents from strangers."

"That's just it. It's because I knew you weren't that I gave it to you."

"But you're a stranger to me."

"I didn't look at it in just that way."

"I know nothing of you."

"I'm sorry. I thought you knew what kind of man I am, as I know what kind of woman you are—and am glad to know it. If it's my record you'd like to be acquainted with, I'm ready to set forth the life and adventures of Ezra G. Huhn at full length whenever you've an hour or two or a day or two to spare. Or I can refer you for them to my lawyer, or to my banker, or to my doctor, according to what part of me it is on which you'd like to have accurate information."

She could not hint that she would like to listen to a chapter or two of his adventures there and then, though some such idea was at the back of her mind. While she was groping for words he stood up, repeating his original suggestion.

"Come with me into the Casino."

She rose also. Not because she wished to; but because—such was the confusion of her mental processes—she found it easier to agree than to differ. They moved across the square. The flat leather case was in her hand.

"Have you found the locket?"

"Yes."

She blushed; but she was a continual blush.

"Good portrait of me, isn't it?"

"Excellent."

"I had it done for my mother. When she was dying I wanted it to be buried with her. But she wouldn't have it. She said I was to give it to—someone else one day. Then I didn't think there ever would be a someone else. But when I met you I sent it to New York and had it mounted in that bracelet—for you."

It was absurd what a little self-control she had. Instead of retorting with something smart, or pretty, or sentimental, she was tongue-tied. Her eyes filled with tears. But he did not seem to notice it. He went on.

"You'll have to give me one of yours."

"I—I haven't one."

"Then we'll have to set about getting one. I'll have to look round for someone who'll be likely to do you justice, though it isn't to be expected that we shall find anyone who'll be able to do quite that."

It was the nearest approach to a compliment he had paid her; probably the first pretty thing which had been said to her by any man. It set her trembling so that, for a moment, she swayed as if she would fall. They were passing through the gate into the Casino grounds. He looked at the case which she still had in her hand.

"Put that in your pocket."

"I haven't one."

She was the personification of all meekness.

"Then where did you have it?"

"Inside my jacket."

"Put it back there. I can't carry it. That's part of the burden you'll have to carry, henceforward, all alone."

She did not stop to think what he meant. She simply obeyed. When the jacket was buttoned the case showed through the cloth. Even in the midst of her tremors she was aware that his eyes kept travelling towards the tell-tale patch. For some odd reason she was glad they did.

They passed from the radiance of the autumn afternoon into the chamber of the "little horses." The change was almost dramatic in its completeness. From this place the sunshine had been for some time excluded. The blinds were drawn. It was garishly lighted. Although the room was large and lofty, owing to the absence of ventilation, the abundance of gas, the crowd of people, the atmosphere was horrible. There was a continual buzz; an unresting clatter. The noise of people in motion; the hum of their voices; the strident tones of the *tourneur,* as he made his various monotonous announcements; all these assisted in the formation of what, to an unaccustomed ear, was a strange cacophony. She shrank towards Mr. Huhn as if afraid.

"What are they doing?" she asked.

Instead of answering he led her forward to the dais on which the nine little horses were the observed of all observers, where the *tourneur* stood with his assistant with, in front and on either side of him, the tables about which the players were grouped. At the moment the leaden steeds were whirling round. She watched them, fascinated. People were speaking on their right.

"*C'est le huit qui gagne.*"

"*Non; le huit est mort. C'est le six.*"

Someone said behind her, in English:—

"Jack's all right; one wins. Confound the brute, he's gone right on!"

The horses ceased to move.

"*Le numéro cinq!*" shouted the *tourneur,* laying a strong nasal stress upon the numeral.

There were murmurs of disgust from the bettors on the columns. Miss Donne perceived that money was displayed upon baize-covered tables. The croupiers thrust out wooden rakes to draw it towards them. At the table on her right there seemed to be only a single winner. Several five-franc pieces were passed to a woman who was twiddling a number of them between her fingers.

"Are they gambling?" asked Miss Donne.

"Well, I shouldn't call it gambling. This is a little toy by means of which the proprietor makes a good and regular income out of public contributions. These are some of the contributors."

Miss Donne did not understand him—did not even try to. She was all eyes for what was taking place about her. Money was being staked afresh. The horses were whirling round again. This time No. 7 was the winning horse. There were acclamations. Several persons had staked on seven. It appeared that that particular number was "overdue." Someone rose from a chair beside her.

Mr. Huhn made a sudden suggestion.

"Sit down." She sat down. "Let's contribute a franc or two to the support of this deserving person's wife and family. Where's your purse?" She showed that her purse—a silver chain affair—was attached to her belt. "Find a franc." Whether or not she had a coin of that denomination did not appear. She produced a five-franc piece. "That's a large piece of money. What shall we put it on?"

Someone who was seated on the next chair said:—

"The run's on five."

"Then let's be on the run. That's it, in the centre there. That's the particular number which enables the owner of this little toy to keep a roof above his head."

As she held the coin in front of her with apparently uncertain fingers, as if still doubtful what it was she had to do, her neighbour, taking it from her with a smile, laid it upon five.

"*Le jeu est fait!*" cried the *tourneur*. "*Rien ne va plus!*"

He started the horses whirling round.

Then with a shock, she seemed to wake from a dream. She sprang from her chair, staring at her five-franc piece with wide-open eyes. People smiled. The croupiers gazed at her indulgently. There was that about her which made it obvious that to such a scene she was a stranger. They supposed that, like some eager child, she could not conceal her anxiety for the safety of her stake. Although surprised at her display of a degree of interest which was altogether beyond what the occasion seemed to warrant, Mr. Huhn thought with them.

"Don't be alarmed," he murmured in her ear. "You may take it for granted that it's gone, and may console yourself with the reflection that it goes to minister to the wants of a mother and her children. That's the philosophical point of view. And it may be the right one."

Her hand twitched, as if she found the temptation to snatch back her stake before it was gone for ever almost more than she could bear. Mr. Huhn caught her arm.

"Hush! That sort of thing is not allowed."

The horses stopped. The *tourneur* proclaimed the winner.

"*Le numéro cinq!*"

"Bravo!" exclaimed the neighbour who had placed the stake for her. "You have won. I told you the run was on five."

"Shorn the shearers," commented Mr. Huhn. "You see, that's the way to make a fortune, only I shouldn't advise you to go further than the initiatory lesson."

The croupier pushed over her own coin and seven others. Her neighbour held them up to her.

"Your winnings."

She drew back.

"It's not mine."

Her neighbour laughed outright. People were visibly smiling. Mr. Huhn took the pile of coins from the stranger's hand.

"They are yours; take them." Him she obeyed with the docility of a child. "Come let us go."

He led the way to the door which opened on to the terrace. She followed, meekly. It seemed that the eight coins were more than she could conveniently carry in one hand; for, as she went, she dropped one on to the floor. An attendant, picking it up, returned it to her with a grin. Indeed, the whole room was on the titter, the incident was so very amusing. They asked themselves if she was mad, or just a simpleton. And, in a fashion, considering that her first youth was passed, she really was so pretty! Mr. Huhn was more moved than, in that place, he would have cared to admit. Something in her attitude in the way she looked at him when he bade her take the money, had filled him with a sense of shame.

Between their going in and coming out the sky had changed. The shadows were lowering. The autumnal day was drawing to a close. September had brought more than a suggestion of winter's breath. A grey chill followed the departing sun. They went up, then down, the terrace, without exchanging a word; then, moving aside, he offered her one of the wicker-seated chairs which stood against the wall. She sat on it. He sat opposite, leaning on the handle of his stick. The thin mist which was stealing across the leaden sea did not invite lounging out of doors. They had the terrace to themselves. She let her five-franc pieces drop with a clinking sound on to her lap. He, conscious of something on her face which he was unwilling to confront, looked steadily seaward. Presently she gave utterance to her pent-up feelings.

"I am a gambler."

Had she accused herself of the unforgivable sin she could not have seemed more serious. Somewhere within him was a laughing sprite. In view of her genuine distress he did his best to keep it in subjection.

"You exaggerate. Staking a five-franc piece—for the good of the house—on the *petits chevaux* does not make you that, any more than taking a glass of wine makes you a drunkard."

"Why did you make me, why did you let me, do it?"

"I didn't know you felt that way."

"And yet you said you knew me!"

He winched. He had told a falsehood. He did know her—there was the sting. In mischievous mood he had induced her to do the thing which he suspected that she held to be wrong. He had not supposed that she would take it so seriously, especially if she won, being aware that there are persons who condemn gambling when they or those belonging to them lose, but who lean more towards the side of charity when they win. He did not know what to say to her, so he said nothing.

"My father once lost over four hundred pounds on a horse-race. I don't quite know how it was, I was only a child. He was in business at the time. I believe it ruined him, and it nearly broke my mother's heart. I promised her that I would never gamble—and now I have."

He felt that this was one of those women whose moral eye is single—with whom it is better to be frank.

"I confess I felt that you might have scruples on the point; but I thought you would look upon a single stake of a single five-franc piece as a jest. Many American women—and many Englishwomen—who would be horrified if you called them gamblers, go into the rooms at Monte Carlo and lose or win a louis or two just for the sake of the joke."

"For the sake of the joke! Gamble for the sake of the joke! Are you a Jesuit?" The question so took him by surprise that he turned and stared at her. "I have always understood that that is how Jesuits reason—that they try to make out that black is white. I hope—I hope you don't do that?"

He smiled grimly, his thoughts recurring to some of the "deals" in which his success had made him the well-to-do man he was.

"Sometimes the two colours merge so imperceptibly into one another that it's hard to tell just where the conjunction begins. You want keen sight to do it. But here you're right and I'm wrong; there's no two words about it. It was I who made you stake that five-franc piece; and I'd no right to make you stake buttons if it was against your principles. Your standard's like my mother's. I hope that mine will grow nearer to it. I ask you to forgive me for leading you astray."

"I ought not to have been so weak."

"You had to—when I was there to make you."

She was still; though it is doubtful if she grasped the full meaning his words conveyed. If he had been watching her he would have seen that by degrees something like the suggestion of a smile seem to wrinkle the corners of her lips. When she spoke again it was in half a whisper.

"I'm sorry, I should seem to you to be so silly."

"You don't. You mustn't say it. You seem to me to be the wisest woman I ever met."

"That must be because you've known so few—or else you're laughing. No one who has ever known me has thought me wise. If I were wise I should know what to do with this."

She motioned towards the money on her lap.

"Throw it into the sea."

"But it isn't mine."

"It's yours as much as anyone else's. If you come to first causes you'll find it hard to name the rightful owner—in God's sight—for any one thing. There's been too much swapping of horses. You'll find plenty who are in need."

"It would carry a curse with it. Money won in gambling!"

He looked at his watch.

"It's time that you and I thought about dinner. We'll adjourn the discussion as to what is to be done with the fruit of our iniquity. I say 'our,' because that I'm the principal criminal is as plain as paint. Sleep on it; perhaps you'll see clearer in the morning. Put it in your pocket."

"Haven't I told you already that I haven't a pocket? And if I had I shouldn't put this money in it. I should feel that that was half-way towards keeping it."

"Then let me be the bearer of the burden."

"No; I don't wish the taint to be conveyed to you." He laughed outright. "There now you are laughing!"

"I was laughing because—" he was on the verge of saying "because I love you;" but something induced him to substitute— "because I love to hear you talking."

She glanced at him with smiling eyes. His gaze was turned towards what was now the shrouded sea. Neither spoke during the three minutes of brisk walking which was required to reach the Hotel de Paris, she carrying the money, four five-franc pieces, gripped tightly in either hand.

In his phrase, she slept on it, though the fashion of the sleeping was a little strange. The next morning she sallied forth to put into execution the resolve at which she had arrived. It was early, though not so early as she would have wished, because, concluding that all Dieppe did not rise with the lark, she judged it as well to take her coffee and roll before she took the air. It promised to be a glorious day. The atmosphere was filled with a golden haze, through which the sun was gleaming. As she went through the gate of the Port d'Ouest she came upon a man who was selling little metal effigies of the flags of various nations. From him she made a purchase— the Stars and Stripes. This she pinned inside her blouse, on the left, smiling to herself as she did so. Then she marched straight off into the Casino.

The *salle de jeu* had but a single occupant, a *tourneur* who was engaged in dusting the little horses. To enable him to perform the necessary offices he removed the steeds from their places one after the other. As it chanced he was the identical individual who had been responsible for the *course* which had crowned Miss Doone with victory. With that keen vision which is characteristic of his class the man recognised her on the instant. Bowing and smiling he held out to her the horse which he was holding.

"*Vlà madame, le numéro cinq! C'est lui qui a porté le bonheur à madame.*"

It was, indeed, the horse which represented the number on which she had staked her five-franc piece. By an odd accident she had arrived just as its toilet was being performed. She observed what an excellent model it was with somewhat doubtful eyes, as if fearful of its being warranted neither steady nor free from vice.

"I have brought back the seven five-franc pieces which I—took away with me."

She held out the coins. As if at a loss he looked from them to her.

"But, madame, I do not understand."

"I can have nothing to do with money which is the fruit of gambling."

"But madame played."

"It was a misunderstanding. A mistake. It was not my intention. It is on that account I have come to return this money."

"Return?—to whom?—the administration? The administration will not accept it. It is impossible. What it has lost it has lost; there is an end."

"But I insist on returning it; and if I insist it must be accepted; especially when I tell you it is all a mistake."

The *tourneur* shrugged his shoulders.

"If madame does not want the money, and will give it to me, I will see what I can do with it." She handed him the coins; he transferred them to the board at his back. Then he held out to her the horse which he had been dusting. "See, madame, is it not a perfect model? And feel how heavy—over three kilos, more than six English pounds. When you consider that there are nine horses, all exactly the same weight, you will perceive that it is not easy work to be a *tourneur.* That toy horse is worth much more to the administration than if it were a real horse; it is from the Number Five that all this comes."

He waved his hand as if to denote the entire building.

"I thought that public gambling was prohibited in France and in all Christian countries, and that it was only permitted in such haunts of wickedness as Monte Carlo."

"Gambling? Ah, the little horses is not gambling! It is an amusement."

A voice addressed her from the other side of the table. It was Mr. Huhn.

"Didn't I tell you it wasn't gambling? It's as this gentleman says—an amusement; especially for the administration."

"Ah, yes—in particular for the administration."

The *tourneur* laughed. Miss Donne and Mr. Huhn went out together by the same door through which they had gone the night before. They sat on the low wall. He had some towels on his arm; he had been bathing. Already the sea was glowing with the radiance of the sun.

"So you've relieved yourself of your ill-gotten gains?"

"I have returned them to the administration."

"To the —— did that gentleman say he would hand those five-franc pieces to the administration?"

"He said that he would see what he could do with them."

"Just so. There's no doubt that that is what he will do. So you did sleep upon that burning question?"

"I did."

"Then you got the better of me; because I didn't sleep at all."

"I am sorry."

"You ought to be, since the fault was yours."

"Mine! My fault that you didn't sleep!"

"Do you see what I've got here?"

He made an upward movement with his hand. For the first time she noticed that in his buttonhole he had a tiny copy of the Union Jack.

"Did you buy that of the man outside the town gate?"

He nodded.

"Why, it was of that very same man that I bought this."

From the inside of her blouse she produced that minute representation of the colours he knew so well. They looked at each other, and . . . .

When some time after they were lunching, he forming a fourth at the small table which belonged of right to Mr. and Mrs. Palmer, he said to Annie Moriarty, that was:—

"Since you're an old friend of Miss Donne you may be interested in knowing that there's likely soon to be an International Alliance."

He motioned to the lady at his side and then to himself, as if to call attention to the fact that in his buttonhole was the Union Jack, while on Miss Donne's blouse was pinned the American flag. But keen-witted Mrs. Palmer had realized what exactly was the condition of affairs some time before.

"Skittles"

CHAPTER I

MR. PLUMBER was a passable preacher. Not an orator, perhaps—though it is certain that they had had less oratorical curates at Exdale. His delivery was not exactly good. But then the matter was fair, at times. Though Mr. Ingledew did say that Mr. Plumber's sermons were rather in the nature of reminiscences—tit-bits collated from other divines. According to this authority, listening to Mr. Plumber preaching was a capital exercise for the memory. His pulpit addresses might almost be regarded in the light of a series of examination papers. One might take it for granted that every thought was borrowed from some one, the question—put by the examiner, as it were—being from whom? On the other hand, it must be granted that Mr. Ingledew's character was well understood in Exdale. He was one of those persons who are persuaded that there is no such thing as absolute originality in the present year of grace. From his point of view, all the moderns are thieves. He read a new book, not for the pleasure of reading it, but for the pleasure of finding out, as a sort of anemonic exercise, from whom its various parts had been pilfered. He held that, nowadays, nothing new is being produced, either in prose or verse; and that the only thing which the latter day writer does need, is the capacity to use the scissors and the paste. So it was no new thing for the Exdale congregation to be informed that the sermon which they had listened to had been preached before.

Nor, Mrs. Manby declared, in any case, was that the point. She wanted a preacher to do her good. If he could not do her good out of his own mouth, then, by all means, let him do her good out of the mouths of others. All gifts are not given to all men. If a man was conscious of his incapacity in one direction, then she, for one, had no objection to his availing himself, to the best of his ability, of his capacity in another. But—and here Mrs. Manby held up her hands in the manner which is so well known to her friends—

when a man told her, from the pulpit, on the Sunday, that life was a solemn and a serious thing, and then on the Monday wrote for a comic paper—and such a comic paper!—that was the point, and quite another matter entirely.

How the story first was told has not been clearly ascertained. The presumption is, that a proof was sent to Mr. Plumber in one of those wrappers which are open at both ends in which proofs sometimes are sent; and that on the front of this wrapper was imprinted, by way of advertisement, the source of its origin: *"Skittles: Not to mention the Beer. A Comic Croaker for the Cultured Classes."*

The presumption goes on to suggest that, while it was still in the post office, the proof fell out of the wrapper,—they sometimes are most insecurely enclosed, and the thing might have been the purest accident. One of the clerks—it is said, young Griffen— noticing it, happened to read the proof—just glanced over it, that is—also, of course, by accident. And then, on purchasing a copy of a particular issue of the periodical in question, this clerk— whoever he was—perceived that it contained the, one could not call it poem, but rhyming doggerel, proof of which had been sent to the Reverend Reginald Plumber. He probably mentioned it to a friend, in the strictest confidence. This friend mentioned it to another friend, also in the strictest confidence. And so everybody was told by everybody else, in the strictest confidence; and the thing which was meant to be hid in a hole found itself displayed on the top of the hill.

It was felt that something ought to be done. This feeling took form and substance at an informal meeting which was held at Mrs. Manby's in the guise of a tea, and which was attended by the churchwardens, Mr. Ingledew, and others, who might be expected to do something, when, from the point of view of public policy, it ought to be done. The *pièces de conviction* were not, on that particular occasion, actually produced in evidence, because it was generally felt that the paper, *"Skittles: Not to mention the Beer, etc."* was not a paper which could be produced in the presence of ladies.

"And that," Mrs. Manby observed, "is what makes the thing so very dreadful. It is bad enough that such papers should be allowed to appear. But that they should be supported by the contributions of our spiritual guides and teachers, opens a vista which cannot but fill every proper-minded person with dismay."

Miss Norman mildly hinted that Mr. Plumber might have intended, not so much to support the journal in question, either with his contributions or otherwise, as that it should aid in supporting him. But this was an aspect of the case which the meeting simply declined to even consider. Because Mr. Plumber chose to have an ailing wife and a horde of children that was no reason, but very much the contrary, why, instead of elevating, he should assist in degrading public morals. So the resolution was finally arrived at that, without loss of time, the churchwardens should wait upon the Vicar, make a formal statement of the lamentable facts of the case, and that the Vicar should then be requested to do the something which ought to be done.

So, in accordance with this resolution, the churchwardens waited on the vicar. The Rev. Henry Harding was, at that time, the Vicar of Exdale. He was not only an easy-going man and possessed of large private means, but he was also one of those unfortunately constituted persons who are with difficulty induced to make themselves disagreeable to any one. The churchwardens quite anticipated that they might find it hard to persuade him, even in so glaring a case as the present one, to do the something which ought to be done. Nor were their expectations, in this respect, doomed to meet with disappointment.

"Am I to understand," asked the vicar, when, to a certain extent, the lamentable facts of the case had been laid before him, and as he leaned back in his easy chair he pushed his spectacles up on his forehead, "that you have come to complain to me because a gentleman, finding himself in straitened circumstances, desires to add to his income by means of contributions to the press?"

That was not what they wished him to understand at all. Mr. Luxmare, the people's warden, endeavoured to explain.

"It is this particular paper to which we object. It is a vile, and a scurrilous rag. Its very name is an offence. You are, probably, not acquainted with its character. I have here——"

Mr. Luxmare was producing a copy of the offensive publication from his pocket, when the vicar stopped him.

"I know the paper very well indeed," he said.

Mr. Luxmare seemed slightly taken aback. But he continued—.

"In that case you are well aware that it is a paper with which no decent person would allow himself to be connected."

"I am by no means so sure of that." Mr. Harding pressed the tips of his fingers together, with that mild, but occasionally exasperating, air of beaming affability for which he was peculiar. "I have known some very decent persons who have allowed themselves to become connected with some extremely curious papers."

As the people's warden, Mr. Luxmare, was conscious of an almost exaggerated feeling of responsibility. He felt that, in a peculiar sense, he represented the parish. It was his duty to impress the feelings of the parish upon the vicar. And he meant to impress the feeling of the parish upon the vicar now. Moreover, by natural constitution he was almost as much inclined to aggressiveness as the vicar was inclined to placability. He at once assumed what might be called the tone and manner of a prosecuting counsel.

"This is an instance," and he banged his right fist into his left palm, "of a clergyman—a clergyman of our church, the national church, associating himself with a paper, the avowed and ostensible purpose of which is to pander to the depraved instincts of the lowest of the low. I say, sir, and I defy contradiction, that such an instance in such a man is an offence against good morals."

Mr. Harding smiled—which was by no means what the people's warden had intended he should do.

"By the way," he said, "has Mr. Plumber been writing under his own name?"

"Not he. The stuff is anonymous. It is inconceivable that any one could wish to be known as its author?"

"Then may I ask how you know that Mr. Plumber is its author?"

Mr. Luxmare appeared to be a trifle non-plussed—as did his associate. But the people's warden stuck to his guns.

"It is common report in the parish that Mr. Plumber is a contributor to a paper which would not be admitted to a decent house. We are here as church officers to acquaint you with that report, and to request you to ascertain from Mr. Plumber whether or not it is well founded."

"In other words, you wish me to associate myself with vague

scandal about Queen Elizabeth, and to play the part of Paul Pry in the private affairs of my friend and colleague."

Mr. Luxmare rose from his chair.

"If, sir, you decline to accede to our request, we shall go from you to Mr. Plumber. We shall put to him certain questions. Should he decline to answer them, or should his replies not be satisfactory, we shall esteem it our duty to report the matter to the Bishop. For my own part, I say, without hesitation, that it would be a notorious scandal that a contributor to such a paper as *Skittles* should be a minister in our beloved parish church."

The vicar still smiled, though it is conceivable that, for once in a way, his smile was merely on the surface.

"Then, in that case, Mr. Luxmare, you will take upon yourself a great responsibility."

"Mr. Harding, I took upon myself a great responsibility when I suffered myself to be made the people's warden. It is not my intention to attempt to shirk that responsibility in one jot or in one tittle. To the best of my ability, at any cost, I will do my duty, though the heavens fall."

The vicar meditated some moments before he spoke again. Then he addressed himself to both his visitors.

"I tell you what I will do, gentlemen. I will go to Mr. Plumber and tell him what you say. Then I will acquaint you with his answer."

"Very good!" It was Mr. Luxmare who took upon himself to reply. "At present that is all we ask. I would only suggest, that the sooner your visit is paid the better."

"Certainly. There I do agree with you; it is always well to rid oneself of matters of this sort as soon as possible. I will make a point of calling on Mr. Plumber directly you are gone."

Possibly, when his visitors had gone, the vicar was inclined to the opinion that he had promised rather hastily. Not only did he not start upon his errand with the promptitude which his own words had suggested, but even when he did start, he pursued such devious ways that several hours elapsed between his arrival at the curate's and the departure of the deputation.

Mr. Plumber lived in a cottage. It might have not been without its attractions as a home for a newly-married couple, but as a residence for a man of studious habits, possessed of a large and noisy family, it had its disadvantages. It was the curate himself who opened the door. Directly he did so the vicar became conscious that, within, there was a colourable imitation of pandemonium. Some young gentlemen appeared to be fighting upstairs; other young gentlemen appeared to be rehearsing some unmusical selections of the nature of a Christy Minstrel chorus on the ground floor at the back; somewhere else small children were crying; while occasionally, above the hubbub, were heard the shrill tones of a woman's agitated voice, raised in heartsick—because hopeless,—expostulation. Mr. Plumber seemed to be unconscious of there being anything strange in such discord of sweet sounds. Possibly he had become so used to living in the midst of a riot that it never occurred to him that there was anything in mere uproar for which it might be necessary to apologise. He led the way to his study—a small room at the back of the house, which was in uncomfortable proximity to the Christy Minstrel chorus. Small though the room was, it was insufficiently furnished. As he entered it, the vicar was struck, by no means for the first time, by an unpleasant sense of the contrast which existed between the curate's study and the luxurious apartment which was his study at the vicarage. The vicar seated himself on one of the two chairs which the apartment contained. A few desultory remarks were exchanged. Then Mr. Harding endeavoured to broach the subject which had brought him there. He began a little awkwardly.

"I hope that you know me well enough to be aware, Mr. Plumber, that I am not a person who would wish to thrust myself into the affairs of others."

The curate nodded. He was standing up before the empty fireplace. A tall, sparely-built man, with scanty iron-grey hair, a pronounced stoop, and a face which was a tragedy—it said so plainly that he was a man who had abandoned hope. Its careful neatness accentuated the threadbare condition of his clerical costume—it was always a mystery to the vicar how the curate contrived to keep himself so neat, considering his slender resources, and the life of domestic drudgery which he was compelled to lead.

"Are you acquainted with a publication called *Skittles?*"

Mr. Plumber nodded again; Mr. Harding would rather he had spoken.

"May I ask if you are a contributor to such a publication?"

"May I inquire why you ask?"

"It is reported in the parish that you are. The parish does not relish the report. And you must know yourself that it is not a paper"—the vicar hesitated—"not a paper with which a gentleman would wish it to be known that he was associated."

"Well?"

"Well, without entering into questions of the past, I hope you will give me to understand that, at any rate, in the future, you will not contribute to its pages."

"Why?"

"Is it necessary to explain? Are we not both clergymen?"

"Are you suggesting that a clergyman should pay occasional visits to a debtor's prison rather than contribute to the pages of a comic paper?"

"It is not a question of a comic paper, but of this particular comic paper."

The curate looked intently at the vicar. He had dark eyes which, at times, were curiously full of meaning. Mr. Harding felt that they were very full of meaning then. He so sympathised with the man, so realised the burdens which he had to bear, that he never found himself alone with him without becoming conscious of a sensation which was almost shyness. At that moment, as the curate continued to fixedly regard him, he was not only shy, but ashamed.

"Mr. Harding you are not here of your own initiative."

"That is so. But that will not help you. If you take my advice, of two evils you will choose what I believe to be the lesser."

"And that is?"

"You will have no further connection with this paper."

"Mr. Harding, look here." Going to a cupboard which was in a corner of the room, the curate threw the door wide open. Within were shelves. On the shelves were papers. The cupboard seemed full of them, shelf above shelf. "You see these. They are MSS.—my MSS. They have travelled pretty well all round the world. They have been rejected everywhere. I have paid postage for them which I could very ill afford, only to have them sent back upon my hands, at last, for good. I show them to you merely because I wish you to understand that I did not apply to the editor of *Skittles* until I had been rejected by practically every other editor the world contains." The Vicar fidgetted on his chair.

"Surely, now that reading has become almost universal, it is always possible to find an opening for good work."

"For good work, possibly. Though, even then, I suspect that the thing is not so easy as you imagine. But mine is not good work. Very often it is not even good hack work, as good hack work goes. I may have been capable of good work once. But the capacity, if it ever existed, has gone—crushed perhaps by the burdens which have crushed me. Nowadays I am only too glad to do any work which will bring in for us a few extra crumbs of bread."

"I sympathise with you, with all my heart."

"Thank you." The curate smiled, the vicar would almost have rather he had cried. "There is one other point. If the paper were a bad paper, in a moral or in a religious sense, under no sense of circumstances would I consent to do its work or to take its wage. But if any one has told you that it is a bad paper, in that sense, you have been misinformed. It is simply a cheap so-called humorous journal. Perhaps not over-refined. It is intended for the *olla podrida*. It is printed on poor paper, and the printing is not good. The illustrations are not always in the best of taste and are sometimes simply smudges. But looking at the reading matter as a whole, it is probably equal to that which is contained, week after week, in some of the high-priced papers which find admission to every house."

"I am bound to say that sometimes when I have been travelling I have purchased the paper myself, and I have never seen anything in it which could be justly called improper."

"Nor I. I submit, sir, that we curates are already sufficiently cribbed, cabined, and confined. If narrow-minded, non-literary persons are to have the power to forbid our working for decent journals to which they themselves, for some reason, may happen to object, our case is harder still."

The vicar rose from his chair.

"Quite so. There is a great deal in what you say—I quite realise it, Mr. Plumber. The laity are already too much disposed to trample on us clerics. I will think the matter over—think the matter over, Mr. Plumber. My dear sir, what is that?"

There was a crashing sound on the floor overhead, which threatened to bring the study ceiling down. It was followed by such a deafening din, as if an Irish faction fight was taking place upstairs, that even the curate seemed to be disturbed.

"Some of the boys have been making themselves a pair of boxing gloves, and I am afraid they are practising with them in their bedroom."

"Oh," said the vicar. That was all he did say, but the "Oh" was eloquent.

"To think," he told himself as he departed, "that a scholar and a gentleman should be compelled to live in a place like that, with a helpless wife and a horde of unruly lads, and should be driven to scribble nonsense for such a rag as *Skittles* in order to provide himself with the means to keep them all alive—it seems to me that it must be, in some way, a disgrace to the English Church that such things should be."

He not only said this to himself, but, later on, he said it to his wife. His words had weight with Mrs. Harding, but not the sort of weight which he desired. The fact is Mrs. Harding had views of her own on the subject of curates. She held that curates ought not to marry. Vicars, rectors, and the higher clergy might; but curates, no. For a poor curate to marry was nothing else than a crime. Had she had her way, Mr. Plumber would long ago have vanished from Exdale. But though the vicar was ruled to a considerable extent by his wife, there was a point at which he drew the line. That a man should be turned adrift on to the world to quite starve simply because he was nearly starving already was an idea which actually filled him with indignation.

If he supposed that his interview with Mr. Plumber had resulted in a manner which was likely to appease those of his parishioners who had objections to a curate who wrote for comic papers, he was destined soon to learn his error. The following morning one of his churchwardens paid another visit to the vicarage— the duty-loving Mr. Luxmare. Mr. Harding was conscious of an uncomfortable twinge when that gentleman's name was brought to him; he seemed to be still more uncomfortable when he found himself constrained to meet the warden's eye. The story he had to tell was not only in itself a slightly lame one, its lameness was emphasised by the way in which he told it. It was plain that it was not going to have the effect of inducing Mr. Luxmare to move one hair's breadth from the path which he felt that duty required him to tread.

"Am I to understand, Mr. Harding, that Mr. Plumber, conscious of his offence, has promised to offend no more? In other words, has he undertaken to have no further connection with this off-scouring of the press?"

Mr. Harding put his spectacles on his nose. He took them off again. He fidgetted and fumbled with them with his fingers.

"The fact is, Mr. Luxmare—and this is entirely between ourselves—Mr. Plumber is in such straitened circumstances——"

"Quite so. But because a man is a pauper, does that justify him in becoming a thief?"

"Gently, Mr. Luxmare, let us consider our words before we utter them. Here is no question of anything even distantly approaching to felony. To be frank with you, I think you are unnecessarily hard on this particular journal. The paper is merely a vulgar paper——"

"And Mr. Plumber is merely an ordained minister of the Established Church. Are we, then, as churchmen, to expect our clergy to encourage, not only passively, but, also, actively, the already superabundant vulgarity of the public press?"

The vicar had the worst of it; when he was once more alone he felt that there was no sort of doubt upon that point.

Whether, intentionally or not, Mr. Luxmare managed to convey the impression that, in his opinion, the curate, while pretending to save souls with one hand, was doing his best to destroy them with the other, and that, in that singular course of procedure, he was being aided and abetted by the vicar. Mr. Harding had strong forebodings that the trouble, so far from being ended, was only just beginning. Those forebodings became still stronger when, scarcely an hour after Mr. Luxmare had left him, Mrs. Harding, entering the study like a passable imitation of a hurricane, laid a printed sheet in front of her husband with the air almost of a Jove hurling thunderbolts from the skies.

"Mr. Harding, have you seen that paper?"

It was the unescapable *Skittles*. The vicar groaned in spirit. He regarded it with weary eyes.

"A copy of it now and then, my dear."

"I have just discovered its existence with feelings of horror. That such a thing should be permitted to be is a national disgrace. Mr. Harding, you will be astounded to learn that the curate of Exdale is one of its chief contributors."

"Scarcely, I think, one of its chief contributors."

Mrs. Harding struck an attitude.

"Is it possible that you are already aware that your ostensible colleague in the great task of snatching souls from the burning has all the time been doing Satan's work?"

"My dear!—really!"

"You know very well that I have objected to Mr. Plumber from the first. I have suspected the man. Now that my suspicions are more than verified, it is certain that he must go. The question is, when? Of course, before next Sunday."

"You move too fast, Sophia."

"In such a matter as this it is impossible to move too fast. Read that."

Turning over a page of the paper, Mrs. Harding pointed to a "copy of verses."

"Thank you, my dear, but, if you will permit me, I prefer to remain excused. I have no taste for that species of literature just now."

"So I should imagine—either now or ever! The shameful and shameless rubbish has been written by your curate. I am told that it has been cut out and framed, and that it at present hangs in the taproom of 'The Pig and Whistle,' with these words scrawled beneath it: 'The Curate's Latest! Real Jam!' Is that the sort of handle which you wish to offer to the scoffers? I shall not leave this room until you promise me that before next Sunday Exdale Parish Church shall have seen the last of him."

He did not promise that, but he promised something—with his fatal facility for promising. He promised that a meeting should be held at the vicarage before the following Sunday. That Mr. Plumber, the churchwardens, and the sidesmen should be invited to attend. That certain questions should be put to the curate. That he should be asked what he had to say for himself. And, although the vicar did not distinctly promise, in so many words, that the sense of the meeting should then be allowed to decide his fate, the lady certainly inferred as much.

The meeting was held. Mr. Harding wrote to the curate, explaining matters as best he could—he felt that in trusting to his pen he would be safer than in trusting to word of mouth. Probably because he was conscious that he really had no choice, Mr. Plumber agreed to come. And he came. Besides the clergy and officers of the church, the only person present was the aforementioned Mr. Ingledew. He was a person of light and leading in the parish, and when he asked permission to attend, the vicar saw no sufficient ground to say him nay.

CHAPTER II

THAT was one of the unhappiest days of Mr. Harding's life. He was one of those people who are possessed of the questionable faculty of being able to see both sides of a question at once. He saw, too plainly for his own peace of mind, what was to be said both for and against the curate. He feared that the meeting would only see what was only to be said against him. That the man would come prejudiced. And he felt—and that was the worst of all!— that, for the sake of a peace which was no peace, he was giving his colleague into the hands of his enemies, and shifting on to the shoulders of others the authority which was his own.

The churchwardens were the first to arrive. It was plain, from the start, that, so far as the people's warden was concerned, the curate's fate was already signed and sealed. The sidesmen followed, one by one. The vicar had had no personal communication with them on the matter; but he took it for granted, from his knowledge of their characters, that though they lacked his power of expression, they might be expected to think as Mr. Luxmare thought. Mr. Ingledew's position was not clearly defined, but everybody knew the point of view from which he would judge the curate. He would pose as a critic of Literature—with a capital L!—and Mr. Harding feared that, in that character, the unfortunate Mr. Plumber might fare even worse with him than with the others.

The curate was the last to arrive. He came into the room with his hat and stick in his hand. Going straight up to the vicar, he addressed to him a question which brought the business for which they were assembled immediately to the front.

"What is it that you would wish to say to me, sir?"

"It is about your contributions to the well-advertised *Skittles*, Mr. Plumber. There seems to be a strong feeling on the subject in the parish. I thought that we might meet together here and arrive at a common understanding."

Mr. Plumber bowed. He turned to the others. He bowed to them. There was a pause, as if of hesitation as to what ought to be done. Then Mr. Luxmare spoke.

"May I ask Mr. Plumber some questions?"

The vicar beamed, or endeavoured to.

"You had better, Mr. Luxmare, address that inquiry to Mr. Plumber."

Mr. Luxmare addressed himself to Mr. Plumber—not genially.

"The first question I would ask you, sir, is, whether it is true that you are a contributor to the paper which the vicar has named. The second question I would ask you, sir——"

The curate interrupted him.

"One moment, Mr. Luxmare. On what ground do you consider yourself entitled to question me?"

"You are one of the parish clergy. I am one of its churchwardens. As such, I speak to you in the name of the parish."

"I fail to understand you. Because I am one of the parish clergy it does not follow that I am in any way responsible for my conduct to the parish. My life would be not worth living if that were so. I am responsible to my vicar alone. So long as he is satisfied that I am doing my duty to him, you have no concern with me, and I have none with you."

"Quite right, Mr. Plumber," struck in the vicar. "I have hinted as much to Mr. Luxmare already."

The people's warden listened with lowering brows.

"Then why have you brought us here, sir?—to be played with?"

"The truth is, Mr. Luxmare—and you must forgive my speaking plainly—you have an exaggerated conception of the magnitude of your office. A churchwarden has certain duties to perform, but among them is not the duty of sitting in judgment on his clergy."

"Then am I to understand that Mr. Plumber declines to answer my questions?"

"It depends," said Mr. Plumber, "upon what your questions are. I trust that I may be always found ready, and willing, to respond to any inquiries, not savouring of impertinence, which may be addressed to me. I have no objection, for instance, to inform you, or any one, that I am, or rather, I have been, a contributor to *Skittles*."

"Oh, you have, have you! May I ask if you intend to continue to contribute to that scandalous rag?"

"Now you go too far. I am unable to bind myself by any promise as to my future intentions."

"Then, sir, I say that you ought to be ashamed of yourself."

"Mr. Luxmare!" cried the vicar.

But the people's warden had reached the explosive point; he was bound to explode.

"I am not to be put down, nor am I to be frightened from doing what I conceive to be my bounden duty. I tell you again, Mr. Plumber, sir, that you ought to be ashamed of yourself. And I say further, that it is to me a monstrous proposition, that a clergyman is to be at liberty to contribute to the rising flood of public immorality, and that his parishioners are not to be allowed to offer even a word of remonstrance. You may take this from me, Mr. Plumber, that so long as you continue one of its clergy, the parish church will be deserted. You will minister, if you are to minister at all, to a beggarly array of empty pews. And, since the parish is not to be permitted to speak its mind in private, I will see that an opportunity is given it to speak its mind in public. I will see that a public meeting is held. I promise you that it will be attended by every decent-minded man and woman in Exdale. Some home truths will be uttered which, I trust, will enlighten you as to what is, and what is not, the duty of a parish clergyman."

"Have you quite finished, Mr. Luxmare?"

The vicar asked the question in a tone of almost dangerous quiet.

"Do not think," continued Mr. Luxmare, ignoring Mr. Harding, "that in this matter I speak for myself. I speak for the whole parish." He turned to his colleague, "Is that not so?"

The vicar's warden did not seem to be completely at his ease. He looked appealingly at the vicar. He shuffled with his feet. But he spoke at last, prefacing his remarks with a sort of deprecatory little cough.

"I am bound to admit that I consider it somewhat unfortunate that Mr. Plumber should have contributed to a publication of this particular class."

Mr. Luxmare turned to the sidesmen.

"What do you think?"

The sidesmen did not say much, but they managed, with what they did say, to convey the impression that they thought as the churchwardens thought.

"You see," exclaimed the triumphant Mr. Luxmare, "that here we are unanimous, and I give you my word that our unanimity is but typical of the unanimous feeling which pervades the entire parish."

"Has anybody else anything which he would wish to say?"

The vicar asked the question in the same curiously quiet tone of voice. Mr. Ingledew stood up.

"Yes, vicar, I have something which I should rather like to say. I am not pretending to have, in this matter, any *locus standi*. Nor do I intend to assail Mr. Plumber on the lines which Mr. Luxmare has followed. To me it seems to be a matter of comparative indifference to which journal a man, be he cleric or layman, may choose to send his contributions. Journals nowadays are very much of a muchness, their badness is merely a question of degree. There is, however, one point on which I should like to be enlightened by Mr. Plumber. I am told that he is the author of some verses which were published in the issue of *Skittles*, dated July 11th, and entitled 'The Lingering Lover.' Is that so, Mr. Plumber?"

As Mr. Ingledew asked his question, the curate, for the first time, showed signs of obvious uneasiness.

"That is so," he said.

Mr. Ingledew smiled. His smile did not seem to add to the curate's comfort.

"I do not intend to criticise those verses. Probably Mr. Plumber will admit that by no standard of criticism can they be adjudged first rate. But, in this connection, I would make one remark—and here I think you will agree with me, vicar—that even a clergyman should be decently honest."

"Pray," asked the vicar, who possibly had noticed Mr. Plumber's uneasiness, and had, thereupon, become uneasy himself, "what has honesty to do with the matter?"

"A good deal, as I am about to show. Mr. Luxmare asked Mr. Plumber if he intended to continue to contribute to *Skittles*. Mr. Plumber declined to answer that question. I could have answered it; and now do. No more of Mr. Plumber's contributions will appear in *Skittles*."

The curate started—indeed, everybody started—vicar, churchwardens, sidesmen and all.

"What do you mean?" stammered Mr. Plumber.

"I base my statement on a letter which I have this morning received from the editor of *Skittles*. In it that great man informs me that he will take care that no more of Mr. Plumber's contributions appear in the paper which he edits."

Mr. Plumber went white to the lips.

"What do you mean?" he repeated.

Mr. Ingledew looked the curate full in the face. As Mr. Plumber met his glance, he cowered as if Mr. Ingledew's words had been so many blows with a stick.

"Can you not guess my meaning, Mr. Plumber? Were you not aware that there are such things as literary detectives? In future, I would advise you to remember that there are. Directly I saw those verses I knew that you had stolen them. I happened to have the original in my possession. I sent that original to the editor of *Skittles*. The letter to which I have referred is his response. The verses which you sent to him as yours are no more yours than my watch is. Are you disposed contradict me, Mr. Plumber?"

The curate was silent—with a silence which was eloquent.

"Mr. Plumber has given a sufficient answer," said Mr. Ingledew, as the curate continued speechless. He turned to the vicar. "This is not one of those cases of remote plagiarism which abound: it is a case of clear theft, which are not so frequent. Mr. Plumber sent to this paper what was, to all intents and purposes, a copy of another man's work. He claimed it as his own. He received payment for it as if it had been his own. If he chooses, the editor of *Skittles* can institute against him a criminal prosecution. If he does, Mr. Plumber will certainly be sentenced to a turn of imprisonment. As an example of impudent pilfering the affair is instructive. Perhaps, vicar, you would like to study it. Here are what Mr. Plumber calls his verses, and here are the verses from which his verses are stolen. As you will perceive, from a literary point of view, Mr. Plumber has merely perpetrated a new edition of another man's crime. Which is the worse, the original or the copy, is more than I can say. Here are the verses as they appeared in the peculiarly named paper of which you have, perhaps, already heard too much, and which, while it professes to be humorous, at least succeeds in being vulgar."

Mr. Ingledew handed Mr. Harding what was evidently a marked copy of the paper which, no doubt, has its attractions for those who like that kind of thing. Mr. Plumber remained silent. He leant on his stick. His eyes were fixed on the floor. The vicar seemed almost afraid to glance in his direction.

"And this," continued the softly speaking gentleman, who in spite of his carefully modulated tones, seemed destined to work the curate more havoc than the noisy parish mouthpiece, "is the publication in which the verses originally appeared. As you will see, it is a copy of a once-talked-of University magazine which is long since dead and done for. Possibly Mr. Plumber relied upon that fact to shield him from exposure."

The vicar received the second paper with an air of what was unmistakably amazement. He stared at it as if in doubt that he was not being tricked by his eyes, or his spectacles, or something.

"What—what's this?" he said.

Mr. Ingledew explained,

"It is a copy of *Cam-Isis*; a magazine which was edited and written by a body of Camford undergraduates some forty years ago."

The more the vicar stared at the paper, the more his amazement seemed to grow. He was beginning to turn quite red.

"Good gracious!" he exclaimed.

"The original of Mr. Plumber's verses you will find on the page which I have marked. They are quite equal to their title, 'The Lass and the Lout.'"

The Vicar's hand which held the paper dropped to his side. He looked up at the ceiling seemingly in a state of mind approaching stupefaction. As if unaware, words came from his lips.

"It's a judgment."

Mr. Ingledew rubbed his chin. He seemed to be pleased.

"It certainly is a judgment, and one for which, I am afraid, Mr. Plumber was not prepared. But I flatter myself that no man, if the thing comes within my cognisance, is able to print another man's works as his own without my being able to detect and convict him of his guilt. I have not been on the look out for plagiarists all my life for nothing."

The vicar's glance came down. He seemed all at once to become conscious of his surroundings. He looked about him with a startled air, as if he had been roused from a trance. He seemed quite curiously agitated. The words which he uttered were spoken a little wildly, as if he himself was not quite certain what it was that he was saying.

"I have to thank you for all that you have said, gentlemen, and I can only assure you that the remarks which you have made demand, and shall receive, my most serious consideration. With regard to the papers"—he glanced at the two papers which he still was holding—"with regard to these papers, with your permission, Mr. Ingledew, I will retain them for the present. They shall be returned to you later." The owner of the papers nodded assent. "And now that all has been said which there is to say, I have to ask you, gentlemen, to leave me, and—and I wish you all good-day."

The vicar himself opened the study door. He seemed almost to be hustling his visitors out of the room, his anxiety to be rid of them was so wholly undisguised. It is possible that both Mr. Luxmare and Mr. Ingledew would have liked to have made a few concluding observations, but neither of them was given a shred of opportunity. When, however, Mr. Plumber made a movement as if to go, Mr. Harding motioned to him with his hand to stay. And the vicar and the curate were left alone.

A stranger would have found it difficult to decide which of the two seemed the more shame-faced. The curate still stood where he had been standing all through, leaning on his stick, with his eyes on the ground; while the vicar, with his grasp still on the handle of the door, stood with his face turned towards the wall. It was with an apparent effort that, moving towards his writing table, placing Mr. Ingledew's two papers in front of him, he seated himself in his accustomed chair. Taking off his spectacles, with his hands he gently rubbed his eyes as if they were tired.

"Dear, dear!" he muttered, as if to himself. He sighed. He added, still more to himself, "The Lord's ways are past our finding out." Then he addressed himself to the curate.

"Mr. Plumber!" Although the vicar spoke so softly, his hearer seemed to shrink away from him. "I have a confession which I must make to you." The curate looked up furtively, as if in fear.

"When I was a young man I did many things of which I have since had good reason to be ashamed. Among the things, I used to write what Mr. Ingledew would say correctly enough it would be flattering to call nonsense. I regret to have to tell you that I wrote those verses to which Mr. Ingledew has just called our attention in that dead and gone Camford magazine."

The curate stood up almost straight.

"Sir!—Mr. Harding!"

"I did. To my shame, I own it. I had nearly forgotten them. I had not seen a copy for years and years. I had hoped that there was none in existence. But it seems that that which a man does, which he would rather have left undone, is sure to rise, and confront him, we will trust, by the grace of God, not in eternity, but certainly in time."

Mr. Plumber was trembling. The vicar continued, in a voice, and with a manner, the exquisite delicacy of which was indescribable.

"I have esteemed it my duty to make you this confession in order that you may understand that I, too, have done that of which I have cause to be ashamed. And in making you this confession I must ask you to respect my confidence, as I shall respect yours."

Mr. Plumber made a movement as if to speak. But, possibly his tongue was parched and refused its office. At any rate, he did nothing but stare at the vicar, with blanched cheeks, and strangely distended eyes. When Mr. Harding went on, his glance, which had hitherto been fixed upon the curate, fell—it may be that he wished to avoid the other's dreadful gaze.

"I think, Mr. Plumber, you might prefer to leave Exdale and

seek another sphere of duty. As it chances, I have had a recent inquiry from a friend who desires to know if I am acquainted with a gentleman who would care to accept a chaplaincy at a health resort in the Pyrenees. One moment." The curate made another movement as if to speak; the vicar checked him. "The stipend is guaranteed to be at least £200 a year; and, as there are also tutorial possibilities, on such an income, in that part of the world, a gentleman would be able to bring up his family in decent comfort. If you like, I will mention your name, and, in that case, I think I am in a position to promise that the post shall be place at your disposal."

The curate's hat and stick dropped from his trembling hands. He seemed unconscious of their fate. He moved, or rather, it would be more correct to say, he lurched towards the vicar's table.

"Sir!" he gasped. "Mr. Harding."

It seemed that he would say more—much more; but that still his tongue was tied. His weight was on the table, as if, without the aid of its support, he would not be able to stand. Rising, leaning forward, the vicar gently laid his two hands upon the curate's. His voice quavered as he spoke.

"Believe me, Mr. Plumber, we clergymen are no more immaculate than other men."

The curate still was speechless. But he sank on his knees, and laying his face on the vicar's writing table, he cried like a child.

"Em"

CHAPTER I

THE MAJOR'S INSTRUCTIONS

"Don't tell me, miss; don't tell me, I say."

And Major Clifford stood up, and shook his fist and stamped his foot in a way suggestive of the Black Country and wife beating. But Miss Maynard, who sat opposite to him, meek and mild, being used to his eccentric behaviour, was quite equal to the occasion. When he got very red in the face and seemed on the point of breaking a blood vessel, she just stood up, moved across the room, and put her hands upon his shoulders.

"Uncle," she said, and her face was very close to his, "I'm sure I'm very much obliged to you."

"It's all very well," the Major replied, pretending to struggle from her grasp. "It's all very well, but I say——"

"Of course. That's exactly what you do say."

And she kissed him. Then it was all over.

When a young woman of a certain kind kisses an elderly gentleman of a certain temperament, it soothes his savage breast, like oil upon the troubled waters. And as Miss Maynard was a young woman whose influence was not likely to be ineffective with any man whether young or old, Major Clifford was tolerably helpless in her hands.

Now, they called her "Em." Emily was her name, Emily Maynard, but from her babyhood the concluding syllables had been forgotten, and by general consent among her intimates she was "Em." There could be no doubt whether you called her Em or whether you did not, she was a young woman it was not unpleasant to know.

She was pretty tall and pretty slender, quiet, like still waters running deep. She never made a noise herself, being a model of good behaviour, but she created in some people an irresistible inclination to look upon life as a first-rate joke.

She had a tendency to throw everything into inextricable confusion by the depth of her enthusiasm. She managed many things, and with complete impartiality managed them all wrong. In that unassuming way of hers she took the lead in all well-directed efforts, and had a wonderful genius for setting her colleagues by the ears.

At the present moment things had occurred which were the cause to her of no little sorrow. She was the treasurer of the District Visitor's Fund, and at the same time of the Coal and Clothing Clubs. In that capacity she had taken a view of the duties of her office which had caused some dissatisfaction to her friends.

Being possessed of a bad memory, it had been her misfortune to receive several subscriptions to the District Visitors' Fund, of which she had forgotten to make any entry, and which she had paid away in a manner of which she was totally incapable of giving any account. In moments of generosity, too, she had bestowed the greater portion of the Coal Fund on unfortunate persons who were not of her parish, nor, it was to be feared, of any creed either. And in moments still more generous, the funds of the Clothing Club she had applied to the purchase of books for her Sunday School Library. Therefore, when the quarter ended and a request was made to examine her accounts and rectify them, she was in a position which was not exactly pleasant.

Now there happened to be at St. Giles's a curate who was a Low Churchman. Miss Maynard had a tendency to "High;" and between these two there was no good feeling lost. It was this curate who was causing all the trouble. He had not only made some uncomfortable remarks, but he had gone so far as to suggest that Miss Maynard should resign her office, and on this particular morning he had made an appointment to call in order that, as he said, some decision might be arrived at.

Major Clifford, I regret to say, was no churchgoer. In addition to which he had an unreasonable objection to what he called "parsons," and was wont to boast that he knew none of them, except the vicar, who was a sociable gentleman of a somewhat older school, even by sight. However, when he heard that the Rev. Philip Spooner was calling, and what was the purport of his intended visit, he announced his intention to favour the reverend gentleman with a personal interview, and to present him with a piece of his mind. Hence the strong words which head this chapter.

Miss Maynard was not at all unwilling that he should see the Rev. Spooner, but she was exceedingly anxious that he should not wait for him as he would for a deadly enemy.

"Uncle, promise me that you will be calm and gentle."

"Calm and gentle!" cried the Major, banging his fist upon the table. "Calm and gentle! Do you mean to say, miss, that I would harm a fly!"

"But I am afraid, uncle, that Mr. Spooner will not understand you so well as I do."

"Then," said the Major, "if the man doesn't understand me, he must be a fool!"

In which Miss Maynard begged to differ, so put her hands upon his shoulders, which was a favourite trick of hers, and said:

"Uncle, you do love me, don't you? And I am sure you wouldn't hurt my feelings. You will be kind to Mr. Spooner for my sake, won't you?"

CHAPTER II

HIS NIECE'S WOOING

IT was a warm morning in a pleasant country lane, and a young gentleman, with a very broad brimmed hat, a very long frock-coat, and a very small, stiff shirt collar, was pacing meditatively to and fro, evidently waiting for someone. Every now and then he glanced up the lane which seemed deserted by ordinary passengers, and if he had not been a clergyman would no doubt have whistled.

At last his patience was rewarded. Over the top of the low hedge a coquettish hat appeared sailing along, and presently a young woman came meekly round the corner, enjoying the fresh country air. It was Miss Maynard. The young gentleman advanced. He seemed to know her, for taking off his broad-brimmed hat, he kissed her, much in the same fashion as a short time before she had kissed the Major, only much more forcibly, and apparently with much enjoyment.

"Em, I thought you were never coming."

"I don't know," she said, and sighed. "I don't know. It's all vanity. I was thinking of your last Sunday's sermon," she continued as they wandered on, seemingly unconscious that his arm was round her waist. "It was so true."

They walked on till they reached a gate which opened into a little woodland copse. Here, under the mighty trees, the shade was pleasant, and the grass cool and refreshing to the eye. They sat at the foot of a great old oak.

"Em," said Mr. Roland—by the way, the Rev. John Roland was the young gentleman's name—"these meetings are very pleasant."

"Yes," said Em, who was always truthful, "they are."

"Therefore, I am afraid to run the risk of ending them."

"What do you mean?" cried she.

To be candid, four mornings out of five were taken up by these pleasant little meetings, and to end them would be to rob her of one of her most important occupations.

"Em, you know what I mean."

"I don't," said she.

"You do," said he.

"I do not," she said, and looked the other way.

"Then I'll tell you." And he told her. "Em, I can keep silence no longer. I must tell your uncle all. And if he forbids me—"

"I don't mind saying," she observed, taking advantage of the pause, "that I don't care if he does."

"What do you mean?"

"John," she whispered.

"Call me Jack."

"No; it's so undignified for a clergyman." Some people would call it undignified for a young woman to lay her hand on a clergyman's shoulder. "What do I care if he says no? He never does say what he means the first time. I can just turn him round my finger. Whatever he said to you he would never dare to say no to me; at least, when I had done with him."

"Let us hope so," said Mr. Roland. "But whatever happens, I feel that I have already been too long silent."

"I don't know," murmured Em, with a saintlike expression in her eyes. "I rather like meeting you upon the sly."

Mr. Roland, as a curate and so on, perceived this to be a sentiment in which, under any circumstances, it was impossible for him to acquiesce—at least, verbally.

"No," he declared; "it must not be. This is a matter in which delay is almost worse than dangerous. I must go to him at once and tell him all."

Miss Maynard yielded. She was not disinclined to have their little mutual understanding publicly announced, if only to gratify Miss Gigsby and one or two other young ladies.

"Yes, Em," he continued, "I will go at once, and doubt will be ended."

They went together to the end of the lane, then she departed to do a few little errands in the town, and the Rev. John Roland went on his visit to Major Clifford.

CHAPTER III

THE LADY'S LOVER

THE Major waited for his visitor—waited in a mood which, in spite of his promise to Miss Maynard, promised unpleasantness for Mr. Spooner. Time passed on, and he did not come. The Major paced up and down stairs, to and from the windows, and from room to room. Finally, he took a large meerschaum pipe from the mantelshelf in the smoking-room and smoked it in the drawing-room, a thing he would not have dared to do—very properly—if Miss Maynard had been at home.

"I promised young Trafford I'd go and see what I thought of that new gun of his," growled the Major, "and here's that jackanapes keeping me in to listen to his insulting twaddle."

The Major probably forgot that at any rate the jackanapes in question had no appointment with him.

At last he threw open the window, and thrusting his head out, looked up and down the street to see if he could catch a glimpse of the expected Spooner.

"The fellow's playing with me!" he told himself considerably above a whisper. "Like his confounded impudence!"

Suddenly he caught sight of a shovel hat and clerical garments turning the street corner, and re-entering the room with some loss of dignity, commenced reading the "Broad Arrow" upside down. Presently there was a knock at the street door, and a stranger was shown upstairs unannounced.

"I have called," he began.

The Major rose.

"I am perfectly aware why you have called," said he. "My niece is not at home."

"No," said the visitor. "I am aware—"

"But," continued the Major, who meant to carry the thing with a high hand, and give Mr. Spooner clearly to understand what his opinions were, "she has commissioned me to deal with the matter in her name."

The Rev. John Roland—for it was the Rev. John Roland—looked somewhat mystified. He failed to see the drift of the Major's observation, and also did not fail to see that, for some reason, his reception was not exactly what he would have wished it to be.

"I regret," he began, with the Major standing bolt upright, glancing at him with an air of a martinet lecturing an unfortunate sub for neglect of duty, "that it is my painful duty—"

"Sir," said the Major, stiff as a poker, "you need regret nothing."

The Rev. John Roland looked at him. It was very kind of him to say so, but a little premature.

"I was about to say," he went on, feeling more awkward than he had intended to feel, "that owing to circumstances——"

"On which we need not enter," said the Major. "Quite so—quite so!"

He rose upon his toes, and sank back on his heels. Mr. Roland began to blush. He was not a particularly shy man, but under the circumstances the Major was trying.

"But I was about to remark that——"

"Sir," said the Major, shooting out his right hand towards Mr. Roland in an unexpected manner, "once for all, sir, I say that I know all about it—once for all, sir! And the sooner we come to the point the better."

"Really," murmured Mr. Roland, "I am at a loss—"

"Then," cried the Major, suddenly flaring up in a way that

was even startling, "let me tell you that I wonder you have the impertinence to say so. And I may further remark that the sooner you say what you have to say, and have done with it, the better for both sides."

Thereupon he went stamping up and down the room with heavy strides. Mr. Roland was so taken aback, that for a moment he was inclined to think that the Major had been drinking.

"Major Clifford," he said, with an air of dignity which he fondly hoped would tell, "I came here to speak to you on a matter intimately connected with your niece's future happiness."

"What the dickens do you mean by your confounded impudence? Do you mean to insinuate, sir, that my niece's happiness can be affected by your trumpery nonsense?"

"Sir," said Mr. Roland. "Major!"

There was no doubt about it, the Major must be intoxicated. It was painful to witness in a man of his years, but what could you expect from a person of his habits of life? He began to wish he had postponed his visit to another day.

"Don't Major me! Don't attempt any of your palavering with me! I'm not a fool, sir, and I am not an idiot, sir, and that's plain, sir!"

"Major," he said—"Major Clifford, I will not tell you——"

"You will not tell me, sir! What the dickens do you mean by you will not tell me? Do you mean to insult me in my own house, sir?"

Mr. Roland was disposed to think that the insult was all on the other side, and inclined to fancy that a man who abused another before he knew either his name or errand, could be nothing but a hopeless lunatic.

"This pains me," he observed—"pains me more than I can express."

"Well, upon my life!" shouted the Major. "A fellow comes to my house with the deliberate intention of insulting me and mine, and yet he has the confounded insolence to tell me that it pains him!"

"Major," Mr. Roland was naturally beginning to feel a little warm, "you are not sober."

"Sober!" roared the Major. "Not sober! Confound it! this is too much!"

And before the curate knew what was coming, the Major took him by the collar of his coat, led him from the room, and—let us say, assisted him down the stairs. The front door was flung open, and, in broad daylight, the astonished neighbours saw the Rev. John Roland, M.A., of Caius College, Cambridge, what is commonly called "kicked-out," of Major Clifford's house.

CHAPTER IV

THE MAJOR'S SORROW

AFTER the Major had disposed of his offensive visitor, he went upstairs to think the matter over. It began to suggest itself to him that, upon the whole, he had not, perhaps, been so kind and gentle as Miss Maynard had advised. But then, as he phrased it, the fellow had been so confoundedly impertinent.

"Bully me, sir! Bully me!" cried the Major, taking a strong view of Mr. Roland's, under the circumstances, exceedingly mild deportment. "And the fellow said I wasn't sober! I never was so insulted in my life."

The Major felt the insinuation keenly, because—for prudential reasons only—he was rigidly abstemious.

When Miss Maynard returned, she was met at the door by the respected housekeeper, Mrs. Phillips, and her own maid, Mary Ann.

"Oh, Miss," began Mrs. Phillips, directly the door was opened, "such goings on I never see in all my life—never in all my days. I thought I should have fainted."

Miss Maynard turned pale. She thought of the mild, if aggravating, Spooner, and was fearful that her affectionate relative might in some degree have forgotten her emphasised directions.

"Oh, Miss Em!" chimed in Mary Ann. "Whatever will come to us I don't know. If the police were to come and lock us all up, I shouldn't be surprised. Not a bit, I shouldn't."

"Pray shut the door," observed Miss Maynard, who was still

upon the doorstep. "Come in here, Phillips, and tell me what is the matter."

Miss Maynard looked disturbed. Mr. Spooner was bad enough before, but he might make things very unpleasant indeed if anything had occurred to annoy him further.

"Oh, Miss Em, Mr. Roland has been here."

"Mr. Roland!"

"Yes, miss. And there was the Major and he a-shouting at each other, and the next thing I see was the Major dragging of him downstairs and a-shoving of him down the front steps."

Miss Maynard sank upon a chair. She seemed nearly fainting.

"Mrs. Phillips, this is awful."

"Awful ain't the word for it, miss. It's a case for the police."

"Mrs. Phillips, this is worse than you can possibly conceive. I must see the Major."

"The Major's in the drawing-room. Can't you hear him, miss?"

Miss Maynard could hear him stamping overhead as though he were doing his best to bring the ceiling down.

"Thank you; I will go to him."

She did go to him. But first she went to her own room, shutting the door carefully behind her. Going to the dressing-table she put her arms upon it and hid her face within her hands.

"Oh!" she said, "whatever shall I do?" Then she cried. "It's the most dreadful thing I ever heard of. Oh, how could he find it in his heart to treat me so?" She ceased crying and dried her eyes, "Never mind, it's not over yet. If he drives me to despair he shall know it was his doing."

Then she stood up, took off her hat and coat, washed her face and eyes, and entered the drawing-room in her best manner.

The Major was alone. He was perfectly aware that Miss Maynard had returned. He had seen her come up the street, he had heard her enter the house, but for reasons of his own he had not gone to meet her with that exuberant warmth with which, occasionally, it was his custom to greet her. He was in a towering passion. At least, he fully intended to be in a towering passion, but at the same time he was fully conscious that, under the circumstances, a towering passion was a very difficult thing to keep properly towering. And when Miss Maynard entered with the expression of her countenance so sweet and saintlike, he knew that there was trouble in the air. He looked at his watch.

"Five-and-twenty minutes to two. Five-and-twenty minutes to two. And we lunch at half-past one. Those servants are disgraceful!"

And he crossed the room to ring the bell.

"Please don't ring," said Miss Maynard, quite up to the manœuvre. "I wish to speak to you."

"Oh, oh! Then perhaps you'll remember it is luncheon-time, and when we're likely to have any regularity in this establishment, perhaps you'll let me know."

Miss Maynard drew herself up.

"Pray don't attack me," she observed. "I don't wish to be kicked out of the house."

The Major turned crimson. It was true that someone had been so kicked that morning, but it was unkind of Miss Maynard to insinuate that he had any desire to kick her.

"Look here!" he cried, actually shaking his fist at her.

"Don't threaten me," remarked Miss Maynard.

"Threaten you! You leave me at home to meet a scoundrel!"

"How dare you!" exclaimed Miss Maynard, who had momentarily forgotten whom it was she had left him there to meet.

"How dare I. Well, upon my soul, this is a pretty thing!"

"I had never thought that in a matter in which my happiness was so involved, my existence so bound up, you could have treated me so cruelly!"

The Major stared. Like Mr. Roland, he was a little puzzled.

"You tell me that your existence is bound up in that fellow's?"

"Fellow! The fellow is worth twenty thousand such gentlemen as you!"

The Major was astounded. The remark amazed him. He really thought Miss Maynard must be demented, not knowing that Mr. Roland had thought the same thing of him not long before.

"Oh, Major Clifford, when I am broken-hearted, and you follow me, if you ever do, to a miserable tomb, then—then may you never know what it is to be a savage!"

The Major began to be alarmed. He feared Miss Maynard must be seriously unwell.

"Eh! ah! you—you're not well. You—you don't take enough care. It's—it's indigestion."

"Indigestion!" cried Miss Maynard, and she sank upon the couch. "Indigestion! He breaks my heart, and he says it's indigestion!"

She burst into a flood of tears. The Major was terrified.

"Mrs. Philips!" he shouted. "Mary Ann!"

"Don't!" exclaimed Miss Maynard. "Call no one. Let me die alone! You have robbed me of the man I love!"

"Love!" cried the Major, racking his brains to think where the tinge of insanity came in the family. "You love Spooner!"

"Spooner!" replied Miss Maynard with contempt. "I love John Roland."

"John Roland!" yelled the Major, thinking that he must be going mad as well. "Who the deuce is he?"

"He asks me who he is, and he kicked him from his house this morning!"

"I kicked him!" cried the Major, indignant at the charge. "I kicked Spooner!"

"You did not!" persisted Miss Maynard between her tears. "You kicked Roland!"

"I kicked Spooner!" said the Major.

"Do you mean to say," enquired Miss Maynard, on whom a light was dimly breaking, "that you didn't know the gentleman you kicked was Mr. Roland?"

"Roland!" exclaimed the Major, staggered. "Roland! I swear I thought the man was Spooner."

"Oh!" gasped Miss Maynard, overwhelmed by the discovery, "Major Clifford, what have you done?"

"Heaven knows!" groaned the Major as he sank into a chair. "Chanced six months' hard labour."

There was silence for a few moments then the Major spoke again:

"I know what I'll do, I'll write."

Miss Maynard was agreeable. Getting pens, ink and paper he sat down and commenced his composition.

"My Dear Sir,

"As an unmitigated idiot and an ungentlemanly ruffian, I am only too conscious that I am an ass——"

"I don't think I would put unmitigated idiot and ungentlemanly ruffian," suggested Miss Maynard mildly. "Perhaps Mr. Roland would not care to marry into a family which contained such characters as that."

"Marry?" said the Major, arresting his pen.

"Yes," replied Miss Maynard. "I think I would put it in this way: 'My Dear Mr. Roland——'"

"But I never saw the man before. I don't know him from Adam."

"Never mind," said Miss Maynard; "I do."

So the Major wrote as he was told.

"My Dear Mr. Roland,

"I have to apologise for my conduct of this morning, which was entirely owing to a gross misconception on my part. If you will kindly call at your earliest convenience I will explain fully. I may say that your proposition has my heartiest approval——"

"But I don't know what his proposition is," protested the Major.

"Mr. Roland's proposition is that he should marry me," explained Miss Maynard. There was silence. Miss Maynard prepared to raise her pocket-handkerchief to her eyes. "Of course, if you wish to break my heart——"

Then the Major succumbed, and Miss Maynard continued her dictation.

——"and I shall have the greatest pleasure in welcoming you as my nephew.

"Believe me, with repeated apologies,

Very faithfully yours,

"Arthur Clifford."

Miss Maynard possessed herself of the epistle, and while the Major was addressing the envelope, added a postscript of her own:

"My Dear Jack,

"You see, I call you Jack for once—my silly old uncle has made a goose of himself. Please, please come this instant to your own Em, because—I will not say I want to kiss you. It would be most unseemly in the afternoon.

"Ever, ever your own

"EM."

This choice epistle, containing additions of which he was

unconscious, the Major packed into an envelope, and, under Miss Maynard's supervision, dispatched to its destination by a maid. Then they went down, models of propriety, to luncheon.

It was after that meal, when they were again in the drawing-room, that there came a knock at the street door. Steps were heard coming up the stairs.

"It is he!" cried Miss Maynard, with that intuition bestowed upon true love preparing to receive him in her arms.

Fortunately, however, he eluded her embrace, because the visitor happened to be Mr. Spooner.

"Mr. Spooner!" cried Miss Maynard.

"Miss—Miss Maynard," said Mr. Spooner, "I—I beg your pardon."

"The Rev. William Spooner—Major Clifford."

Miss Maynard introduced them. The gentlemen looked at each other. At least, the Major looked at Mr. Spooner. Mr. Spooner, after the first shy glance, seemed to be studying the pattern of the carpet.

"With regard to the purport of your visit," went on Miss Maynard, using her finest dictionary words, "I have to place in your hands my resignation of the offices I have hitherto so unworthily held. With reference to the unfortunately mismanaged—er—book-keeping, to make that all right"—it was rather a comedown—"Major Clifford wishes to present you with a donation of," she paused, "of twenty-five guineas."

"Fifty," growled the Major, much disgusted. "For goodness sake, make it fifty while you are about it!"

"Just so," said Miss Maynard blandly. "The Major is particularly anxious to make it fifty guineas."

The Major glared at her. If they had been alone, and the circumstances had been different, he would no doubt have given her a small piece of his mind. As it was—well, discretion is the better part of valour.

Mr. Spooner began his speech:

"I—I am sure we shall be very happy; I—I should say we shall exceedingly; that is, no doubt the donation is—is— At the same time, Miss—Miss Maynard's services, though—though—"

He went blundering on, Miss Maynard looking at him stonily,

raising not a finger to his help. The Major took his bearings. He was a tall, thin young gentleman with a white face—which, however, was just now pinkish—white hair upon the top of his head, and a faint suspicion of more white hair upon his upper lip. It would have been cruel to apply assault and battery to one so innocent.

While Mr. Spooner was still stammering, and stuttering there came another knock at the street door. Miss Maynard gave a slight jump. There was no mistake about it this time. Somebody came bolting up the stairs apparently three steps at a time. The door was thrown open. Somebody entered the room, and in about two seconds in spite of the assembled company Miss Maynard and the Rev. John Roland were locked breast to breast. To do the young man justice it was not his idea of things at all. He was plainly taken a little aback. But the young woman's enthusiasm was not to be restrained.

"This," explained Miss Maynard, holding Mr. Roland by his coat sleeve, "this is the Rev. John Roland. John, this is my uncle."

There was a striking difference between the tones in which she made the two announcements. The two gentlemen bowed. They had had the pleasure of meeting before. One, if not both, felt a little awkward. But Miss Maynard did not care two pins how they felt. She transferred her attentions to Mr. Spooner.

"I am going to leave St. Giles's," she observed; "the service is too low. I am going to St. Simon Stylites. I suppose, John, I may as well tell Mr. Spooner that you are going to be my husband."

John was silent. So was Mr. Spooner. The latter was gentleman amazed not to say indignant. In his heart of hearts he had been persuaded that Miss Maynard was consumed by a hopeless passion for William Spooner.

"Perhaps Miss Maynard will become treasurer of the Clothing Club at St. Simon Stylites."

Had it not been a case of two clergyman, Mr. Roland might possibly have liked to have had a try at knocking Mr. Spooner down. As it was he refrained.

"If Miss Maynard does so honour us, she at least need fear no insults from the clergy."

Miss Maynard favoured him with a lovely smile, and Mr. Spooner was annihilated.

Since then Mr. Roland and Miss Maynard have been united in the bonds of holy matrimony. The ceremony was performed at St. Simon Stylites, and the Rev. William Spooner was, after all, one of the officiating clergy. Mr. Roland is at present Vicar of a parish in the neighbourhood of Stoke-cum-Poger, of which parish Mrs. Roland is also Vicaress. He is very "High," and it is darkly whispered that certain courts possessing very nicely defined spiritual powers have their eyes upon him. Of that we know nothing, but we do know that he is possessed of a promising family, and that, not so very long ago, Mrs. Roland presented him with a second Em.

A Relic of the Borgias

CHAPTER I

VERNON'S door was opened, hastily, from within, just as I had my hand upon the knocker. Someone came dashing out into the street. It was not until he had almost knocked me backwards into the gutter that I perceived that the man rushing out of Vernon's house was Crampton.

"My dear Arthur!" I exclaimed. "Whither away so fast?"

He stood and stared at me, the breath coming from him with great palpitations. Never had I seen him so seriously disturbed.

"Benham," he gasped, "our friend, Vernon, is a scoundrel."

I did not doubt it. I had had no reason to suppose the contrary. But I did not say so. I held my tongue. Crampton went on, gesticulating, as he spoke, with both fists clenched; dilating on the cause of his disorder with as much freedom as if the place had been as private as the matters of which he treated; apparently forgetful that, all the time, he stood at the man's street door.

"You know he stole from me my Lilian—promised she should be his wife! They were to have been married in a month. And now he's jilted her—thrown her over—as if she were a thing of no account. Made her the laughing stock of all the town! And for whom do you think, of all the women in the world? Mary Hartopp—a widow that should know better! It's not an hour since I was told. I came here straight. And now Mr. Vernon knows something of my mind."

I could not help but think, as he went striding away, as if he were beside himself with rage—without giving me a chance to say a word—that all the world would quickly learn something of it too.

The moment seemed scarcely to be a propitious one for interviewing Decimus Vernon. He would hardly be in a mood to receive a visitor. But, as the matter of which I wished to speak to him was of pressing importance, and another opportunity might not immediately occur, I decided to approach him as if unconscious of anything untoward having happened.

As I began to mount the stairs there came stealing, rather than walking down them, Vernon's man, John Parkes. At sight of me, the fellow started.

"Oh, Mr. Benham, sir, it's you! I thought it was Mr. Crampton back again."

I looked at Parkes, who seemed sufficiently upset. I had known the fellow for years.

"There's been a little argument, eh, Parkes?"

Parkes raised both his hands.

"A little argument, sir! There's been the most dreadful quarrel I ever heard."

"Where is Mr. Vernon?"

"He's in the library, sir, where Mr. Crampton left him. Shall I go and tell him that you would wish to see him?"

Parkes eyed me in a manner which plainly suggested that, if he were in my place, he should wish to do nothing of the kind. I declined his unspoken suggestion, preferring, also, to announce myself.

I rapped with my knuckles at the library door. There was no answer. I rapped again. As there was still no response, I opened the door and entered.

"Vernon?" I cried.

I perceived at a glance that the room was empty. I was aware that, adjoining this apartment was a room which he fitted up as a bedroom, and in which he often slept. I saw that the door of this inner room was open. Concluding that he had gone in there, I went to the threshold and called "Vernon!"

My call remained unanswered. A little wondering where the man could be, I peeped inside. My first impression was that this room, like the other, was untenanted. A second glance, however, revealed a booted foot, toe upwards, which was thrust out from the other side of the bed. Thinking that he might be in one of his wild moods, and was playing me some trick, I called out to him again.

"Vernon, what little game are you up to now?"

Silence. And in the silence there was, as it were, a quality which set my heart in a flutter. I became conscious of there being, in the air, something strange. I went right into the room, and I looked down on Decimus Vernon.

I thought that I had never seen him look more handsome than he did then, as he lay on his back on the floor, his right arm raised above his head, his left lying lightly across his breast, an expression on his face which was almost like a smile, looking, for all the world as if he were asleep. But I was enough of a physician to feel sure that he was dead.

For a moment or two I hesitated. I glanced quickly about the room. What had been his occupation when death had overtaken him seemed plain. On the dressing table was an open case of rings. Three or four of them lay in a little heap upon the table. He had, apparently, been trying them on. I called out, with unintentional loudness—indeed, so loudly, that, in that presence, I was startled by the sound of my own voice.

"Parkes?"

Parkes came hurrying in.

"Did you call, sir?"

He knew I had called. The muscles of the fellow's face were trembling.

"Mr. Vernon's dead."

"Dead!"

Parkes' jaw dropped open. He staggered backwards.

"Come and look at him."

He did as I told him, unwillingly enough. He stood beside me, looking down at his master as he lay upon the floor. Words dropped from his lips.

"Mr. Crampton didn't do it."

I caught the words up quickly.

"Of course he didn't, but—how do you know?"

"I heard Mr. Vernon shout 'Go to the devil' to him as he went downstairs. Besides, I heard Mr. Vernon moving about the room after Mr. Crampton had gone."

I gave a sigh of relief. I had wondered. I knelt at Vernon's side. He was quite warm, but I could detect no pulsation.

"Perhaps, Mr. Benham, sir," suggested Parkes, "Mr. Vernon has fainted, or had a fit, or something."

"Hurry and fetch a doctor. We shall see."

Parkes vanished. Although my pretensions to medical knowledge are but scanty, I had no doubt whatever that a doctor would pronounce that Decimus Vernon was no longer to be numbered with the living. How he had come by his death was another matter. His expression was so tranquil, his attitude, as of a man lying asleep upon his back, so natural; that it almost seemed as if death had come to him in one of those commonplace forms in which it comes to all of us. And yet——

I looked about me to see if there was anything unusual which might catch the eye. A scrap of paper, a bottle, a phial, a syringe— something which might have been used as a weapon. I could detect no sign of injury on Vernon's person; no bruise upon his head or face; no flow of blood. Stooping over him, I smelt his lips. There are certain poisons the scent of which is unmistakable, the odour of some of those whose effect is the most rapid lingers long after death has intervened. I have a keen sense of smell, but about the neighbourhood of Decimus Vernon's mouth there was no odour of any sort or kind. As I rose, there was the sound of some one entering the room beyond.

"Decimus?"

The voice was a woman's. I turned. Lilian Trowbridge was standing at the bedroom door. We exchanged stares, apparently startled by each other's appearance into momentary speechlessness. She seemed to be in a tremor of excitement. Her lips were parted. Her big, black eyes seemed to scorch my countenance. She leaned with one hand against the side of the door, as if seeking for support to enable her to stand while she regained her breath.

"Mr. Benham—You! Where is Decimus? I wish to speak to him."

Her unexpected entry had caused me to lose my presence of mind. The violence of her manner did not assist me in regaining it. I stumbled in my speech.

"If you will come with me into the other room, I will give you an explanation."

I made an awkward movement forward, my impulse being to conceal from her what was lying on the floor. She detecting my uneasiness, perceiving there was something which I would conceal, swept into the room, straight to where Vernon lay.

"Decimus! Decimus!"

She called to him. Had the tone in which she spoke, then, been in her voice when she enacted her parts in the dramas of the mimic stage, her audiences would have had no cause to complain that she was wooden. She turned to me, as if at a loss to comprehend her lover's silence.

"Is he sleeping?" I was silent. Then, with a little gasp, "Is he dead?" I still made no reply. She read my meaning rightly. Even from where I was standing, I could see her bosom rise and fall. She threw out both her arms in front of her. "I am glad!" she cried, "I am glad that he is dead!"

She took me, to say the least of it, aback.

"Why should you be glad?"

"Why? Because, now, she will not have him!"

I had forgotten, for the instant, what Crampton had spluttered out upon the doorstep. Her words recalled it to my mind. "Don't you know that he lied to me, and I believed his lies."

She turned to Vernon with a gesture of scorn so frenzied, so intense, that it might almost have made the dead man writhe.

"Now, at any rate, if he does not marry me, he will marry no one else."

Her vehemence staggered me. Her imperial presence, her sonorous voice, always were, theatrically, among her finest attributes. I had not supposed that she had it in her to display them to such terrible advantage. Feeling, as I did feel, that I shared my manhood with the man who had wronged her, the almost personal application of her fury I found to be more than a trifle overwhelming. It struck me, even then, that, perhaps, after all, it was just as well for Vernon that he had died before he had been compelled to confront, and have it out with, this latest illustration of a woman scorned.

Suddenly, her mood changed. She knelt beside the body of the man who so recently had been her lover. She lavished on him terms of even fulsome endearment.

"My loved one! My darling! My sweet! My all in all!"

She showered kisses on his lips and cheeks, and eyes, and brow.

When the paroxysm had passed—it was a paroxysm—she again
stood up.

"What shall I have of his, for my very own? I will have
something to keep his memory green. The things which he gave
me—the things which he called the tokens of his love—I will grind
into powder, and consume with flame."

In spite of herself, her language smacked of the theatre. She
looked round the room, as if searching for something portable,
which it might be worth her while to capture. Her glance fell upon
the open case of rings. With eager eyes she scanned the dead man's
person. Kneeling down again, she snatched at the left hand, which
lay lightly on his breast. On one of the fingers was a cameo ring. On
this her glances fastened. She tore, rather than took it from its place.

"I'll have that! Yes! That!"

She broke into laughter. Rising she held out the ring towards
me. I regarded it intently. At the time, I scarcely knew why. It was,
as I have said, a cameo ring. There was a woman's head cut in
white relief, on a cream ground. It reminded me of Italian work
which I had seen, of about the sixteenth century. The cameo was
in a plain, and somewhat clumsy, gold setting. The whole affair
was rather a curio, not the sort of ring which a gentleman of the
present day would be likely to care to wear.

"Look at it. Observe it closely! Keep it in your mind, so that
you may be sure to know it should you ever chance on it again.
Isn't it a pretty ring—the prettiest ring you ever saw? In memory
of him"—she pointed to what was on the floor behind her—"I will
keep it till I die!"

Again she burst into that hideous, and, as it seemed to me,
wholly meaningless laughter. Her bearing, her whole behaviour,
was rather that of a mad woman, than a sane one. She affected
me most unpleasantly. It was with feelings of unalloyed relief that
I heard footsteps entering the library, and turning, perceived that
Parkes had arrived with the doctor.

CHAPTER II

WHEN Vernon's death became generally known, a great hubbub

arose. Mrs. Hartopp went almost, if not quite, out of her senses. If I remember rightly, nearly twelve months elapsed before she was sufficiently recovered to marry Phillimore Baines. The cause of Vernon's death was never made clear. The doctors agreed to differ; the post-mortem revealed nothing. There were suggestions of heart-disease; the jury brought it in valvular disease of the heart. There were whispers of poison, which, as no traces of any were found in the body, the coroner pooh-poohed. And, though there were murmurs of its being a case of suicide, no one, so far as I am aware, hinted at its being a case of murder.

To the surprise of many people, and to the amusement of more, Arthur Crampton married Lilian Trowbridge. He had been infatuated with her all along. His infatuation even survived her yielding to Decimus Vernon—bitter blow though that had been— and I have reason to believe that, on the very day on which Vernon was buried, he asked her to be his wife. Whether she cared for him one snap of her finger is more than I should care to say; I doubt it, but, at least, she consented. At very short notice she quitted the stage, and, as Mrs. Arthur Crampton, she retired into private life. Her married life was a short, if not a merry one. Within twelve months of her marriage, in giving birth to a daughter, Mrs. Crampton died.

I had seen nothing since their marriage either of her or her husband. I was therefore the more surprised when, about a fortnight after her death, there came to me a small package, accompanied by a note from Arthur Crampton. The note was brief almost to the point of curtness.

Dear Benham,—

My wife expressed a wish that you should have, as a memorial of her, a sealed packet which would be found in her desk.

I hand you the packet precisely as I found it.

Yours sincerely,

Arthur Crampton.

Within an outer wrapper of coarse brown paper was an inner covering of cartridge paper, sealed with half a dozen seals. Inside the second enclosure was a small, duodecimo volume, in a tattered binding. Half a dozen leaves at the beginning were missing. There was nothing on the cover. What the book was about, or why Mrs.

Crampton had wished that I should have it, I had not the faintest notion. The book was printed in Italian—my acquaintance with Italian is colloquial, of the most superficial kind. It was probably a hundred years old, and more. Nine pages about the middle of the volume were marked in a peculiar fashion with red ink, several passages being trebly underscored. My curiosity was piqued. I marched off with the volume there and then, to a bureau of translation.

There they told me that the book was an old, and possibly, valuable treatise, on Italian poisons and Italian poisoners. They translated for me the passages which were underscored. The passages in question dealt with the pleasant practice with which the Borgias were credited of having destroyed their victims by means of rings—poison rings. One passage in particular purported to be a minute description of a famous cameo ring which was supposed to have belonged to the great Lucrezia herself.

As I read a flood of memory swept over me—what I was reading was an exact description, so far as externals went at any rate, of the cameo ring, which I had seen Lilian Trowbridge remove after he was dead from one of the fingers of Decimus Vernon's left hand. I recalled the frenzied exultation with which she had thrust it on my notice, her almost demoniac desire that I should impress it on my recollection. What did it mean? What was I to understand? For three or four days I was in a state of miserable indecision. Then I resolved I would keep still. The man and the woman were both dead. No good purpose would be served by exposing old sores. I put the book away, and I never looked at it again for nearly eighteen years.

The consciousness that his wife had spoken to me, with such a voice from the grave, did not tend to increase my desire to cultivate an acquaintance with Arthur Crampton. But I found that circumstances proved stronger than I. Crampton was a lonely man, his marriage had estranged him from many of his friends; now that his wife had gone he seemed to turn more and more to me as the one person on whose friendly offices he could implicitly rely. I learned that I was incapable of refusing what he so obviously took for granted.

The child, which had cost the mother her life, grew and

flourished. In due course of time she became a young woman, with all her mother's beauty, and more than her mother's charms: for she had what her mother had always lacked—tenderness, sweetness, femininity. Before she was eighteen she was engaged to be married. The engagement was in all respects an ideal one. On her eighteenth birthday, it was to be announced to the world. A ball was to be given, at which half the county was expected to be present, and the day before, I went down, prepared to take my share in the festivities.

In the evening, Crampton, his daughter, Charlie Sandys, which was the name of the fortunate young gentleman, and I were together in the drawing-room. Crampton, who had vanished for some seconds, re-appeared, bearing in both his hands, with something of a flourish, a large leather case. It looked to me like an old-fashioned jewel case. Which, indeed, it was. Crampton turned to his daughter.

"I am going to give you part of your birthday present to-day, Lilian—these are some of your mother's jewels."

The girl was in an ecstacy of delight, as what girl of her age would not have been? The case contained jewels enough to stock a shop. I wondered where some of them had come from—and if Crampton knew more of the source of their origin than I did. Wholly unconscious that there might be stories connected with some of the trinkets which might not be pleasant hearing, the girl, girl-like, proceeded to try them on. By the time she had finished they were all turned out upon the table. The box was empty. She announced the fact.

"There! That's all!"

Her lover took up the empty case.

"No secret repositories, or anything of that sort? Hullo!—speak of angels!—what's this?"

"What's what?"

The young girl's head and her lover's were bent together over the empty box. Sandys' fingers were feeling about inside it.

"Is this a dent in the leather, or is there something concealed beneath it?"

What Sandys referred to was sufficiently obvious. The bottom of the box was flat, except in one corner, where a slight protuberance suggested, as Sandys said, the possibility of there being something concealed beneath. Miss Crampton, already excited by her father's gift, at once took it for granted that it was the case.

"How lovely!" she exclaimed. She clapped her hands. "I do believe there's a secret hiding-place."

If there was, it threatened to baffle our efforts at discovery. We all tried our hands at finding, it, but tried in vain. Crampton gave it up.

"I'll have the case examined by an expert. He'll soon be able to find your secret hiding-place, though, mind you, I don't say that there is one."

There was an exclamation from young Sandys.

"Don't you? Then you'd be safe if you did, because there is!"

Miss Crampton looked eagerly over his shoulder.

"Have you found it? Yes! Oh, Charlie! Is there anything inside?"

"Rather, there's a ring. What a queer old thing! Whatever made your mother keep it hidden away in there?"

I knew, in an instant. I recognised it, although I had only seen it once in my life, and that once was sundered by the passage of nineteen years. Mr. Sandys was holding in his hand the cameo ring which I had seen Lilian Trowbridge remove from Decimus Vernon's finger, and which was own brother to the ring described in the tattered volume, which she had directed her husband to send me—"as a memory"—as having been one of Lucrezia Borgia's pretty playthings. I was so confounded by the rush of emotions occasioned by its sudden discovery, that, for the moment, I was tongue-tied.

Sandys turned to Miss Crampton.

"It's too large for you. It's large enough for me. May I try it on?"

I hastened towards him. The prospect of what might immediately ensue spurred me to inarticulate speech.

"Don't! For God's sake, don't! Give that ring to me, sir!"

They stared at me, as well they might. My sudden and, to them, meaningless agitation was a bolt from the blue. Young Sandys withdrew from me the hand which held the ring.

"Give it to you?—why?—is it, yours?"

As I confronted the young fellow's smiling countenance, I felt myself to be incapable, on the instant, of arranging my thoughts in sufficient order to enable me to give them adequate expression. I appealed for help to Crampton.

"Crampton, request Mr. Sandys to give me that ring. I implore you to do as I ask you. Any explanation which you may require, I will give you afterwards."

Crampton looked at me, open-mouthed, in silence. He never was quick-witted. My excitement seemed to amuse his daughter.

"What is the matter with you, Mr. Benham?" She turned to her lover. "Charlie, do let me see this marvellous ring."

I renewed my appeal to her father.

"Crampton, by all that you hold dear, I entreat you not to allow your daughter to put that ring upon her finger."

Crampton assumed a judicial air—or what he intended for such.

"Since Benham appears to be so very much in earnest—though I confess that I don't know what there is about the ring to make a fuss for—perhaps, Lilian, by way of a compromise, you will give the ring to me."

"One moment, papa: I think that, as Charley says, it is too large for me."

I dashed forward. Mr. Sandys, mistaking my purpose, or, possibly, supposing I was mad, interposed; and, in doing so, killed the girl he was about to marry. Before I could do anything to prevent her, she had slipped the ring upon her finger. She held out her hand for us to see.

"It is too large for me—look."

She touched the ring with the fingers of her other hand. In doing so, no doubt, unconsciously, she pressed the cameo. A startled look came on her face. She gazed about her with a bewildered air. And she cried, in a tone of voice which, long afterwards, was ringing in my ears.

"Mamma!"

Ere we could reach her, she had fallen to the ground. We bent over her, all three of us, by this time, sufficiently in earnest. She lay on her back, her right hand above her head; her left, on one of the fingers of which was the ring, resting lightly on her breast. There was the expression of something like a smile upon her face, and she looked as if she slept. But she was dead.

THE END

www.ingramcontent.com/pod-product-compliance
Lightning Source LLC
Chambersburg PA
CBHW011354010726
47494CB00008B/2311